"Why are you calling him a victim?"

Olivia frowned. Was this cop some recent hire looking to impress the chief? He was as fresh of face and as awkward of body as a preadolescent boy, but his speech was clipped and laced with arrogance. "I chose that term because unless that man buried himself up to the neck and then somehow found a way to cover his head with a bucket, someone *else* performed those actions for him."

Reddening, the eager policeman tried to regain his composure. He studied the sheet on the clipboard again . . .

As Olivia walked around the rear of her vehicle, the medical examiner's female assistant came scampering over the dunes.

"You won't believe this, Bobby!" She pulled on the officer's sleeve in a familiar gesture. The ME's assistant used her free hand to brush a lock of dark from her heart-shaped face while giving Bobby's shirt another excited tug. "The vic was buried holding a little plastic sand shovel. A green one, just like the bucket that covered his head. He's got nothing else on him, and I mean *nothing*!"

"No wallet? No ID?"

"Don't you get what I'm saying? There'd be no place to hide personal effects!" she exclaimed and waved for him to follow her. "The guy was buried buck ass naked!"

Berkley Prime Crime titles by Ellery Adams

A KILLER PLOT
A DEADLY CLICHÉ

A BOOKS
BY THE BAY
MYSTERY

A Deadly Cliché

ELLERY ADAMS

BERKLEY PRIME CRIME, NEW YORK

THE BERKLEY PUBLISHING GROUP
Published by the Penguin Group
Penguin Group (USA) Inc.
375 Hudson Street, New York, New York 10014, USA
Penguin Group (Canada), 90 Eglinton Avenue East, Suite 700, Toronto, Ontario M4P 2Y3, Canada
(a division of Pearson Penguin Canada Inc.)
Penguin Books Ltd., 80 Strand, London WC2R 0RL, England
Penguin Group Ireland, 25 St. Stephen's Green, Dublin 2, Ireland (a division of Penguin Books Ltd.)
Penguin Group (Australia), 250 Camberwell Road, Camberwell, Victoria 3124, Australia
(a division of Pearson Australia Group Pty. Ltd.)
Penguin Books India Pvt. Ltd., 11 Community Centre, Panchsheel Park, New Delhi—110 017, India
Penguin Group (NZ), 67 Apollo Drive, Rosedale, North Shore 0632, New Zealand
(a division of Pearson New Zealand Ltd.)
Penguin Books (South Africa) (Pty.) Ltd., 24 Sturdee Avenue, Rosebank, Johannesburg 2196,
South Africa

Penguin Books Ltd., Registered Offices: 80 Strand, London WC2R 0RL, England

A DEADLY CLICHÉ

A Berkley Prime Crime Book / published by arrangement with the author

PRINTING HISTORY
Berkley Prime Crime mass-market edition / March 2011

Copyright © 2011 by Ellery Adams.
Excerpt from *The Last Word* by Ellery Adams copyright © by Ellery Adams.
Cover illustration by Kimberly Schamber.
Cover design by Rita Frangie.
Interior text design by Tiffany Estreicher.

ISBN: 978-0-425-24023-6

BERKLEY® PRIME CRIME
Berkley Prime Crime Books are published by The Berkley Publishing Group,
a division of Penguin Group (USA) Inc.,
375 Hudson Street, New York, New York 10014.
BERKLEY® PRIME CRIME and the PRIME CRIME logo are trademarks of Penguin Group (USA) Inc.

PRINTED IN THE UNITED STATES OF AMERICA

10   9   8   7   6   5   4   3   2   1

To the Cozy Chicks, my sisters in crime:

Deb Baker
Lorraine Bartlett
Kate Collins
Maggie Sefton
Leann Sweeney
Heather Webber

(Love) is easily the most empty cliché, the most useless word, and at the same time the most powerful human emotion—because hatred is involved in it, too.

—Toni Morrison

Chapter 1

There are some things you learn best in
calm, and some in storm.
—WILLA CATHER

"Storm's comin'," the fisherman said, stroking the pewter whiskers of his beard. He glanced at the small television mounted above the espresso machine, squinting at the green radar image of circulating clouds.

Olivia Limoges followed his gaze. She looked at the irregular shape of the low-pressure system forming in the Caribbean, listening closely as the meteorologist showed the storm's projected path should it gather strength and become more than a tropical disturbance. The slick-haired weatherman assured his viewing audience that although the storm was likely to organize and grow in force, it would remain out at sea, allowing for a perfect Labor Day weekend for those heading to the beach.

"Jackass," the fisherman's voice rumbled like distant thunder. He rubbed a calloused, leathery hand over his lined face as though he could wipe away the other man's erroneous words. "Don't matter how much fancy equipment these boys get. They don't understand a damned thing 'bout balance. We're due for a big one and we're witnessin' her beginnin' right here and now on that TV screen. I feel it in my bones. It's a comin'."

Olivia nodded in agreement, for she and the man beside her shared an understanding. The ocean lived inside them. Like the merfolk of legend, their blood seemed to be mixed with salt water and their hearts filled with cresting waves. There was a rhythm, like the pull of a tide, within their souls. Since birth, they'd been schooled to respect the currents and the shallows and the cold depths where no light penetrated. As adults, they were still awed by each powerful swell and surge.

In return for their reverence, the sea offered them gifts. The fisherman, whose name was Fergusson, had been granted three decades of nets brimming over with brown, white, and pink shrimp. With every haul, the captain counted his blessings. The ocean fed his family and gave him purpose. He was a man satisfied with his lot in life. Olivia had been given trinkets, pushed onto shore by frothy wavelets, and a fresh start, white and gleaming as a strip of sand in the moonlight.

She and the taciturn shrimp boat captain had been the first customers in the casual eatery. At six thirty in the morning, they'd taken black coffees and bagels with cream cheese to a café table to talk business over breakfast. Olivia had met Captain Fergusson over the summer, and after serving his shrimp to the patrons of her five-star restaurant, The Boot Top Bistro, she would order from no other shrimper. Not only did his catches taste as fresh as the moment they'd been lifted from the ocean, but the captain was also a sharp businessman who treated both his crew and his customers with equal fairness.

The grizzly fisherman and the tall, elegant restaurateur launched into a round of pleasant haggling. Olivia's standard poodle, Captain Haviland, slept at their feet, his belly replete with a breakfast of eggs and bacon made especially for him by the doting coffeehouse proprietor.

An hour later, their business complete, the two residents of Oyster Bay, North Carolina, sat together in comfortable silence. Slowly, other residents of the small coastal town trickled in, followed by a few bleary-eyed tourists who'd just discovered that the kitchen in their costly vacation rental home lacked a working coffeemaker.

A man sporting a Yankees cap and a fresh sunburn complained to Wheeler, the octogenarian owner of Bagels 'n' Beans, as he ordered several complicated espresso creations. "I'm shelling out five grand a week for that freaking house! Do they expect me to drink that instant crap they left in the pantry?"

Wheeler issued a noncommittal grunt, scowling slightly as he skimmed the foam from the surface of the pitcher of steamed milk. Olivia knew the old man resented having to make what he referred to as "girly drinks" for his customers, but he knew enough about profit margins to realize he couldn't have turned the slab of concrete behind the store into a cozy eating area without the revenue generated by tourists such as this one.

"I know better than to order bagels this far away from New York, so I hope you've got something else I like." The man scrutinized the selection of baked goods and then pointed at his hat. "You guys just don't have the right water. That's the real difference." Adopting a splayed-leg stance, he pointed at the pastry display. "I'll take those caramel apple turnovers off your hands. They don't look too bad." His eyes gleamed as he watched Wheeler slip the sweets into a brown bag. Unconsciously rubbing his formidable paunch, he told Wheeler to add a few chocolate chip cookies as well.

"He ain't gonna live to see seventy," Captain Fergusson

muttered as the tourist stuffed one of the cookies in his mouth. While the vacationer chewed greedily, he stirred six sugar packets into his mocha latte.

"Might not see tomorrow," Olivia agreed. "If he comes to The Boot Top tonight, it will seal the deal. Michel's specials for this evening include lobster-stuffed ravioli in a vodka cream sauce and an almond and Parmesan crusted salmon steak in a lemon-thyme sauce. Most of my patrons will need to be rolled out the door on dollies."

The pair smiled at one another, picturing bloated tourists being wheeled down the restaurant's handicapped ramp.

As they cleared the dishes from their table and brought them to the counter, the tourist turned to them. "You were brave enough to eat the bagels, huh?"

Fergusson barely held his sneer in check. "Everythin' Wheeler sells is good."

The man snorted and brushed away the cookie crumbs clinging to his chin. "You gotta be a local. Everybody knows you can't eat bagels, pizza, or cold cuts this far south." He scrutinized the seaman, his red, fleshy face dismissive as he peered at Olivia over the shrimper's shoulder.

"*You* don't look like you're from around here," he told her, his gaze traveling down her body, examining her black sundress and silver sandals. "You look like a city girl."

Olivia narrowed her eyes at the man. "I grew up in Oyster Bay. I left for a time, but I came back. This is my home."

He gaped at her over his coffee cup. "Why the hell would you *come back*? Woman with your looks? You could have snagged yourself a rich husband and been set up in style in New York or Palm Beach. Anywhere but here! This place is okay for a week, but that is *it*." He sidestepped the fisherman. "If you were my gal, you wouldn't have to lift a finger. You could sit around all day watching soap operas."

Olivia gave him a frosty smile. "What a tempting offer." She then gestured at his wedding ring. "Your wife is a *such* a lucky woman." Her smile became genuine as she said good-bye to Fergusson. At the snap of his mistress's fingers, the sleeping poodle detached himself from the shadows beneath the table and leapt to his feet, barking once to illustrate that he was fully awake.

"What the—" the tourist spluttered and coffee dribbled onto his shirt.

Fergusson grinned, displaying a mouthful of tobacco-stained teeth. "Look out, mister. That dog's a black devil. He'll bite your hand off if you take another step closer to Olivia. You'd best keep your distance."

Olivia smiled, pausing at the fixings bar near the front door. The tourist turned to Fergusson, mistakenly assuming that Olivia had left the café when, in fact, she had decided to add another splash of cream to her to-go cup.

"What does she do in this podunk town?" the tourist asked, his back to the door. "A fine woman like that?"

"Owns most of it," Fergusson replied, knowing full well that Olivia was listening. He then pivoted away from the man and began to converse with Wheeler about the storm.

However, the tourist refused to be ignored. "That harmless front isn't heading in this direction at all. Why worry about it? Didn't you guys listen to the weather report?"

Fergusson put a lid on his takeout cup. "Oh, it's comin' all right. Too bad you'll be gone."

Wheeler tried not to smile as the seaman headed for the restroom. The tourist stared after him in befuddlement and the slightest tinge of anxiety. "Pffah! He's nuts. What are they going to do? Run out and buy batteries and bottled water?"

"Not Fergusson," Wheeler answered as though the question hadn't been laced with sarcasm. "But Miss Olivia will prepare." He winked at Olivia over the tourist's head. "Chances are she'll be good and ready for any storm. Wouldn't be like her not to have a plan."

Again, the dismissive snort. "Come on! What would a woman like that know about weathering a major storm?"

Pausing in the act of drying a mug with his dishtowel, Wheeler gestured at the television. Once again, the channel featured a radar image of the tropical disturbance. "She knows plenty, my friend. A hurricane is gonna form while you're lyin' on the beach this weekend. I know of one that started just like this one." He lowered his voice, but the words seemed to burn their way into Olivia's ears.

"It came through Oyster Bay when Miss Olivia was a little girl. That storm was a monster." Wheeler was lost in the memory. "It kicked and screamed and howled and when all was said and done, a child had lost her mama. A few other folks got killed too. Most of 'em died 'cause they didn't respect the storm." He finished drying the cup and picked up another. "I s'pect this one'll claim her share of lives too. That's the way of things 'round these parts. You either bend to nature's power or she'll force you to your knees."

Mumbling under his breath that the local population was made up of inbred lunatics, the tourist gathered his pastries, his coffees, and his impenetrable arrogance and left.

He walked right past Olivia without realizing she was still standing there, trying to fit the lid on her cup with trembling fingers.

Olivia and Haviland walked three blocks south to the hardware store. The streets were crowded now. Female vacationers in swim suits and sheer cover-ups shopped for sunscreen and folding beach chairs while their husbands hunted for newspapers and ice for their coolers.

Hampton's Hardware had occupied a prime spot on Main Street since Olivia was a toddler. Back then, when there were no parking meters and a horse-drawn trolley shuttled people from the two downtown churches to a parking and picnic area near the docks, Hampton's also housed the town's only post office. With the recent influx of cash into Oyster Bay's municipal coffers, however, a new post office had been built at the end of the block and Hampton's began stocking souvenirs instead of stamps. Cheap T-shirts, plastic sand toys, tacky postcards, salt-water taffy, and plaster replicas of the local lighthouse filled the large front window and the area surrounding the checkout.

At first, the townsfolk regarded Hampton's new wares with a critical eye, but he displayed the brightly colored trinkets so creatively that they'd not only grown used to his Made in Taiwan section, but had even come to anticipate what he'd do next to sell his cornucopia of mass-produced items.

In celebration of the new school year, Hampton had built a trio of giant, wooden apples and had rigged the tops with mechanical pulleys so that they opened like treasure chest lids, revealing the rotund faces of Cabbage Patch dolls. Each doll brandished a souvenir perfect for stuffing a child's new backpack. From rulers and lunchboxes decorated with beach scenes to pencil cases and hemp purses stamped with the slogan, "I got an A+ in Beach Bumming," the plump dolls seemed to be daring each shopper to grab a school-related item from an apple.

Hampton's Labor Day weekend display had certainly caught the interest of a pair of toddler boys. One had a pudgy fist clamped onto the arm of a Cabbage Patch girl with auburn pigtails as he attempted to wrestle an iridescent pencil from her grasp. The second boy, a mirror reflection of the first, was doing his best to climb into the apple already occupied by a Cabbage Patch boy dressed in denim overalls and a red baseball cap. The wooden lid on the apple was just about to clamp down on the toddler's head of wild brown curls when his mother rescued him.

"Oh, Olivia!" The young woman smiled as she pulled her son out of the apple. "Hi, there!"

Her lovely face flushed with exertion of having to hold one wriggling child while yanking his brother away from the apple filled with thousands of colorful pencils, Laurel Hobbs shot Olivia a look of apology. "Let me just buckle them into the stroller, then I might actually be able to speak in complete sentences to you."

"By all means, strap away." Olivia eyed the three-point canvas belt system that seemed similar to a parachute harness. Haviland gave an impatient whine and sniffed the nearest Cabbage Patch Kid. He issued a disdainful grunt.

"They have the look of mutated mushrooms about them, don't they?" Olivia stroked the poodle's head. She watched in amazement as her petite friend wrestled her twins into the double stroller, handed them each a snack bag of cheese crackers, and then fastened her long, wheat-blond hair into a perfectly smooth ponytail. Sighing with relief, she put her hands on her narrow hips, looking exactly like the high school cheerleader she once was, and waved for Olivia to follow her down the tool aisle.

"I am *so* behind in critiquing Harris's chapter!" she exclaimed and then dropped her voice. "One of my neighbors was robbed and I've been a mess ever since! I feel like I need to buy a big knife and keep it under my mattress." She touched one of the teeth on a shiny handsaw and then hastily withdrew her fingers.

Not so long ago, Olivia wouldn't have been the slightest

bit interested in Laurel's trials and tribulations, but over the past few months, the oak-barrel heiress and the stay-at-home mom had become friends. In fact, Olivia counted all four of the Bayside Book Writers as friends. She was still trying to get used to the experience.

"Was anyone hurt?" she inquired as they walked deeper into the store.

Laurel pried a hammer out of Dermot's hand. Or was it Dallas? Olivia couldn't tell the two boys apart and she'd forgotten which child tended to wear shades of green and which one favored blue. "No, thank heavens, but they took *everything* of value. Jewelry, silver, art, electronics."

Olivia placed several battery-powered lanterns in her cart. "Do your neighbors have a burglar alarm?"

Laurel nodded. "Yes. Most of the people in my neighborhood do." She chewed her lip for a moment. "It might not have been turned on though. I mean, this happened in the middle of the day! I don't put mine on to run out to the grocery store. And these guys must have been *real* professionals. There was no sign of a break-in and they didn't even make a mess. Left some food on the kitchen counter but that's it." She glanced at Olivia with admiration. "I bet you never get scared, even though you live out on the Point all by yourself."

Haviland whined petulantly.

"Oh! I wasn't even thinking!" Laurel's hands fluttered over her mouth as she received a withering stare from Olivia's poodle. "Of course you don't need to worry with such a magnificent guard dog watching over you!"

Appeased, Haviland resumed his thorough examination of the scents lingering around the battery and flashlight end cap.

"It's just that Steve goes out of town all the time for dental conferences and seminars and I keep thinking about being alone in the house. The only weapon I know how to wield is a nail file."

"Do your sons have wooden blocks? I bet they'd make excellent projectiles." Olivia selected several packages of batteries. "Seriously, though. If you'll feel better about having company, ask your in-laws to stay over. I'm sure they'd be delighted."

Laurel rolled her eyes. "I'd rather be attacked by burglars." Her pale blue eyes gleamed. "Actually, this topic gives me an idea for my next chapter."

Olivia arched her brows. "Your duchess is going to be ravished by a handsome highwaymen?"

"*No.* I'm trying to avoid clichés, remember? But what if she's captured by someone of the wrong class and grows to love him? A rogue with a Robin Hood complex. Things could get very complicated and *very* steamy."

It was always a delight to see how animated Laurel became when she spoke of her writing. Olivia smiled. "And what of the poor, cuckolded duke?"

"He shouldn't have taken his wife for granted!" Laurel declared heatedly and Olivia couldn't help but wonder if they were still discussing a fictional couple or if the conversation had suddenly entered the realm of autobiography.

One of the twins crushed a cracker in his fist and scattered orange crumbs across the floor. "Now we won't get lost," he told his brother, who immediately followed suit.

"Boys!" Laurel balled her fists in frustration. "Mommy has told you *not* to leave trails when we're *inside*."

Olivia could see how the little boys might view their surroundings as being similar to an enchanted forest. They were in an aisle at the back of the store where the overhead lights failed to successfully illuminate the space. As a result, shadows hid in the crevices between lines of lawn rakes, brooms, shovels, and mops. From the perspective of the small boys, looking up into the steel and plastic rake tines and the bushy mop heads must have been akin to glancing up through the branches of a strange, magical wood.

Grabbing two glow sticks from her cart, Olivia cracked them until they radiated a phosphorescent yellow light and handed one to each twin. "These work better than breadcrumbs," she whispered conspiratorially. The boys accepted the gift and stared at her in awe.

"You are *so* good with children," Laurel gushed. "I can't see why you don't want any of your own."

Olivia laughed, a sound rich and deep as the tolling of a bell in the distant sea. "I'm good with yours for about thirty seconds, but that's only because they're yours. Besides, one doesn't have to know much about children to recognize intelligence. Your boys are smart and imaginative and I must admit, I enjoy the glint of mischief in their eyes."

"It's more than a glint," Laurel murmured, but she was clearly pleased by the compliment. "Why are you filling your cart with emergency supplies?" she asked as they headed toward the checkout.

"I like to be prepared," Olivia answered cryptically. Laurel had enough on her mind without having to worry about an impending storm. As Laurel tried to maneuver her stroller through the narrow checkout space, she looked very young and vulnerable to Olivia.

Unaware of their mother's struggle, the twins giggled, sticking their glow sticks under their shirts and watching in scientific delight as the material in the center of their chests changed hue. It was as if their hearts had turned into little moons. Olivia reached out toward their firefly glow and tickled their chubby legs.

"Laurel," she said, ignoring the cashier who waited for her to sign her credit card receipt. "When you get home, call a locksmith and find out if there's anything you can do to make your home safer. Don't take any chances."

Clearly surprised by Olivia's serious tone, Laurel hesitated, but she must have recognized the concern on her friend's face, because she nodded and then pushed the stroller out the door.

"She'd be better off buyin' a gun," the man in line behind Olivia remarked. "Doesn't her man have one?" he queried, making it apparent that any man who did not possess a firearm wasn't a genuine male.

"Her husband's a dentist. I believe he prefers other weapons." Olivia accepted her bags from the cashier and flashed a wry grin at the man behind her. "But don't worry. I could always loan her my rifle. I've got a Browning and she's a beauty."

As Olivia stepped outside, she heard the man murmur, "Damn, now *that's* my kind of lady."

As the sun hit her face, Olivia gave a slight smile. Some men loved a woman with her own weapon.

Chapter 2

*If you must speak ill of another, do not
speak it, write it in the sand near the
water's edge.*
—NAPOLEON HILL

The Saturday before Labor Day promised to be sultry
with a scattering of feathery clouds in a denim blue
sky. The beaches of Oyster Bay would be packed with children and sun-worshippers, the harbor would be crammed
with boats heading out for fishing trips or pleasure cruises,
and every space in The Boot Top's reservation log would
be full.

Olivia was grateful to have the beach to herself this
morning. She lived north of town and there was nothing but
the lighthouse to capture the interest of vacationers. Even
then, they had to be willing to traverse the gravel road leading to the landmark and pay a small fee for the privilege of
being able to climb up the winding stairs to the main gallery.

From here, the view was spectacular. The ocean stretched
endlessly into the distance until it blurred into a thin, blue
line where it kissed the horizon. Ships of all sizes passed
slowly across the water, and dark shadows indicative of large
schools of fish provided contrast to the glittering surface
waves.

This was the beauty of the lighthouse in the daytime, but only a select number of locals knew that its true magnificence was revealed when a storm front moved in or when the sun set and night fell over the ocean.

As a child, Olivia had often nicked the key from the absentminded keeper and had climbed the stairs to the watch. She would bring a book and an old towel to sit on and read as a million stars were born in the inky blackness overhead. When the sea had turned as dark as the sky, the water seemed to be pushing stars in Olivia's direction and she felt cherished by the offering.

On other days, she'd crouch on the balcony, her blue eyes wide as heavy thunderclouds bore down upon the Point. She had traveled across the world, but never had she seen a sight more electrifying than forks of lightning bursting across the sky, endeavoring, or so it seemed, to pierce the very heart of the ocean.

Now, at a quarter past eight in the morning, the beach was deserted. The lighthouse didn't open until ten and Olivia's closest neighbors lived two miles up the beach and rarely ventured outside.

"What do you think we'll find today, Captain?" she asked Haviland and lowered the Bounty Hunter Discovery 3300 metal detector to the ground.

The poodle shook his black ears and shot forward, unwilling to wait as his mistress fiddled with her noisy machine. There were gulls and sandpipers to chase and crabs that needed to be sent scuttling back into their sandy burrows.

Olivia adjusted the metal detector's volume and began to walk, sweeping the disc in a slow and constant arc as she moved forward. After years of hunting for assorted treasures deposited onto the shore by generous waves, Olivia knew how to differentiate between the high bleeps signaling useless items like nails or bottle caps and the higher-pitched sounds indicating the presence of jewelry or coins.

She paused after half a mile and removed a bottle of water and a folding trench shovel from her backpack. After taking several swallows of water, she dug through the moist sand and uncovered two tokens for a children's arcade located several towns away.

"Nothing exciting," she told Haviland as he trotted over to examine her find. Still, she pocketed the tokens. Later, she would clean them with the same precision she'd apply to a priceless coin.

Olivia kept all her finds in jumbo pickle jars. Each one was labeled with the season and the year. During the winter months, she liked to sit on the floor of her cavernous living room and spill the contents onto her Aubusson rug. In front of a crackling fire in the wide stone hearth, Olivia would run her fingers over shotgun shells, rings, coins, and belt buckles, wondering about the lives of the owners as the salty smell of the sea drifted over the carpet.

Since childhood, Olivia had received gifts from the ocean. These days she had to search for them, but the long, quiet walks gave Olivia's restless soul a measure of peace, and the steady whisper of the waves kept her company. The sea had taken her father from her, but that was the only time it had claimed anything belonging to her. Last summer, the currents had even delivered several clues that allowed her to assist the local police in solving a murder case.

As Olivia thought back on the violent death of her friend and fellow writer, she rounded a bend at the tip of the Point and hesitated. Normally, she'd turn back after this distance, driven by hunger and a desire for a second cup of coffee, but something urged her onward. The waves near her feet abruptly retreated, as though the tide had yanked them backward in order to let her pass. Up ahead, Olivia saw the glint of sunlight on metal.

"Haviland!" Olivia called and the poodle raced toward the twinkle, barking happily. "That dog loves a mystery," she muttered to herself with a smile.

Her expression changed as Haviland's bark became agitated. The poodle darted toward what appeared to be a child's plastic bucket and then rapidly jumped away again. The large green bucket was planted in the sand as though someone was preparing to build the first of several castle turrets but had suddenly been called away.

"What is it, Captain?" Olivia watched her dog carefully. He was clearly repelled by the scent emanating from beneath the bucket, and as Olivia drew closer, the breeze shifted and she was nearly flattened by the stench.

"Holy Hell!" she covered her mouth and nose with her hand and winced. "What's *in* there?"

Setting the metal detector on the ground, she approached the bucket warily.

"Did some kid trap a horseshoe crab?" She looked at Haviland, but he answered with an urgent bark. It was not a horseshoe crab.

Olivia searched for a stick. There were none by the water's edge, so she climbed up the dunes and came back with a dried reed stalk. She paused to tie a bandana around the bottom half of her face, her breathing becoming shallower out of trepidation. The smell spoke of death and rot and things not meant to be exposed to the harsh light of the morning sun.

As she eased the reed under the lip of the bucket, it snapped in two. Olivia cursed, wanting to jump away from the odor and the scent of her own fear. Haviland was barking frantically now, driving Olivia to react quickly and decisively. She put a hand on each side of the bucket and whipped it off, releasing a fresh burst of putrid air.

Gagging, she stumbled backward, losing her footing and falling onto the sand with a soft thud. Haviland whined and rushed to her, his snout exploring her partially hidden face.

"I'm not hurt, Captain," she said, turning away from the horrible thing on the beach. She lowered her mouth to the sand and breathed deeply. Once she had a lungful of air, she had to look back, to try to comprehend the atrocity she'd uncovered.

For surely that's what it was. No other word could adequately describe the loose, waxy flesh, the torn pieces of skin, the drooping eyes, or the presence of half a dozen crabs, creeping over what was once a nose, a mouth, a cheek.

Fighting back the nausea rising in her throat, Olivia fixed her gaze at the ocean. It was there, pulsing and swelling, a symbol of constancy and saneness. The gurgle of the waves eventually gave her the strength to take a step closer.

The sight was just as gruesome as it had been at first glance. It was not a Halloween prop or a practical joke. It was a human head. Male, from what Olivia could tell, and it was rapidly decomposing in the heat and with assistance from the crabs.

"We need to get help," Olivia told Haviland in a hoarse croak, her eyes flicking toward the incoming tide.

After a moment's pause, she put the bucket back where she'd found it. There, in the middle of the pristine beach, it was almost possible to believe she'd imagined the horror it disguised. Yet the odor was not, *could* not, be concealed.

Death saturated the air, tainting the salt-laden wind. The decay was incongruent with the cloudless blue sky and sparkling sea and yet it was almost possible to imagine tendrils of stench, gray and puckered as octopus tentacles, creeping out from beneath the bucket.

Knowing time was against her, Olivia left her metal detector and backpack on the baking sand and began to run.

Chief Rawlings stared down at the distorted head with pity.

Olivia was certain that the sight and the smell of the thing repulsed him, but she knew that he was able to look beyond the horror and recall that what had been revealed after the removal of the green bucket was a human being. Was he thinking of the people who cared about this person, this misshapen memory of a man? A mother, a sister, a wife, or even a child. She wondered if Rawlings prayed that the victim was not anyone's father. She could picture the chief walking slowly up a front path and stepping gingerly over a skateboard or a jump rope to knock on the door, his fist heavy on the wood. How much must it hurt him each time he was forced to crush a family under the weight of his news.

From her vantage point in the lee of a dune, Olivia noticed Rawlings stood back a ways from the team assisting the medical examiner, watching as they painstakingly removed the sand from the head, exposing a neck and finally, a set of shoulders.

"We got a whole body in here, Chief!" one of his officers shouted in excitement, as though Rawlings hadn't reached the same conclusion. But the chief nodded in encouragement. He ruled the Oyster Bay Police Department with a mixture of gentleness and an unyielding demand for excellence. The men and women working under him stood up a fraction straighter and vowed to work a little harder whenever they were in his presence. In his late forties, Rawlings had a pleasant face and a bit of a paunch, which he tried to disguise under Hawaiian shirts when he wasn't on the job.

Rawlings put his hand on his hips as his officers continued to scoop sand away from the body and then he turned and walked toward the dunes where Olivia and her black poodle sat waiting and watching.

"I'm sorry you had to be the one to find him," Rawlings said.

Olivia put a hand on Haviland's back. "Better me than some tourist," she answered, her eyes searching the chief's face. "Are there any clues as to why he was buried here?"

"We haven't found anything around the body yet," Rawlings admitted. "Why don't you go on home? You've seen enough."

He smiled warmly at her, but Olivia knew she was being given an order. "I'll be at Grumpy's critiquing Harris's chapter in case you need me." She stood, her body throwing a long, lean shadow over the hot sand.

Rawlings nodded. "I hope I have the opportunity to read his chapter before our meeting. Enjoy your late breakfast." He paused and then added, "One of these days, I'd like to share a meal with you, Miss Limoges." He looked at Haviland and dipped his chin. "And you too, Haviland. But for now, I'll wish you both good morning."

As the chief walked back to his men, Olivia saw him pull a handkerchief from his pocket and dab the perspiration from his forehead. She liked that Sawyer Rawlings was the type of man who would carry a handkerchief. He was old fashioned and believed strongly in traditions, but he was also a man of contradictions. He created beautiful paintings and read poetry, yet wore those dreadful

Hawaiian shirts and ate junk food, letting his middle-aged body turn soft about the waist and hips. Olivia studied him for another minute, wondering exactly what it was about the man she found so intriguing.

"He is not as he appears. There are many layers to Chief Rawlings," she explained defensively to Haviland, but the poodle didn't share her interest in the lawman. Haviland growled and jerked his snout toward the road. He was hungry and had grown tired of breathing in the rank smell adrift on the air.

Olivia gave him a sympathetic pat on the head. "It is awful, Captain. We can go."

The closest police cruiser was parked with its windows open and a sun protector stretched across the windshield. A young officer leaned against the driver's side door and read a sheet of paper attached to a clipboard. He looked up as Olivia approached.

"Chief said you should stop by the station to give your official statement." He tapped on the clipboard and then cast a sideways glance at Olivia. "You sure you've never seen that guy before? He's not someone from your workplace or maybe a neighbor?"

"I don't recognize him," she answered. "I've only met my closest neighbors, the Eflands, twice. They're an older couple and don't spend much time outside and certainly not when it's this hot. From what I could see, the victim's at least twenty years younger than Mr. Efland."

A predatory glint appeared in the officer's eyes. "Why are you calling him a victim?"

Olivia frowned. Was this cop some recent hire looking to impress the chief? He was as fresh of face and as awkward of body as a preadolescent boy, but his speech was clipped and laced with arrogance. "I chose that term because unless that man buried himself up to the neck and then somehow found a way to cover his head with a bucket, someone *else* performed those actions for him."

Reddening, the eager policeman tried to regain his composure. He studied the sheet on the clipboard again. "You stated that you were out on a walk with your dog and a metal detector," he said as though she had been doing something indecent. "Find anything of interest near the crime scene?"

Olivia narrowed her eyes. She was quickly losing patience. "I didn't waste time combing the surrounding area for jewelry or rare coins once I'd lifted up that bucket. However, your department is more than welcome to borrow my Bounty Hunter if you think it would be of use to the investigation."

Like a child being offered a sweet, the young cop brightened. "Really? That would be great!" He immediately suppressed his exuberance. "We'll return it to you as soon as we're done here."

"That won't be necessary," Olivia assured him tersely. "I'll collect it when I come to the station to sign my statement." Without waiting to be dismissed, she opened the passenger door of her Range Rover to let Haviland hop inside. As she walked around the rear of her vehicle, the medical examiner's female assistant came scampering over the dunes.

"You won't believe this, Bobby!" She pulled on the officer's sleeve in a familiar gesture. The two uniformed twentysomethings looked alike and were probably cousins to some degree. Most of the older Oyster Bay families were related in one way or another. The ME's assistant used her free hand to brush a lock of dark hair from her heart-shaped face while giving Bobby's shirt another excited tug. "The vic was buried holding a little plastic sand shovel. A green one, just like the bucket that covered his head. He's got nothing else on him and I mean *nothing*!"

"No wallet? No ID?"

"Don't you get what I'm saying? There'd be no place to hide personal effects!" she exclaimed and waved for him to follow her. "The guy was buried buck-ass naked!"

Olivia was met at the front door of Grumpy's Diner by a roller-skating dwarf. Dixie Weaver was the manager, bookkeeper, hostess, and head waitress of the eatery bearing the same name as her husband. Grumpy, the gifted fry cook, was actually quite pleasant, but he was a man of so few words that people assumed he was unfriendly. He'd earned the moniker early in life, and when it came time to choose a name for the diner, Dixie assured him that "Grumpy's" would soon become a household word in Oyster Bay. As usual, she was right.

"You're late this mornin'!" The diminutive proprietor put her hands on her hips and glared at Olivia. "I can't hold your table on a Labor Day weekend,"

"Believe me, I hadn't expected to be delayed by the police . . ." Olivia trailed off. Rawlings wouldn't be pleased if the news that a body was found on the Point traveled around town before he even made it back to the station.

Unfortunately, Olivia could see that she had said too much. Dixie's eyes lit up and she practically forced the customer seated at the end of counter to topple from his stool. Scooping up his check and his money without a thought to providing change, she pushed him toward the front door and called out, "Have a nice day now, ya hear!"

Flying back to the counter to wipe the area clean, Dixie stood as tall as she could on her white roller skates and patted the stool. "I'm gonna get you some fresh coffee, but if you expect to taste a single drop, you'd best be prepared to finish that sentence."

She returned with a bowl of water for Haviland and a clean coffee cup for Olivia. Dangling a steaming carafe from her free hand, Dixie batted her false eyelashes. "Come on, lady. I don't have all day. Those folks in the *Evita* booth want a refill."

"Blackmailing me with java." Olivia scowled in disapproval. "That is low, even for you."

Dixie dumped the coffeepot on the counter and tugged at a pair of Hello Kitty arm warmers. "Is that a height joke?"

"Of course not." Olivia wiggled her index finger so that Dixie would skate closer. "You have to swear on all twelve of your children not to breathe a word of this until it's become a matter of public record."

Dixie smirked. "My kids ain't eggs. I don't have a dozen. Last count it was five. Six at the most." She poured the coffee. "But you have my word."

"I found a body on the beach this morning. About a mile and a half north of the lighthouse keeper's cottage," Olivia whispered. She watched Dixie absorb the startling information.

Oddly, Dixie's expression was not of curiosity, but of concern. "Are you okay?"

"I am, thank you. I didn't know the man, but I pity him. His death was no accident." Olivia clammed up. "Have you heard of any locals that have gone missing? A wife complaining about a wayward husband for example?"

Ignoring the waving hands coming from the *Evita* booth, Dixie thought about the question. "I haven't, but I'll keep my ears open and my mouth shut. Can I at least tell Grumpy? I'll explode like an overstuffed turkey if I can't share this with somebody!"

Olivia nodded. She knew Grumpy was no gossip. "Ask him the same question. He might hear talk among his friends about someone not turning up at home or at work. Maybe we can help the police identify the dead man."

"We aren't gonna be able to help unless he's in the damned restaurant business." Dixie plastered on her best waitress smile and signaled to the man holding his coffee cup in the air. "*Most* folks have three whole days off, 'Livia. The dead guy probably didn't have to be anywhere 'til Tuesday, the lucky bastard."

Recalling the grotesque visage and foul odor of the corpse, Olivia frowned. "Trust me, he was not lucky." She reached into her purse for the chapter she needed to critique by that evening. "And if ever he was, then every ounce of that ran out." She uncapped her pen to signal that the subject was now closed.

While Dixie skated from the kitchen to tables with platters of three-egg omelets, cinnamon French toast, or double bacon cheeseburgers for those ordering an early lunch, the hum of conversation brought Olivia a sense of calm. She didn't come to Grumpy's for the atmosphere, nor did she share Dixie's deep admiration for Andrew Lloyd Webber. Every booth paid homage to one of his musicals, and though Olivia was amused by the displays showcasing *Starlight Express*, *Cats*, or *Phantom of the Opera*, she preferred to sit at the sole window booth and work on her writing projects.

Olivia ate at the diner at least once a week. Upon returning to Oyster Bay, Dixie had become her first true friend. Olivia was fond of the smaller woman's feisty personality and sharp wit. Dixie also adored Haviland and had Grumpy prepare special meals for the coddled poodle while requesting items not found on the regular menu for Olivia. This morning, she skated to the counter with a frittata made of fresh spinach and shredded provolone and a bowl of honeydew melon squares.

"Those folks at the *Jesus Christ Superstar* table are drivin' me hog wild!" Dixie said through gritted teeth. "They wanna know if our bacon is local. Shoot, I told them we've got more pig farms in this state than gas stations." She whipped a compact from her apron pocket and applied a fresh coat of pink frosted lip gloss. "Don't think they cared for that answer, but I reckon they're lousy tippers anyhow. All those yoga-twistin', garbage-recyclin' tree huggers are tightwads."

"It's the booth decor, Dixie," Olivia said after swallowing a bite of frittata. "It makes some people uncomfortable. Maybe you should replace Jesus with a poster of Glenn Close from *Sunset Boulevard*."

"That right there is blasphemy!" Dixie presented Haviland with a plate of gently cooked ground beef mixed with rice and greens. He gave her his most sincere canine smile and then turned his attention to his second meal of the morning. "Maybe *Joseph and the Technicolor Dreamcoat* would make people more at ease. I'll have a look-see on eBay tonight."

Using the green pen Harris had given to his fellow writers, Olivia circled a typo in the first line of the second chapter of his work in progress, a science fiction novel entitled, *The Chosen One*.

Having critiqued the first chapter, Olivia knew that the story's heroine, Zenobia, had been safely evacuated from her dying planet, Zulton. However, upon arriving at her new home on the Planet Remus, Zenobia discovered that the ship carrying her parents and most of the other government officials was destroyed in an inexplicable collision with a floating prison colony.

Olivia didn't care for science fiction as a rule, but she was interested in Zenobia's fate, proving that Harris knew how to create a strong, complicated female character.

However, his writing was often bogged down by too many details concerning space travel or the complicated names and nuances of alien races. His minor characters also spoke in dialogue riddled with clichés.

"Let's see what will happen to Zenobia now," Olivia murmured, took a sip of coffee, and began to read.

Zenobia stepped out of the healing bath, her aching muscles and sore joints restored to normal. If only she could dip her feelings in the warm, medicinal waters and resurface without the knife twists of grief. Practicing her fighting technique in the simulation room allowed her to concentrate on something else for a little while, but when it was over and her score flashed on the wall screen, she was still filled with rage.

She'd punched the bare wall with her fists until her knuckles were shredded and dripping blood. Now, looking down at them, they were merely a little redder than the rest of her skin. She turned her hand over and touched the tattoo on her palm. It was only a few pinpricks of blue, creating a constellation known as the Hunter. The very first Chosen Ones hailed from a galaxy where the Hunter was one of the most prominent constellations in the sky. For the past one thousand years, all Chosen Ones were tattooed with this star formation at birth as a sign of their superior physical and mental prowess. The children of Chosen Ones entered into marriage contracts by the time they were five years old, but Zenobia's betrothed, a man named Halydyn, was dead, killed in a devastating space collision with a drifting prison colony.

"Everyone's dead!" Her words echoed like a rushing river in the close chamber. She put her hands over her ears, trying to shut out the strangeness of her own voice.

A message appeared on the wall screen by the door. The Regent was summoning her. There were decisions to be made, a memorial service to plan, judicial cases to be heard. He expected her to sit beside him in one of the crystal thrones beneath the Sky Dome within the hour.

"I didn't ask for this," Zenobia muttered at the silent screen as she dressed in loose pants and a blue tunic. She fastened her weapon belt, holstered her photon pistol, and twisted her fiery red hair into a Samurai's knot. "Damn it all! Why did this have to happen?"

She traced the stars of her tattoo again, as if they could somehow take her through a wormhole, to another time before the tragedy. She was sixteen years old and all alone. Her parents, her closest friends, and the man she was meant to marry were gone.

Chosen Ones were not supposed to cry. Zenobia's pride stopped the tears from coming, but there was a yawning emptiness in her chest, like a part of her had been carved out and jettisoned into deep space. She felt lost in the sparkling new palace and she wanted to run, but there was nowhere for her to go.

The deaths of the other Chosen Ones would follow her like a thousand shadows.

Olivia stopped reading, pausing to write comments here and there on Harris's word choice. The book's tone seemed to grow heavier with each sentence, but Olivia was unsure if it was the content or her experience earlier that morning that made her reticent to read any more.

"I know that look," Dixie said, appearing at her side. "You need somethin' sweet."

Save for two tables of tourists struggling to finish every morsel of their copious brunches, the diner had cleared out.

Dixie laid checks down at both booths and then slid a plate containing a slice of warm apple bread in front of Olivia. She performed an ungainly climb onto the next stool and sighed. "This is the only time I feel like I'm the same size as everybody else, but it's a right pain to get up here."

"Your brain makes up for your lack of height," Olivia replied with a smile. "And you have an uncanny gift for knowing exactly what I need to eat. My mother used to make bread like this for my first day of school and she always packed an extra slice for my teacher."

Dixie twirled a strand of her feathered hair around her finger. "I should do that. Might save me a few trips to the principal's office. I was there so much last year that I got to know all about his secretary's love life. Lord, but that woman is a tramp!"

Olivia laughed. "Thanks, Dixie. I'm going to finish this life-affirming treat and then head to the restaurant. Maybe if I watch over Michel's shoulder while he cooks I can take my mind off what I saw on the beach."

"He's a chef, 'Livia. You hang over his shoulder and you're liable to get a cleaver in the face. Go see that man of yours. If those eyes and that bod don't make you think of somethin' else besides a dead stranger, then nothin' will."

After placing a twenty on the counter, Olivia stepped out into the sunlight. Instead of walking to her car or in the direction of her lover's bookstore, she and Haviland headed for the docks. There was a decrepit building on the waterfront she'd had her eye on for some time. It was a mess, requiring months of work at enormous expense, but it was for sale. Only someone with very deep pockets and a love of old buildings would consider purchasing the dilapidated warehouse.

It was perfect for Olivia

"I couldn't do anything to help the man on the beach,"

she said to Haviland. She shielded her eyes against the sun's glare and studied the building. "But I can rescue this place. Restore a piece of Oyster Bay's history and create some new jobs. I'm in the mood for a new project. Don't you think The Bayside Crab House has a nice ring to it?"

The poodle barked his assent.

Chapter 3

We were put here as witnesses to the
miracle of life. We see the stars, and we
want them. We are beholden to give back
to the universe . . . If we make landfall
on another star system, we become
immortal.
—RAY BRADBURY

Olivia wondered if Chief Rawlings would be able to push away the images of the crime scene photos and the scant facts written on the whiteboard in the station's conference room before knocking on the door of the lighthouse keeper's cottage. But it took only a glance for her to see that the details of the investigation clung to him like cigarette smoke. His hazel eyes, which were tinged with green and gold in direct sunlight, were murky as shallows in the marshes, and the skin of his face was pinched.

Rawlings stepped forward to greet the other writers, but Olivia blocked his path and placed a tumbler of scotch whiskey in his hand.

The chief was surprised by the act. Olivia had generously refurbished the neglected building for the use of their writers' club and other community organizations, but her charitable gestures did not typically include the sharing of her twenty-five-year-old Chivas Regal. True, the cottage refrigerator was regularly stocked with beer and white wine and Olivia supplied her friends with the same bottles of fine merlot and cabernet blends featured on The Boot Top's wine list, but everyone knew better than to reach for her scotch.

"Thank you." Rawlings took a grateful sip. The night was warm, but the amber liquid felt good sliding down his throat. It settled in the pit of his empty stomach, blended with his blood, and eased the tension from his knotted neck and shoulder muscles. "A few more swallows and I might actually make some intelligent comments this evening."

Before Olivia could reply, Laurel took the chief by the arm and pulled him over to the sofa. "Are you having any luck cracking the robbery case? It happened in my neighborhood, you know."

Rawlings looked stunned for a moment, as though the loss of a well-to-do suburbanite's material possessions was the furthest thing from his mind.

"I know you're out of uniform during these meetings, but I can't stop thinking about guys in ski masks creeping around my subdivision. I haven't slept well since it happened." Laurel's anxiety was obvious.

The chief had only made it to two critique nights thus far. His schedule was unpredictable and demanding and he'd been late on both occasions. At first, the other writers had peppered him with questions concerning his whereabouts until he'd chided them for acting like a suspicious wife. He had insisted upon being allowed to leave his job behind when he stepped over the threshold into the cottage's cozy living room.

Olivia watched the lawman with interest. She knew Rawlings was a voracious reader, but he had turned out to be a skilled critic as well. Most of his comments were phrased as questions, and she wondered if he interrogated suspects with the same gentleness he'd displayed when pointing out flaws in the other writers' work. She sensed he was eager to turn his attention to Harris's chapter but was too much of a gentleman to leave Laurel's question unanswered.

"I can't say that I am aware of any updates regarding the burglaries," Rawlings finally replied.

"Burglaries?" Laurel's eyes went wide. "There's been more than one?"

"We have two open cases. One in your neighborhood and another that occurred in Sandpiper Shores several weeks ago. Similar items were taken and there was no sign of forced entry." He gave Laurel's hand a paternal pat. "We'll apprehend the thieves, don't you worry. Just keep your doors locked and your eyes open."

"The chief's got more serious bad guys to chase than a few TV-swiping cat burglars, right, Chief?" This from Millay, the Asian American bartender who wrote young adult fantasy. Millay was an exotic beauty, with full lips, dark brown eyes, and tea-hued skin. The girl seemed to deliberately mar her loveliness with brow piercings, hair tint, and heavy makeup. Tonight, for example, she wore her customary knee-length leather boots, thigh-high striped socks, a metallic miniskirt, and a T-shirt bearing a "Little Miss Sunshine" iron-on. Her hair was gelled into sharp points that hovered over her shoulder, and each tip had been dyed an electric plum. Her eyes were rimmed with black eyeliner and she wore a thick coating of lipstick in a dark cherry shade. Examining her chipped nail polish, she gave the chief a falsely nonchalant glance. "Heard something pretty nasty washed up on the Point today."

Rawlings clearly knew that he was being baited but

couldn't prevent the corners of his mouth from pulling down in irritation. "Has one of my men been tweeting about life on the Oyster Bay police force again?"

He tried to keep his voice light, but Millay shook her head. "Nah. I heard it standing in line behind some grandma in Stop 'n' Shop. She was whispering about it to one of her bingo buddies. It's gotta be all over town by now. Those biddies don't have anything better to do with their time." She tossed her skull-covered messenger bag onto the sofa. "She also told me I looked like a child of Satan and asked me if my mom knew I dressed like this."

Instead of claiming the gossip to be false, Rawlings fixed Millay with a soft gaze. "We haven't been able to ID the man. Will you keep an ear open to the talk circulating in Fish Nets over the next few days and let me know if anyone mentions a local having gone missing?" He leaned forward slightly, as though he and Millay were the only people in the room. "That woman may not understand your fashion sense, but I know you're bright and observant no matter what you wear. I could use your help. Unofficially, of course."

"Yeah, sure. No sweat." Millay's eyes twinkled. She was clearly pleased to be given the chief's trust but didn't want to let it show. The patrons of her smoke-filled drinking den weren't as loose-tongued as the senior citizens shopping at Stop 'n' Shop, but they often shared confidences with Millay. The young woman pretended she was uncomfortable with her role as confidante and chalked it up as an occupational hazard. "Goes with the territory," she'd told them months ago. "I hear stuff their wives, best buddies, and ministers don't even know. You give a man enough to drink and suddenly he's your best friend."

Olivia supposed there was some truth to that, but she also imagined that Millay's beauty had more than a little to do with the number of secrets she became privy to over her eight P.M. to two A.M. shift.

"Did I miss anything?" Harris asked as he walked in and helped himself to a beer.

Olivia pointed at the pages she held in her hand and shot Laurel a warning look. It was time to get down to business. "We were just jawing a bit, but now that you're here we can begin. Grab some food and settle in."

Harris took an unusually large slug of beer and then wiped his mouth with the back of his hand. The science fiction writer was thirty but didn't look a day over twenty-one. Boyishly handsome, he had ginger hair, an angular chin, rose red lips, and a playful laugh. He reminded Olivia of Peter Pan. Harris was more bashful than the leader of the Lost Boys, however, due to a chronic case of rosacea. As a result, he spent too much time alone with only cyber friends as company.

Over the summer Olivia had convinced Harris to try a new laser treatment offered by her aesthetician, with excellent results. The skin on Harris's face now resembled a blush instead of an angry crimson. He'd already attended a few social functions with coworkers from the computer software company where he worked developing background graphics for video games. Harris had another treatment scheduled in two weeks and Olivia hoped he'd continue to fall for the aesthetician's assurances that his treatments were free because she was conducting a clinical trial.

"Should I strap on my suit of armor?" Harris asked the other writers nervously and opened a notebook featuring UFOs on the cover.

As soon as Olivia set a platter of desserts on the coffee table, Harris lurched forward and loaded up on chocolate mousse served in white chocolate cups, miniature key lime pies, and homemade shortbread.

"I'll go first," Olivia began. "As you know, I am not a fan of science fiction. But it doesn't matter that this story is set in the future. What matters is that I am invested in Zenobia. In the beginning of chapter one I found her a little cold—a sheltered and spoiled child. At this point in the narrative, however, I empathize with this young woman and hope she can find a way to grieve while having to represent the calm and controlled face of the nobility. I think you've done a good job illustrating the difficulty she's having managing both her anger and her sorrow. Her loneliness is almost tangible and I think readers will root for her to find genuine companionship in the next few chapters." She paused, scanning over her written comments. "I'm curious about the tattoo on her palm as well. I wonder if the Hunter is based on the Orion constellation."

Harris grinned. "It is. There's a connection to the Chosen Ones and Earth. Of course, Earth has been depleted of all it natural resources, but Zenobia's people have the technology to completely restore the planet. But they won't search for our galaxy in this book. This one concentrates on Zenobia coming into her own and figuring out how to make Zulton the new home of her people."

Millay studied Harris. "I like that your heroine's not some prissy princess type. The martial arts training scene was way cool." Harris flushed a deeper shade of red at the praise. Olivia sensed the young man would do anything to gain the favor of the beautiful barkeep. "But you have *got* to change some of Zenobia's dialogue." Millay traced her hand down a page, looking for the right notation. "For example, Zenobia says she's going to squash her simulation opponent 'flat as a pancake.' I don't see pancakes as a futuristic food and it's a total cliché anyway. You do it again later on. Zenobia's 'seeing red' when she notices the Regent on her father's throne and she tells her advisor not to 'pull her leg.' Those terms don't mesh with your genre at all."

Harris looked horrified. Sticking his hands into his wavy, ginger hair, he moaned. "Ugh, those clichés really stand out now that I'm hearing them aloud."

Laurel gave Harris a kind smile. "You know what you do wonderfully in this chapter?" She held out his pages. "You make me view things through Zenobia's eyes. That scene where she walks into the throne room and looks up at the seven moons and the starry sky through that enormous glass ceiling . . ." She glanced out the cottage window where daytime was fading into twilight. The horizon over the ocean was blurred by the humidity, and the sky was a nearly colorless yellow. "I could see those moons and the star clusters and the nebulae as if they were right out that window. Whenever you described the setting using terms I understood, I was able to get *completely* lost in the scene." She hesitated. Laurel did her best to deliver criticism with a gentle touch. "But whenever you used too many futuristic terms, I couldn't visualize what you were writing about any longer. For example, I got the description of the fighting simulator, but when you started talking about Zenobia's weapons I was totally confused."

"I thought everyone knew about photon laser pistols," Harris answered in genuine surprise.

Rawlings laughed. "At least you're crediting your readers with intelligence. I researched the pistol and the bolt staff on the computer and found a fascinating site on sci-fi weapons that are being developed as prototypes by the army. After looking at drawings, I was able to imagine exactly how Zenobia's weapons operated, but you can't expect that of all your readers. I just happen to be interested in that sort of thing." He gestured around the room. "You've got to do the work for us. It would only take a sentence or two to describe the light and energy of the photon pistol or the burst of concentrated electricity from the bolt staff. Keep it short and simple."

Harris nodded. "I can do that. Would you write down that website for me? It sounds awesome!"

Handing him a piece of paper, Rawlings grinned. "I figured you might ask."

Finishing his beer, Harris sank back against the cushions with a sigh of relief. "That went better than the last chapter. I've really benefitted from our meetings. When I sit down to write, I've got you all in my head, acting like virtual editors. It's exciting to know you're going to help me shape my book into something decent. Before, I was anxious about letting you guys read it. Now, I can't wait until it's my turn again." His eyes shone. "If we keep going like this, we might all be ready to submit to agents in a year's time!"

Laurel clapped her hands and bounced up and down on the sofa. Olivia feared her friend would try to lead them in a spontaneous cheer. "Wouldn't that be something? If one of us actually got a publishing contract? We could say, 'I knew Harris *way* before he made the *New York Times* list.'"

"I don't know about that." Harris's optimism deflated somewhat. "Sci-fi isn't any easy genre to break into. Millay has a better chance with young adult fantasy or the chief here with his thriller."

Rawlings laughed again. "You're assuming my work is actually engaging."

"We'll find out this week, won't we?" Olivia asked. She couldn't wait to read the lawman's chapter. She wondered if yet another side of his complex personality would be revealed in his writing and whether she'd find it as attractive as his paintings or as repellent as the orange Hawaiian shirt he was wearing.

As the other writers packed up and headed out into the warm night, Rawlings lingered. "How are you doing?"

Olivia knew what he meant by the question. "I think I'll be haunted by that man's ruined face for quite a while." She poured them both another splash of scotch and led Rawlings out to the back deck. They settled on wooden rockers and watched Haviland sprint down the beach to the water line. The dunes were covered in shadow as the sky continued to darken. Olivia and Rawlings listened to the buzz of insects and the whisper of the waves. The chief's ability to cherish the silence, to sit and open his senses to the world around him, was, in Olivia's opinion, his finest quality. She knew very few people who didn't feel the need to fill up the quiet with the sound of their own voice.

"I feel angry," she spoke softly. "Over how the victim was turned from a man to a repulsive *thing*. Someone knew that would be the result. Only a person with a cold, deep rage could deliberately do that to another human being."

Rawlings let her words settle around them before replying. "He was also buried in the nude, holding a plastic toy sand shovel. Another degrading act. We couldn't get good prints either, as his fingertips were severely damaged. Too much skin had been sloughed off by the water and wet sand. We'll try to work on dental records come Monday, but I don't think he visited a dentist regularly."

"How old was he?"

"Barely thirty, I'd say. I thought he was older at first, but that effect was created by his rapid decomposition." Rawlings sipped from the tumbler. "I only have the ME's initial report, but the victim seemed to be in good physical condition. Looks like he was drugged before he was buried, but it's unsure at this point whether he became conscious after the killer was done . . . positioning him."

Olivia looked at the chief in horror. "Do you mean he

could have been paralyzed by the drugs or the weight of the sand but cognizant of what was happening?"

Rawlings nodded. "I don't mean to upset you. In fact, I'm only talking to you about the case . . . well, because it helps me. I'm being selfish. You're a smart woman, Olivia, and I trust your discretion. I used to tell my wife details about open investigations because she'd ask a question or make a comment and I was able to see things more clearly. The story would start to unfold, to reveal its beginning and middle. There's always a story behind every crime. And even though I'm there at the ending, it's my job to discover the source. That's how I catch the bad guys."

Haviland bounded up the steps, pressed his wet nose against Olivia's hand, and raised his ears. "You can play for a little longer," she told him and the poodle dashed away again, his black coat blending into the darkness. "There's another thing about this crime that strikes me as odd." She gestured in the direction of the isolated stretch of beach. "Why here? Was the killer counting on a remote spot to avoid the chance of a passerby coming to his victim's aid?"

Rawlings puckered his lips in thought. "I don't believe he chose the Point for that reason. The murderer was very particular. He brought his victim to a place of few inhabitants, but where eventually, the body would be found. He wasn't trying to hide what he'd done. In fact, he staged a scene. He also cleared any traces of his presence from that scene."

"Did the neighbors hear anything? A car or boat motor?" Olivia asked.

"Nothing."

Olivia listened to the ocean's murmur against the shore. The steady rhythm raised another question in her mind. "If he wanted the tableau to be found intact, he took a big risk. The tide would have ruined it had I not set out on my morning walk when I did."

Rawlings grunted and then eased himself out of the rocking chair. He walked to the railing and held on to the wood with both hands. It was the pose of a man searching for answers in the distance and Olivia imagined the chief spent less of his time looking at crime scenes, written reports, and photographs and more of it engaged in active thought. She also realized it was not a job for an impatient man. Like now, Rawlings was forced to wait for clues to come to light.

"The killer might not be a seaman, but I think he's a local. He banked on someone living on the Point to take a walk over the holiday weekend and come across that body." Rawlings turned and stared at Olivia. "I just hope he hasn't been watching that beach, gathering info on who took their strolls and when. I don't like the idea of him hiding somewhere nearby with a pair of binoculars."

Olivia glanced past him to where her poodle was splashing in the shallows. "Me either." She squared her shoulders and rubbed at the raised flesh on her arms. "But even if he did, I don't mean anything to him. I discovered his find. I played my part. He'd have no more use for me."

"We're dealing with a clever and manipulative individual."

"And a very angry one. The murderer hated the man he buried in the sand. He was disgusted with him." She exhaled.

They fell silent after that, each reflecting, and not for the first time that day, on what had provoked the killer and how he had channeled his rage, shaping it into a ruthless and premeditated crime.

"Well, I'd best get going. I could sit here all night, but I'd like to review the few facts I've got in the case file before falling asleep in front of the television." Rawlings smiled at her.

"Of course. I wish I could be of more help." Olivia took his tumbler and walked him to the front door of the cottage, calling for Haviland as she did so.

After the chief had gone, she loaded the soiled plates and glasses into the tiny dishwasher in the cottage's kitchen and turned out the lights. She locked up and then she and Haviland made their way up the sandy path through the dunes to her stone and wood Low Country–style home. Inside the living room, the most noticeable feature was the bank of windows facing the ocean. A few stars burned through the night haze but the moon wasn't visible. Searching for it out the nearest window, Olivia was suddenly aware of being alone.

Usually, she cherished her solitude, but now she felt strangely vulnerable. She knew part of this unfamiliar feeling was a reaction to the murder, but there was something about seeing Chief Rawlings drive away that had her reluctant to face a Saturday evening at home.

Casting a gaze at the clock, she suspected that her lover, Flynn McNulty, would be closing his bookstore right about now. She could picture him counting the cash from the till, switching off the coffeepot, and turning out lights. He'd flip over the hand-painted sign on Through the Wardrobe's front door from "Open" to "Closed" and, jiggling his keys as he hummed or whistled or gave some other evidence of how content he was with life, he would ride his mountain bike home.

Olivia was attracted to Flynn because he was everything she was not. A textbook extrovert, he relished the exchange of small talk and gossip with his customers. He played with their children in the store's puppet theater and bantered with them in area bars and restaurants. He was lively and friendly and fun. Everyone liked him. Men wanted to befriend him, women of all ages flirted with him, and children idolized him.

Olivia rarely saw him in the act of charming members of the general public, as she preferred to call on him once darkness had fallen. They often shared a late meal together or, if it was past dinnertime, had a nightcap on Flynn's patio. Sometimes, they'd dance on the flagstones and Flynn would croon silly songs in her ear.

Afterward, they'd have sex. Their bodies would intertwine as one day gave way to another and then, despite Flynn's protests, Olivia would leave. She couldn't wake up in his bed, the sun streaming through the slats of his blinds. She couldn't begin a new day in his house. Somehow, that would mean too much of her belonged to him. And Olivia Limoges belonged to no man.

For months, Flynn had accepted what Olivia was willing to offer. He let her initiate contact, was always available when she called, and never pried into her past. They lived completely in the present, and even though Flynn was familiar with every curve of Olivia's body, he knew very little about her as a person. In keeping with the parameters of their relationship, he limited communication to the sharing of amusing work anecdotes or the discussion of books. Literature provided the cement for their tenuous connection. They exchanged books, argued about books, and read books aloud to one another.

Without books, without the words penned by others, their relationship would have crumbled almost immediately. Instead, fictional narratives knit them together, loosely, like a mitten that could easily be unwound by tugging on a loose string.

Turning away from the window, the dark sea, and the missing moon, Olivia caught Flynn on his cell phone. He was heading out to pick up a small pizza for dinner and offered to share the pepperoni, sausage, and ham pie.

"I've already eaten," she told him. "But I can bring an excellent Chianti to accompany your gourmet meal."

Flynn loved to be teased. "You think that's fancy? You should have seen what I had for lunch. I could have sailed a paper boat in the river of grease streaming from my hamburger."

"At least you'll give a local cardiologist business in the near future."

Laughing, Flynn said, "I burn it all off when I run. For a middle-aged man-about-town, I'm the picture of health."

Olivia couldn't argue with that statement. "I hope you haven't run *too* far today. You'll need your strength for later tonight."

"Why do you think I ordered all that extra protein on my pie?" Flynn answered huskily and hung up.

Chapter 4

When a man sends you an impudent
letter, sit right down and give it back
to him with interest ten times com-
pounded, and then throw both letters in
the wastebasket.
—ELBERT HUBBARD

The Boot Top Bistro was closed on Mondays, but Olivia often went in to catch up on paperwork. She loved to sit in her small office, which was located off the kitchen near the dry goods pantry, and complete a list of mundane tasks while listening to the radio. When Michel and his team were on the job, the kitchen was filled with noise. Raised voices, the gurgle of boiling water, a knife slapping against a carving board, and the hiss of the door leading to the walk-in refrigerator blended to form the melody of industry. Today, the kitchen was silent, its stainless steel surfaces, pots, and utensils gleaming under the overhead lights.

Olivia inhaled the odors still clinging to the air from last night's meal. She detected cilantro and garlic, rosemary and butter, ground mustard, fresh scallions, and a faint trace of warm apples and nutmeg. Haviland raised his snout high and sniffed eagerly, but the lingering scent of braised lamb chops refused to materialize into lunch.

"I'll whip you up some meat and veggies in a bit, Captain. I've got the budget to balance and this week's menu to review first."

Haviland snorted, displeased to be at the mercy of the whims of his mistress. To illustrate his unhappiness, he refused to keep her company by curling up on the plush dog bed in her office. Instead, he trotted through the kitchen into the lounge and stretched out at the foot of the baby grand. The two companions ignored one another for the better part of an hour before a knock on the rear door startled Haviland into a frenzy of barking.

Assuming that a deliveryman had confused the days of the week, Olivia looked through the door's peephole and then turned to the poodle. "It's okay, Captain. It's Laurel."

Olivia opened the door and stepped aside to let Laurel in. "This is a surprise. How did you ever find me here?"

Laurel pushed a tendril of damp hair from her cheek and blushed prettily. "I've been stalking you since this morning. I drove to your house and then cruised through town, hoping to spot your Range Rover. When I couldn't find your car anywhere, I decided I had nothing to lose by coming to the restaurant. Steve and the twins are at a Labor Day moon bounce party, so I have about twenty minutes left before I have to be back."

"Has something happened?" Olivia led her friend through the kitchen and into the bar. "Do I need to start pouring?"

Laurel waved off the suggestion. "No, it's nothing like that! I wouldn't have bothered you at all, but you're the only woman I'm close to who actually enjoys her work. My other friends prefer to shop, and cook, and do crafty stuff at home . . ." She sighed and pointed at one of the leather club chairs. "Can we sit down?"

Unaccustomed to social visits at the restaurant, Olivia recovered her manners and offered Laurel her pick of refreshments, but the younger woman was only interested in capturing Olivia's full attention. "I woke up this morning and realized I don't like being at home all the time anymore. Actually, I feel a little trapped, and what I want, well . . . I want a job!"

"Here?" Olivia was dumbfounded.

"*No!*" Laurel hastily replied. "No offense, but I'm done with waitressing! I worked at a Mulligans to help pay for college. I will *never* wear suspenders again!" She covered her collarbone with her hands as though to assure herself that the offensive accessory was no longer present.

Olivia gave a soft laugh. "What job would you like?"

"I want to apply for the part-time writer position advertised in yesterday's paper." Laurel's light blue eyes twinkled. "I saw the ad and figured, why wait to become a published writer? I can start small, gain experience, and build a writing résumé. I used to write for my high school paper and I loved it!"

Olivia was impressed. "Sounds like a good opportunity. So what's the quandary?"

Turning pink with embarrassment, Laurel fiddled with the ends of her ponytail. "Steve doesn't support my decision to work part-time and frankly, neither do my in-laws."

"I thought they moved to Oyster Bay to help you with the twins. Let them watch the boys while you work."

Laurel smirked. "If you count buying the most expensive and noisy toys known to man, feeding them junk food, and keeping them up past their bedtime 'helping,' then they're doing *more* than enough, thank you very much!" She shook her head, ashamed of her outburst. "Oh my, that sounds so ungrateful, but whenever I want to do something for myself, they get really busy all of a sudden. If Steve wants to go out, then they're over in a flash, hands filled with choking hazard toys and snacks made of twelve different kinds of sugar. But they never want to babysit if it means I get to do something just for me."

Olivia was at a loss. She'd never had problems like Laurel's. She didn't have children, a husband, or in-laws. Still, her employees often came to her seeking advice concerning personal problems and she always listened intently and gave them honest counsel. Though she was unskilled at delivering her recommendations with gentleness, she made up for her directness with sincerity. In Laurel's case, Olivia decided to be as forthright as always.

"If you want this job, then you should apply for it. This is the modern era, Laurel! You don't need your husband's permission, though it would be nice to have his support." She tried to ease off the judgmental tone. "Aren't the twins doing some preschool kind of thing starting tomorrow?"

"It's just a mom's morning out provided by the church. The boys will go twice a week for two hours and I don't think that would give me enough time to research and write more than one article for the *Oyster Bay Gazette*."

Olivia considered this. "No, you'll certainly need more free time than that." A mischievous glint entered her eyes. "What if you told the in-laws that you needed their babysitting services twice a week so that you could do an activity that would meet with their approval?"

Laurel frowned. "Like what?"

"I remember you telling the Bayside Writers that Steve's mother has always been critical of your culinary skills. Tell her that in order for Steve and the boys to dine on the best possible meals you need to enroll in a cooking class. I bet she'll offer to babysit in a flash." Olivia sat back, feeling smug.

"You think I should *lie*?" Laurel looked aghast.

Olivia shrugged. "If you truly want this job, then you tell your family that you're applying for it and that's that or you're going to have to bend the truth until you're ready to stand up for yourself. They obviously see nothing wrong with *you* dancing like a puppet on strings. You're late nearly every Saturday because you feel guilty leaving your family. Don't be ashamed because you're pursuing a dream, Laurel!" Olivia knew she was being deliberately harsh, but she wanted her friend to gain a measure of freedom. "Are you a puppet or are you a writer?"

Laurel pressed her lips together and then yelled, "I'm a writer! They think they can control everything I do, but I'm my *own* person. I'm *not* just a mother and a wife! I'm *me* too! Laurel! There are things I'm good at, even though I can't smock or cook coq au vin." She nibbled a fingernail. "Um, where *would* I be taking this fictional cooking class?"

Wordlessly, Olivia gestured around the empty restaurant.

"Oh, you're the best!" Laurel did one of her trademark happy hand claps coupled with a great deal of bouncing up and down on the chair. "But what happens when I burn the Thanksgiving turkey again?"

"Leave the culinary dilemmas to me. You march right down to that newspaper and apply for that job." She eyed Laurel's outfit. "But go home and put something else on first. I think you've got maple syrup on your shirt and a piece of pancake mashed into your necklace."

"That would be Dermot." Laurel examined the stains with pride and then rose slowly to her feet. "I've never done anything like this before. I'm about to deceive my family and I know it should feel wrong, but it doesn't. I want this job and I deserve a chance to do something more fulfilling than laundry and grocery shopping!"

Olivia wished her friend good luck and tried not to stiffen when Laurel suddenly embraced her. The younger woman then jogged out to her car, her ponytail swinging like a golden scythe.

Haviland cocked his head and stared at his mistress.

"What are you looking at?" Olivia demanded and the poodle flashed her a toothy smile. "You'd better not give me that 'you're a softie' look if you want lamb with rice and peas! After all, this is how normal people are supposed to act. They're supposed to listen to one another and accept hugs without turning to stone and—"

Haviland cut her off with a quick howl that sounded much like laughter.

"You're right, I'll never be quite like that, but I *am* trying to cast off my Ice Queen image." She opened the walk-in refrigerator and Haviland's ears perked up. "Maybe 'cast off' isn't the best word choice. Perhaps 'defrost' is a better way of putting it. Ah, here's the lamb!"

Pressing his snout against Olivia's palm, Haviland searched for bite-sized cubes of juicy lamb and, sensing they were close at hand, began to shift his front paws in anticipation.

Once Olivia had satisfied her poodle's hunger, she satiated her own by fixing a spinach salad with lamb, feta cheese, and pecan crumbles accompanied by a side of pita wedges toasted with a sprinkling of Parmesan and fresh basil. She never prepared meals like this in her own home, but there was something about the spacious, gleaming kitchen that made her want to cook.

Later, once the budget had been balanced and she'd placed phone orders to the distributors still open for business on Labor Day, she reviewed Michel's menu for the upcoming week. Making a note in the margins that her chef needed to add two more vegetarian selections (Michel, like Haviland, loved his meat), Olivia began to go through Saturday's mail.

She sorted through two pounds of junk mail, including catalogs from restaurant supply companies, credit card and refinancing offers, form letters from big-name banks and insurance companies entreating Olivia to give them her business, and the weekly flyer from Pizza Bay.

Olivia examined the flimsy yellow and red paper featuring the graphic of a smiling fisherman holding a slice of pizza with one hand as he manned the helm with the other. "Best in the Bay!" the ad proclaimed and provided a coupon for two free toppings or a free side of garlic bread sticks. "Why send coupons to a five-star restaurant week after week after week? Do they enjoy wasting paper?" she asked Haviland.

Too full to muster up the strength required to even open an eye, Haviland remained unresponsive. "What would the Pizza Bay delivery boy do if I actually placed an order during business hours? Come right to the hostess podium wearing that hideous electric yellow T-shirt and holding a warming box?" She grinned. "I might have to try that sometime. Teach those Pizza Bay owners a lesson about mass mailing."

The local printing and copy center had obviously not produced the last letter in the pile. Olivia's name and the restaurant's address had been handwritten in black ink on a plain white envelope. The penmanship was childlike and the letters seemed to have been driven into the paper as though a great deal of force had been applied. There was no return address and the post office stamp showed that the letter had originated in Wilmington, which was roughly one hundred and fifty miles south of Oyster Bay.

Her curiosity aroused, Olivia ripped open the letter and pulled out a single sheaf of lined three-hole paper. Picturing the sticker-covered binder of a grade school student, she briefly wondered why some child would be communicating with her.

Then she read the message.

YOUR FATHER IS NOT DEAD. HE HAS BEEN WITH US FOR THIRTY YEARS, BUT NOW HES REAL SICK. IF YOU WANT TO SEE HIM WHILE HES STILL BREETHING, SEND $1000 CASH TO THIS ADRESS. IF YOU TELL ANYONE THE DEALS OFF.

Following these astonishing lines was a street address in Wilmington. Apparently, the cash was to be sent in care of a man named RB.

Olivia hurled the paper onto her desk and shoved her wheeled chair backward so violently that she nearly tipped over. Haviland, jolted out of his full-belly slumber, jumped onto his feet with an alarmed snarl, his brown eyes darting about the room, searching for the source of danger. Anxiously, he sniffed Olivia's hands, but she made no move to comfort him. Her eyes burned as they stared fixedly at the paper on her desk.

"It cannot be true," she whispered. Haviland grew more and more disconcerted by her immobility. He sniffed her again and placed his left front paw on her lap. Absently, she touched the fur on his neck, but her gaze remained on the letter. "It isn't possible."

Olivia never drank alcohol until five thirty in the afternoon, but today she didn't think twice about breaking this custom. She marched out of her office and straight to the bar. Taking down a clean tumbler from Gabe the bartender's neat row of polished glasses, she poured out two fingers of Chivas Regal, drank it in a single gulp, and refilled. This time, she added a splash of water and carried the tumbler back to her office.

Keeping her distance from the letter, she rummaged in a desk drawer until she found a magnifying glass. She then examined every inch of the notebook paper and the envelope from which it came, but found nothing of significance.

Next, she turned to the Internet, calling up a map of the North Carolina coast.

Her father had disappeared on his boat after leaving the mouth of Oyster Bay Harbor and entering Pamlico Sound. He could certainly have motored close enough to Wrightsville Beach or the port area of Wilmington, abandoned the boat, and swum ashore. He could have also hopped aboard another fishing vessel and headed out for a long journey in deep waters, but Olivia had always dismissed that theory because it meant that he didn't want to be found, that he deliberately let his daughter believe that it was the fog and the whiskey and the angry seas that had claimed his life.

She traced the bumpy coastline on the computer screen. Was it possible? *Could* her father be alive? Could he be as close as Wilmington?

"How do you know who I am?" she asked the anonymous writer angrily, jabbing at the paper with her letter opener. The blade landed near one of the holes, slicing it neatly all the way to the edge. It was satisfying, and for a moment, Olivia was tempted to cut the entire letter to shreds, to stab and slice it until she could convince herself that it had never existed.

"But it does exist and I need to decide what to do about it." She put the opener away in the drawer and held the letter under the light. "No Harvard graduate here. Either that, or this writer doesn't proofread." Missing apostrophes, spelling errors, and the use of capital letters throughout seemed to emphasize her initial reaction about the author; that he or she didn't put pen to paper very often.

" 'He's been with us for thirty years,' " she repeated the line aloud. "Who is 'us'?" She took a drink. "Who the *hell* is '*us*'!"

Anger swelled inside her, but she held it in check. She needed to think straight. Why would this person approach her after all this time? Either the letter writer needed money or her father did. When Olivia's grandmother died, leaving the Limoges oak-barrel fortune to her only relative, Olivia, news of the young woman's incredible wealth had been in all the papers.

For years, paparazzi kept tabs on her every move, but she had eventually escaped to the one place they wouldn't bother to track her. She returned home and became a businesswoman, homeowner, and solid member of the community. She no longer jetted around the world, dated famous bachelors, or dressed in haute couture. Therefore, she was no longer interesting to the press, but her name was still well known. People could find Olivia Limoges if they looked hard enough.

"I could risk the money," she said to Haviland, who was giving her his full attention. "That's not a problem. I just don't want to be made a fool of."

Once again, she turned back to the computer. She did a Google search for RB of Wilmington, North Carolina, but found nothing. However, when she typed the address into the search box, she was directed to a Yellow Page listing. RB's address was actually a mailbox located in a UPS store.

"That tells me nothing!" she banged on the keyboard in frustration. Downing the rest of her drink, she stood behind her desk chair and grabbed the cushion until her knuckles turned white. "What can I do?"

The poodle grunted and turned in circles by the door. He was ready to leave and his mistress's edginess was wearing on him.

Noting Haviland's discomfort, Olivia grabbed the letter, shoved it back into the envelope, and turned off the office lights. "There's only one person who can advise me about this enigma. Come along, Captain. Off to the police station."

When they pulled into the police station parking lot, Haviland yipped in excitement. He was very fond of Greta, Oyster Bay's attractive canine officer. The two dogs had met on several occasions and had always exchanged dignified but affectionate sniffs, nose rubs, and tail wags. Olivia sensed that Haviland had been gravely disappointed when they didn't run into Greta on Saturday, as she and her fellow officer were out on patrol.

There was no sign of Greta in the police department's lobby and the female officer manning the reception desk had her hands full with a truculent tourist. The furious man waved a parking ticket while releasing a torrent of insults. Though the officer did her best to remain composed, it was clear that she wouldn't stay calm much longer.

Suddenly, the red-faced man tore the ticket into tiny pieces and threw them on the counter, jabbing his index finger inches away from the woman's face. The officer's eyes blazed with indignation. She picked up her phone and requested backup. Taking advantage of the distraction, Olivia opened the door to a hallway. She and Haviland slipped inside and hurried past office doors until they reached the one bearing Sawyer Rawlings' name in brass.

Olivia knocked and waited.

"This had better be good," Rawlings growled from within. When he saw Olivia and Haviland, a mixture of surprise and delight replaced his sullen expression.

"Don't get up," Olivia said as Rawlings moved to stand. "I'm sorry to interrupt. I know the local press has gotten wind of your case and you must be very busy."

"I wish there was something for me to be busy *doing*." Rawlings was obviously irked. "We still have no ID for our victim and no matching dental records either. I'm going to have to ask for the public's help and I can't tell you how many fruitcakes will call or drop by the second the television announcement runs." He waved at the window. "Everyone with a Superman complex will line up in the lobby."

Without waiting to be asked, Olivia sat in one of the two chairs facing the chief's tidy desk. "I take it the medical examiner's report provided no additional clues."

"Only that our victim wasn't drugged." Rawlings picked up a rubber band and wound it around his thumb and index finger. "There was duct tape residue on his neck, implying that a bag was taped over his head long enough to cause him to lose consciousness. Before burying the victim in the sand, the killer tried to remove all signs of the tape but missed a few pieces."

Olivia tried to push away the picture forming in her mind of a man fighting desperately to breathe, his lips drawing in plastic while his frantic exhalations fogged up the bag, blurring the movements of his attacker. "Run-of-the-mill silver duct tape?"

Rawlings nodded. "Yes. Even if I got a record of every duct tape sale over the last thirty days from Hampton's Hardware, there are still dozens of places across the county to buy the stuff. Grocery stores, auto parts centers, gas stations." He ran a hand over his cheek, pausing to rub an area of stubble he'd missed while shaving that morning.

"I wish I could tell you that I was here because I had useful information, but I don't." Olivia withdrew the envelope from her purse. "My visit is purely selfish. I'd like your opinion on this if you can spare the time."

The lines on Rawlings' forehead deepened as he accepted the letter. He paused, and Olivia knew he was seeing something in her face he'd never seen there before. Sorrow, carefully tucked away for many years, surfaced in her dark blue eyes.

She could feel him nearly reach for her hand, but when

she gazed at the lined paper in his grasp, he turned his attention to the words written in bold black ink.

When he was finished, he didn't speak right away but turned to the window and stared out at the purple crape myrtle trees lining the parking lot.

"The author of this letter is interested in money," he said eventually. "If you give him the initial payment, he will ask for more." He laced his fingers together and looked at Olivia. "Do you think there's a possibility that this claim is true? That your father is alive and possibly unwell?"

Hesitating, Olivia smoothed out the letter's envelope in her lap. She didn't answer for a long time. "I do. I think someone recently discovered that he and I are related and decided to profit from that knowledge. For example, my father could be in a hospital where one of his nurses figured out our connection." She pointed at the letter. "This person wrote me because my father is sick. That strikes me as being the truth."

Rawlings considered this theory. "Not a nurse. Someone with less education." he said. "So we're assuming that your father has been lying low for thirty years?"

"Yes," Olivia answered through tight lips.

"Without filing for taxes or leaving a paper trail of any kind." The chief appeared impressed. "Your grandmother hired a private investigator to search for him, didn't she?"

"Several. They all came up empty-handed. My father's boat was found adrift with all his gear aboard. I don't see how he could make a living without that trawler." Her memory strayed back to the night she'd pushed the little dingy away from the hull of her father's boat, away from his rage and his raised fist, the hate in his black eyes and the stink of whiskey on his breath. "They found several empty liquor bottles on board. Everyone came to the conclusion he'd drowned. He was an alcoholic. He was depressed.

And that night, he was raving. I could see him—have often imagined him—losing his balance and pitching backward into the ocean."

Rawlings sat very still. "Thereby acquiring peace."

Olivia nodded, her throat tight with emotion. "I know he felt responsible for my mother's death. I did too. He couldn't run away from the guilt, but he tried. He took long fishing trips, leaving me alone at home. I preferred to have him at sea, because when he was around, our little house was too small for his grief, the whiskey, and my mother's ghost."

Now Rawlings did come around his desk. He sat down in the chair next to Olivia, his knees touching hers. He put a large, warm hand over her thinner, colder one. "I can see that you want to answer this letter, but as your friend, I have to warn you against doing so. Let's say that your father is alive and you pay thousands of dollars to discover his whereabouts. You rush to his bedside and then what? What are you hoping for?"

"I don't know!" Olivia's reply held anger, but it was not directed at Rawlings. "Maybe I want to have a copy of his medical history so I can see what I've got in store! Maybe I want the chance to call him a bastard to his face before he dies. Maybe I want to spit in his face and ask him what kind of man leaves a little girl all alone day after day and then, one day, abandons her forever!"

Horrified to notice that tears wet her cheeks, Olivia pulled her hand out from under the chief's and turned away.

"You want the truth," he finished her thought, his tone quiet and soothing. "Even if it opens old wounds or causes fresh ones. You want the truth, no matter what the cost."

Her eyes met his. Olivia nodded, grateful for both his words and his gentleness. He understood. He understood everything. "Just promise me one thing," he said. "If this turns out to be a hoax and we're able to track down the letter writer, then you hand him or her over to me. If there ends up being no truth, then I will give you something else. Justice."

She could have kissed him then. His entire body was radiating a righteous authority and his eyes gleamed with conviction, the muddy brown alive with glints of gold. And she knew at that moment that he would do a great deal to defend and to protect her and that something had changed between them on this day.

She had laid herself bare to Rawlings and he had treated her naked emotions with care.

Reclaiming the letter from his desk, Olivia was afraid to look at him again for fear he'd see that she was, at that moment in time, completely in awe of him. Instead, she put her palm on his forearm and let it linger there for a brief second, before rising and pulling open his office door. "I'll see you Saturday, Chief. Thank you for your time."

As she walked away Olivia sensed that she had stirred something inside Rawlings, something that might have been lying dormant in the depths of his heart for a long time.

She wondered, glancing at the purple crape myrtle blooms beneath his window, what would become of this newfound longing between them.

Chapter 5

There is nothing like looking, if you want to find something. You certainly usually find something, if you look, but it is not always quite the something you were after.

—J. R. R. TOLKIEN

Olivia told no one else about the letter. She put it away in a desk drawer at home, beneath a utility bill. Even though it was out of sight, the letter called to her. Whenever she sat down at the desk to work on her manuscript, her concentration was completely ruined by the knowledge of what sat in her bill drawer.

Until she had found the body on the beach, Olivia had been making steady progress on her novel, becoming fully immersed in her fictionalized version of Egypt during the reign of Ramses the Second. But neither her character, a concubine named Kamila, nor the charisma of the famous Nineteenth Dynasty pharaoh could draw Olivia's attention from the letter.

Finally, on Friday, she took the envelope from the drawer, yanked out the single piece of paper, and read the scant lines though she already knew every word by heart.

Her computer screen was covered by images of the clothing and jewelry worn by the nobility of Ancient Egypt, but Olivia closed every website window and began a new search. She knew the pull of her novel wasn't strong enough to distract her from the letter and that she needed to take action. In this case, Olivia required the services of the sharpest private investigator in Wilmington.

After researching several firms, she made a decision, picked up the phone, and asked to speak to the agency's owner. Coming right to the point, Olivia explained that she wanted eyes on a particular mailbox housed in The UPS Store.

"I want photographs of this RB person. I want a background check. I want to know where he lives, the details of his family life, his profession, and what he does in his spare time. I want a week's worth of information on this man so that by the time you've cashed my sizable check, I'll feel like I've known him my whole life," Olivia directed.

When the investigator probed her for more explanation, the only response Olivia gave was, "Let's just say that he's invited me to make an investment, and before I send him money, I need to learn what kind of man I'd be dealing with."

Olivia could tell the PI wasn't convinced, but he was wise enough not to push the matter. It was an easy, low-risk assignment and would bring in much-needed revenue.

"I'll pay you half of your fee up front," Olivia offered quickly. "But I want your promise that you'll handle this job yourself. I read about the profiling classes you took and I want *your* take on this man. No one else's will suffice."

Assurances were given and she was transferred to a secretary who took her credit card number and billing information. Olivia hung up the phone in higher spirits. Hiring the detective had allowed her to regain a sense of control. She folded the letter, tucked it back into its envelope, and walked over to the floor-to-ceiling bookshelves flanking the stone fireplace.

After studying the books for several moments, she took down a hardcover called *Snow Flower and the Secret Fan* and slipped the letter between its pages. Since the novel centered on a series of secret letters written in code on a Japanese fan, Olivia found the book an appropriate hiding place for her troublesome missive.

She then replenished her empty coffee cup and gave Haviland a kiss on his cool black nose, feeling ready to devote her complete attention to her character's dilemma. Kamila's sycophantic aunt had given the young concubine to the pharaoh's sandal bearer as though she were chattel, when in truth she was an intelligent young woman and a skilled dancer. Told by the other concubines that her only chance to secure a future in the palace was to bear Pharaoh a child, Kamila waited to be called to the king's bed.

Olivia had written to the scene where the Living God finally requested Kamila's presence. She now needed to describe the young woman's failure to seduce mighty Ramses.

Kamila had been meticulously prepared for a night of lovemaking with the king. Servants had washed and waxed her, rubbed and oiled her, perfumed her wig, and clothed her in a linen shift so fine that it appeared to have been spun out of filaments of mist.

One of Pharaoh's eunuchs came to collect Kamila. The other concubines and lesser wives tittered excitedly as she was led away, but Kamila trembled behind the giant mute as he led her through the cool passageways. Their shadows rippled on the walls and a thousand fears coursed through Kamila's mind. Would the Living God be gentle or would he pin her down on the sleeping couch, his regal hands encircling her wrists and squeezing, tighter and tighter, as his desire grew? Would her inexperience repulse or delight him? The other girls spoke boldly of Ramses' skill as an adept lover. Surely the act could not be painful if they wanted to repeat it even after bearing the king a son.

Ramses was seated on a gilded stool examining a papyrus drawing when Kamila entered the chamber. She prostrated herself before the Lord of the Two Lands but he quickly bade her rise, dismissed the eunuch, and gestured for her to approach his royal person. He was tall and muscular with a firm jaw and a strong nose. His eyes were dark as night in the dim chamber, but he smiled at her kindly and she was finally able to breathe.

"I have been anxiously awaiting these plans. This is how I shall improve upon the temple of Amun-Re," he told her, gesturing at the scroll. "Would you like to see?"

Kamila crept closer to the man, curiosity overwhelming her unease. She forced her gaze from his noble profile to the drawing laid out before him.

"It is magnificent! The gods will be very pleased!" she declared a trifle too loudly, but Ramses laughed.

"I have lost much sleep over this project." He stared at the plans again. "And because of other cares as well." His eyes slid to her face. "Tell me. How do you find sleep when you are troubled?"

Kamila flushed. She hadn't expected the king to ask her such an intimate question, but she answered truthfully. "I sing to myself, Great One. Always the same tune. It was my mother's favorite song. My voice is not as lovely as hers, but as I grow older I sound more and more like her."

Ramses turned from her and stretched out on the sleeping couch. Folding his arms over his chest, he closed his eyes and commanded, "Sing it for me."

For a moment, Kamila didn't move. This was not what she had expected, but a command was a command. Softly, she began to sing.

"The lotus petals come floating past/ carried in the river's arms/ the reeds whisper a tale to me/ and the ibis flies where I cannot go/ but I have fields to tend and oxen to lead/ the soil is more precious than lapis stones . . ." Kamila trailed off, her mind skipping to the next stanza in which the farmer touches the freshly turned earth and knows he is blessed to be an Egyptian. Omitting the words, she softly hummed the melody instead, seeing that the king had fallen asleep.

She hummed until the candle burned low. Silently, the eunuch reappeared and beckoned for her to exit the chamber. He led her to her own pallet in a room filled with the sighs and stirrings of sleeping women and then left, noiseless as a breath of air.

Kamila's friend, Mery, was a very light sleeper. The moment Kamila curled up on her pallet, Mery sat up on an elbow and whispered, "Well? Did you please him?"

Kamila closed her heavy eyes. "I do not know."

Mery reached over and touched Kamila's hand. "There will be another time. You're one of the most beautiful women in the entire palace."

"I need to be more than that. The king is surrounded by beauty. I must offer him something he does not have in excess, but what do I give that would please one who owns everything?" Kamila asked miserably and then, hearing no reply from her perplexed friend, fell into a troubled sleep.

Olivia's fingers moved swiftly over the keyboard. Ramses sent for Kamila twice more and each night she sang him to sleep, acting the part of nursemaid instead of lover. One day, the king and his retinue abruptly left the palace to meet with a team of architects and stonemasons at Karnak. Unsure of what Kamila would do in the pharaoh's absence, Olivia saved what she'd written and closed the file.

Stretching her arms over her head, she wondered if there was enough time to read the chief's chapter before heading out to her lunch date. She had requested a meeting with an agent from Coastal Realty. The Realtor, a polished, seventy-year-old matron named Millicent Banks, promised to bring Olivia a file folder stuffed with documents pertaining to the crumbling warehouse on the waterfront.

"I could probably critique two pages before I have to go," Olivia said, removing the stapled packet Rawlings had distributed to the Bayside Book Writers last Saturday. The chief had already confessed that his book was yet untitled so she searched for the beginning of chapter one. However, the first two pages were stuck together and as Olivia peeled them apart, she realized they were identical. Flipping through the packet, she noted that every page was a copy of page one.

Pulling up her online address book, she called Harris at work.

"You got fifteen copies of the same page too, huh?" Harris laughed. "I guess we're all busted for putting off our critique homework 'til this late in the week. Millay called me at two in the morning to tell me about the duplicate pages. I figured she'd get a hold of Rawlings and set him straight. Personally, I don't have the guts to dial the chief of police's number just to point out that he screwed up."

"Not phoning a policeman in the middle of the night sounds less like courage and more like self-preservation to me," Olivia remarked.

"I think Millay likes to talk a big game, but I bet she'd do it if someone dared her." Harris was quick to defend the attractive bartender.

Olivia decided to change the subject. "Did Millay happen to mention whether she'd heard about any missing persons? The chief still hasn't been able to identify the body I found on the Point."

Harris yawned loudly. "Sorry. I'm trying to remember what else she said. I was in the middle of this crazy dream where trolls were tearing apart my high school when she called. That's what happens when you create fantasy settings all day long. You start seeing the images in your sleep." He paused. "But no, she hasn't had word from her regulars about anyone having gone AWOL. There's been plenty of talk about the murder though. Even here at work, where most of us are total ostriches and have no idea what's going on in the outside world, people are coming up with all kinds of crazy theories."

"At least the story didn't break until Monday. Most of the tourists were packing up by the time they saw the headlines in the *Gazette*," Olivia said, recalling the media coverage of the past week. The local news channels had done their best to spin the story into as many segments as they could, but by Thursday night, it was clear there was no fresh information to convey.

There was also a hotter news topic to cover, being that Tropical Storm Ophelia was now speeding northeast toward the North Carolina coast. The meteorologists called for rain beginning on Saturday with high wind gusts due in by Sunday morning. A team of experts, all of whom had come up with a bevy of scientific-sounding excuses as to why they'd called for the storm to move northwest into the Atlantic, was now falling all over themselves to predict the height of the storm surge and total amount of rainfall Ophelia would produce.

Despite her own interest in the storm, as she'd have to determine whether to close The Boot Top and plan what she and Havilland would eat once they lost power, Olivia had been wondering if the police department's appeal for help had garnered anything useful. Now, Rawlings' incomplete chapter gave her the perfect excuse to contact the chief.

Olivia realized she hadn't been paying attention to Harris, who was prattling on about his latest software development. She tuned in just in time to hear his description of how the trees he created could come to life and grab video game warriors in their clawlike branches. "Oh! Oh crap!" He sounded alarmed. "I've gotta run! There's a major bug in this code! My tree just ripped an elf in half. Elves are supposed to be immune to nature attacks!"

"Sounds serious," Olivia sympathized and, after wishing Harris good luck, tried to reach the chief. Unfortunately, Rawlings was unavailable and Olivia didn't feel like leaving a message. She sent him a quick e-mail instead, requesting that he send an attachment containing his chapter in its entirety. *Otherwise, tomorrow's meeting will be extremely brief,* she added. She cc'd the rest of the Bayside Book Writers so no one else harassed Rawlings over his missing pages.

As she drove into town for her lunch meeting, Olivia wondered how Laurel's interview had gone. Olivia was surprised by her own interest in the subject. She wasn't used to being intimately involved in other people's personal lives, but she felt protective of Laurel and wanted the younger woman to succeed.

"I guess she didn't get the job or we would have heard from her by now," Olivia said to Haviland.

The poodle glanced at her and then stuck his head back out the open passenger window, his tongue unrolling from between his lips like a length of pink carpet. The humidity had dropped, the powerful September sun was obscured by a thick cloud cover, and the salt-tinged air clearly appealed to Haviland.

"Don't worry, Captain, your day is only going to get better from here on out." Olivia parked in the loading zone in front of Beach Burgers. "Guess where we're having lunch."

Haviland pawed his seat belt and barked. The moment Olivia released the belt, he leapt through the open car window and waited impatiently on the sidewalk for Olivia to collect her purse and briefcase. Prancing beside her, Haviland displayed his best grin to all the passersby, receiving dozens of compliments from the townsfolk. The only person who seemed displeased to see him was Millicent Banks, the Realtor.

"I'd heard that your pooch accompanies you everywhere, but I put that down as rumor," Millicent said as she plastered on her professional smile.

"He goes where I go. Think of him as my benevolent shadow. At least no one will try to steal your purse while he's around." The Realtor unconsciously held on to her Chanel clutch a little tighter as Olivia turned away to tell the café's hostess they'd like a patio table.

Millicent blanched. "Are you sure? It's still rather hot, even though that nice wind from the incoming storm has chased away the humidity."

"Trust me, it's much hotter inside. The kitchen's open and the heat from the fryers has no place else to go but into the dining room," Olivia assured her. "In any case, I try to dine al fresco whenever Haviland is with me. People find it less offensive to eat near an animal when he's outside," she explained. "Haviland probably has better table manners than most of their children, but I try to be discreet about serving him his meal around two-legged patrons."

Millicent curled her lip in distaste but quickly tried

to hide her face with her menu before her client noticed. Olivia knew the Realtor tried to please all prospective clients. Millicent's motto wasn't "You can bank on Millicent!" for nothing. Olivia could only assume Millicent had heard of Olivia's fondness for historic properties and planned to milk that angle for all it was worth. If Olivia wanted to buy a dilapidated warehouse so be it. "I brought all the documents you requested," Millicent said after they'd ordered. She then casually passed Olivia a legal-sized manila folder. "This building has *quite* a colorful past."

"As do all interesting ladies," Olivia said with a wry grin.

Millicent squeezed lemon into her iced tea. "During the late eighteen hundreds, it was a turpentine warehouse. Things were chugging merrily along until a careless foreman started a fire that destroyed half the place and *both* of the neighboring structures. I read an old newspaper clipping stating that *five* men died in the blaze."

"Must have been a difficult conflagration to handle with a bucket brigade," Olivia commented while accepting her pepper jack and barbeque bacon burger from the waitress.

Millicent wasn't going to be sidetracked by Victorian methods of fire fighting. She continued with her history lesson. "The building was repaired and became a cotton mill. It was well maintained right into the next century." She consulted her notes. "In the mid-1950s it housed a plumbing supply business and in the seventies, was sold and divided into various retail spaces. One business bought out most of the leases and didn't close its doors until the year two thousand."

Olivia was hooked. Setting aside her food, she flipped through pages in the folder and felt the excitement of a new project beginning to rise. "I wasn't living in Oyster Bay at that time. What did the most recent retailer sell?"

Blushing, Millicent fiddled with her iced tea spoon. "The

products? Well, they were, ah, goodness!" She clasped her hands primly on the table. "I believe they sold lingerie and, ah, adult toys and things of *that* nature."

"My, my." Olivia was amused. She held up a photograph of the building. "This old lady *does* have a colorful past."

Ignoring the remark, Millicent pushed her fork around her Cobb salad. "The town wanted to convert the structure into a small performing arts center, but in the end, it proved to be less expensive to build something from the ground up." She frowned. "It's a shame the Historic Society couldn't act, but they just don't have much of a budget and there are so many buildings in need of preservation."

Olivia's gaze returned to the photograph of the wood and brick building. The basic shape was perfect—a long rectangle with a giant bank of windows facing the water. She could easily envision an expansive second-story deck filled with wrought-iron tables, potted plants, and fairy lights. A live band could play inside on weekends with acoustic ensembles entertaining patrons during lunch and weekday meals. Before she got too occupied by images of checkered tablecloths and disposable lobster bibs, however, she needed to know whether the building was truly salvageable.

"What happened to the last deal?" she asked Millicent. "When I first examined the building, there was a 'Sold' sign out front. And please be straightforward. The absolute truth is important to me."

Millicent looked affronted. "I wouldn't dream of sugarcoating my reply, Ms. Limoges." She immediately softened her tone. "The warehouse was to be turned into luxury loft apartments, but when the investors saw what it would cost to make the transformation, they backed out. No one felt the permanent residents of Oyster Bay would be willing to spend that kind of money on a monthly lease. They also agreed that the average tourist preferred to rent a vacation home or condo within walking distance to the beach."

The explanation sounded plausible. "So it had nothing to do with the integrity of the building? Did they plan to renovate the original structure or tear it down and start from scratch?"

"As far as I know, they were going to work with what they had." Millicent dabbed her lips with her napkin and pushed her nearly untouched salad bowl away. "But the total estimate was no small sum. Revitalizing this building is not a project for the faint of heart," she said, showing Olivia that she was on her side. "Of course, this isn't your first time handling a major project such as this. Look at how you transformed so many of our empty storefronts. Thanks to you, I now have a new favorite dress shop."

Though the Realtor was laying it on a bit thick, Olivia didn't mind feeling a little pleased when it came to the part she played in reshaping the town. "We've got to collect every hard-earned tourist dollar we can. Something's got to tide us over during the winter months." She removed the bun from a plain hamburger, cut the meat into bite-sized pieces, and set the plate on the ground near her left foot. Haviland, who had been pretending to doze in the shade of Olivia's chair, crept up to the dish and daintily wolfed down his lunch.

"Yes, indeed," Millicent agreed. "At least we have the Cardboard Regatta coming up. Used to be the town was empty from Labor Day to May Day, but I cannot believe how many people will fill up the hotels again just for the chance to race their little handmade boats. I do hope Ophelia has come and gone in time."

Olivia closed the folder and stuffed it in her purse. She took out her wallet and signaled for the waitress. "I'm going to have my contractor go over every inch of this property as soon as the storm passes. Assuming he gives me a good report and the warehouse manages to survive Ophelia, I'll stop by your office and we can draw up an offer." Olivia reached across the table and shook Millicent's hand. "Thank you for joining me for lunch. If I'd known you weren't fond of burgers I would have chosen another venue. This place isn't exactly known for their salads."

"Oh, my salad was *perfectly* fine. I'm just trying to watch my figure," Millicent lied grandly. "I look forward to hearing from you when we're done being battered about by Ophelia."

The Realtor walked away and Olivia imagined the older woman was already dreaming of how she'd spend the sizable commission she'd make off the deal. Olivia didn't mind. In fact, she admired Millicent's ambition and hoped to have the same amount of pluck in thirty years' time.

Olivia decided to let Haviland chase pigeons in the park before hitting the grocery store followed by a latte at Bagels 'n' Beans. She settled on a bench in the shelter of a mammoth magnolia tree and took out her latest purchase from Flynn's bookstore, Sharon Kay Penman's *The Reckoning*. As Haviland explored the fascinating scents at the base of every shrub, tree, and light post, Olivia quickly lost herself in the story of Llewelyn ap Gruffydd, the thirteenth-century Welsh prince.

She was so immersed in the novel that the ringing of her cell phone seemed incongruent with Penman's descriptions of stone castle walls and heavy bed hangings.

"I could chose to ignore you," she warned the phone before checking the caller ID, but seeing that the number belonged to Laurel, Olivia answered. "Do you have news?" she asked her friend.

"Yes!" Laurel managed to encapsulate fear, joy, and exhilaration into a single word. "It's *wonderful*! And it's *horrible*! I'm a mess!"

Olivia grinned. "You got the job."

"I got the job," Laurel squeaked in excitement. "They just told me. But it's only on a provisional basis. I need to prove myself over the next few weeks. How am I going to do that? My silly articles on how to get stains out of your clothes or the best play areas for toddlers will hardly dazzle the editor and they've already got three reporters covering the storm!"

"Why don't you interview your neighbor?" Olivia suggested. "The one who was robbed? Everyone likes to read about local crimes. But you should do it soon. Everyone will be busy preparing for the storm before long."

Laurel gasped. "You're so *brilliant*! They say that crime pays. Let's see if it can get *me* paid too!" She hesitated. "Listen, Olivia, I know it's a lot to ask, but I haven't interviewed anyone since high school and the articles I wrote back then focused on the captains of the sports teams and the homecoming queens. This is *so* much more serious. Will you come with me?"

Normally, Olivia would have turned Laurel down flat without the slightest tinge of regret, but she was curious about the burglary and wanted to hear the victim's account firsthand. "I'll pretend to be your cameraman. Just this once. And, Laurel, we'd better go tomorrow before the rain moves in."

"Thank you, thank you, thank you!" Laurel squealed. "I'll call my friend and set it up." Another pause. "Um, do you have a decent digital camera?"

Olivia let loose a wry chuckle before agreeing to bring a camera with her as well. Laurel obviously recognized she'd pushed her friend far enough and quickly hung up.

Whistling for Haviland, Olivia led him back to the car. "Change of plan, Captain. We're driving to New Bern to buy a congratulations-on-maybe-getting-a-job gift for Laurel, that sweet nitwit."

Haviland panted and rolled his eyes.

Olivia removed a water jug from the back of the Range Rover and filled the poodle's travel dish while Haviland cast a longing glance in the direction of the park. "The squirrels will still be there when we return, Captain. They have an uncanny ability to make it through the worst weather conditions." She gazed at the mothers pushing strollers, the elderly couples reading newspapers on the wooden benches, and the occasional jogger sailing beneath the green canopy of the park's mature trees, and frowned in concern. "I can only hope the people of Oyster Bay are as fortunate."

Chapter 6

But what is the difference between literature and journalism? Journalism is unreadable and literature is not read.
—OSCAR WILDE

No one heard back from Rawlings that Friday, but Olivia and the Bayside Book Writers nearly forgot about their next meeting in light of new concerns regarding the impending storm. Over the course of the night, Ophelia shrugged off her title of tropical storm. Now a category two hurricane, she gained the undivided attention of the residents living on the coasts of North Carolina and Virginia.

Upon waking Saturday morning, Olivia switched on the television and listened to three different updates on Ophelia. She ate breakfast during the hurricane expert's report, fed Haviland while glancing at the amateur footage taken by a resident of the Bahamas, and sank back down in the chair to listen to the Air Force Reserve pilot's exciting narrative as he steered a Lockheed Martin WC-130J into the hurricane's eye.

By nine, Olivia was still unable to tear her gaze away from the slow, spinning wheel of green on the television screen. She sipped her coffee and watched the meteorologist point to the projected path, which was highlighted in red. The crimson hue reminded Olivia of a biblical plague. It seemed that every inch of the state's coastline had been marked by the ominous dye.

The local meteorologists predicted landfall would occur in Oyster Bay late Monday night, depending on whether the hurricane maintained its current velocity. With wind gusts already measuring close to one hundred miles per hour, any nonresidents would soon evacuate and many of the locals would flee too, relocating to the homes of family and friends farther inland.

"We're staying right here," Olivia told Haviland. After all, her girlhood had been punctuated by season after season of tropical storms, hurricanes, and nor'easters. She'd clear out if the hurricane increased to a category four or five, but she wouldn't budge for anything less. Her decision would come across as strange or downright foolish to some, seeing as her own mother was killed in the midst of a hurricane, but Olivia believed hers was a tragedy resulting from a lack of judgment. Her mother had taken an unnecessary risk by driving into town to fetch the puppy she'd gotten her daughter for her birthday and had paid the ultimate price. Olivia would never disrespect the destructive power of a storm by leaving the shelter of her home. Then again, Olivia had no one for whom she would demonstrate such an enormous act of devotion, except perhaps Haviland.

As though summoned by her thoughts, the poodle came to Olivia's side and nudged her leg. He was ready for their morning walk.

She leaned over to kiss him on the bridge of his nose. "Have you forgotten what we found last Saturday?"

Clearly unconcerned by recollections of the fetid odor, Haviland rushed to the sliding glass door leading to the back deck and to the path through the dunes. Olivia let him out and then collected her Bounty Hunter and knapsack from an unlocked outdoor storage closet. She examined her metal detector absently for a moment, recalling how relieved she was when one of Rawlings' officers returned it to her. The tool provided her with a mindless hobby, allowing her to collect many years' worth of interesting trinkets. Very few were valuable, but every one was precious to Olivia.

"I wonder what new treasures the storm will unearth?" she asked the poodle.

Olivia's home was built on a bluff and had been designed to withstand the variety of tempests pushed onshore by the Atlantic Ocean. The raised deck jutted out over a lawn of sharp grass and sand and was supported by reinforced wooden pylons. From roof to floor, the entire structure was anchored into the foundation and the mammoth windows were made of impact glass. The best builders in the region had fitted it with hurricane shutters, exterior doors that opened outward, and a detached garage.

"The only thing that's going to bother us will be cabin fever," Olivia predicted as she and Haviland set out on their stroll.

The morning air felt oddly still. There were no gulls or sandpipers haunting the shore, and the crabs had scuttled back to their burrows hours ago. By this time on a September morning, Olivia was usually in town or working on her novel, but on this Saturday, she meandered up the beach, barely paying attention to the metal detector's chirps and bleeps. Eventually, she discarded the machine altogether, leaving it and her backpack in the lee of a dune.

Haviland spent a great deal of time sniffing the air and Olivia knew he sensed a shift in the weather. Even the waves were strangely subdued, curling gently onto the shore, as though to apologize for the relentless aggressors they were soon to become.

Olivia's cell phone rang from the pocket of her sweatpants. It wasn't her habit to bring it along on walks, but after the discovery of the buried corpse last week, she decided to keep it close.

"Ms. Limoges? Will Hamilton here. I've got some preliminary information for you."

Olivia was impressed. The private investigator worked fast. "My reception isn't great, but please go on."

"The mailbox in question belongs to a Mr. Rodney Burkhart. He has a home T-shirt printing business called Big Rod's Tees and uses The UPS Store mailbox as his company address. I've seen his shirts around town. They all feature fishermen surrounded by busty girls and make a play on the phrase 'big rod.' Word is they're selling like hot cakes all over the country. Burkhart's had to hire a pair of students from UNC Wilmington just to keep up with the orders."

"So it would appear that he's financially secure?" Olivia asked, befuddled. Rodney Burkhart didn't seem like a man in desperate need of cash.

Hamilton said, "I need to do some more digging, ma'am. I haven't gotten a look at our guy's personal life yet, but I'm heading over to his place now. I should have more for you by Monday. I'll do as much recon as I can before Ophelia shuts us down. I'll be in touch."

"Thank you." Olivia put the phone back into her pocket and continued to amble, her mind churning. What connection could a T-shirt printer have to her father? Perhaps Rodney's wife worked in a nursing home or hospital. Maybe *she* was the mastermind behind the blackmail and her husband was merely the messenger.

Her languid mood spoiled by unanswered questions, Olivia abruptly stopped, turned around, and whistled for Haviland to follow her back to where she'd left the Bounty Hunter.

By the time she reached the lighthouse keeper's cottage, she was ready for a midmorning snack but decided to delay satisfying her hunger in order to assess what kind of storm damage the older building might incur when Ophelia got closer.

Unlike Olivia's house, the cottage was built on a rise much closer to the ocean and faced potential flooding if the wind pushed the waves far enough up the beach. Olivia's girlhood home had been completely overhauled last summer and the four-room, shotgun-style structure was now a community meeting place. From Alcoholics Anonymous to the Girl Scouts, all sorts of groups made use of the comfortable living room, kitchen, and conference room. Once a member signed up for a time slot on the town's website, they were told that the key to the front door was kept in the mouth of a ceramic frog near the welcome mat. Truthfully, the place could have remained unlocked. There was nothing to steal except for some kitchenware and a few small appliances, but Olivia didn't want to run the risk of having it vandalized by inebriated teenagers.

Still, she was surprised to find the front door wide open. Someone had raised the living room windows and the sound of muffled music drifted through the holes in the screens. Olivia assumed a member of the Bayside Book Writers was in the cottage, for Saturdays were reserved exclusively for their use. Though their group didn't meet until late afternoon or evening, Olivia found that the cottage provided the perfect blend of industry and tranquility and had therefore opened the space for her writer friends' use.

"Howdy," Millay murmured from the nearest sofa. She had a laptop resting on her knees and a thermos and package of Twinkies on the coffee table. The music abruptly ceased. "Figured I'd try to get my chapter done a week early and e-mail it to everyone, but it isn't happening. My characters are being totally rebellious today and their dialogue sounds like crap. Too bad our master crime fighter couldn't bother to send us the rest of his pages."

"There's been no word from Rawlings?" Olivia was surprised.

Millay unwrapped a Twinkie and studied it as though wondering what its ingredients were. "Maybe another body washed up on the beach," she said. "Or someone got whacked in the grocery store. Jesus, you should see the old women scrambling over each other to buy bread and milk."

Olivia opened the Yellow Pages and looked up the number for Neuse River Storage. "Senior citizens enjoy getting worked up over the weather. Besides, most of them have witnessed the damage these kinds of storms can produce. It can be pretty scary. Preparation helps dull the fear." She glanced away from the phone book's tiny print. "Is this your first hurricane?"

Millay snorted, ignoring the question. "All I know is that Fish Nets is going to be closed and that means I won't be making any tips." She sighed. "Guess I'll be sitting around with Harris, tossing around ideas for the boat he's going to build for the Cardboard Regatta. At least he'll feed me. My pantry has one package of ramen noodles and a jar of mustard."

Olivia found the business listing and circled it in pencil. "Harris really likes you."

"I know." Millay's voice grew small. "I wish I felt the same. I've gone out with dozens of guys who aren't half as cool as Harris, but I don't want to get serious with anyone. I don't think I'm wired to stick with just one guy." She took a big bite of Twinkie and chewed. "I go out with some dude, we have fun for a while, and then I get out. I can't stick with anyone, you know?"

Phone in hand, Olivia thought of Flynn and the many

other men before him. "*I* understand, but Harris wouldn't. You should be careful with him."

Millay's eyes fixed on her laptop, her face bathed by the screen's soft glow. "There must be something wrong with me, something missing . . ." she mused almost inaudibly, but Olivia heard the words and glanced over at the lovely young woman. Millay came across as steely and unfeeling, but her characters were bursting with powerful emotion, revealing the true depth and complexity of their creator.

Olivia knew all too well about denying one's own vulnerability. It had led her to a life of solitude. She sensed Millay wouldn't flourish in a home of empty rooms, but her fellow writer hadn't been looking for advice, so she turned her attention to the voice answering her call to Neuse River Storage.

"I'd like two rooms worth of furniture to be collected and stored until Ophelia is gone. Can you send men out by the end of the day?" Olivia waited while the manager coughed and spluttered a series of excuses. "I'll double your regular fee," she stated flatly and in a flash, arrangements were made.

Millay was watching her curiously. "You really think we're going to get slammed by this thing, don't you?"

"Yes. And since we don't have any work to review tonight, we might as well make this a social occasion. A pre-storm party," Olivia suggested.

"A drink-'em-while-you-got-'em theme?" Millay grinned.

Olivia smiled in return. "Exactly."

After a lunch of turkey, brie, and apple slices on pumpernickel, Olivia dressed in tan slacks and a crisp white blouse. She tucked a notebook and Laurel's new camera into a leather tote bag and headed to her friend's house.

Laurel's subdivision, like so many of the new housing developments, had been given a ridiculous name. Olivia frowned as she passed the gold lettered sign for Blueberry Hill Estates.

"There may have been wild blueberry bushes here at one point, but there was *never* a hill," she informed Haviland. Despite the silly name, the neighborhood was comprised of tasteful homes of brick or clapboard. Most were Georgian or American colonial, interspersed with a few Spanish villas and colorful Victorians.

Laurel's house was situated on a small cul-de-sac off Elderberry Drive. It was a spacious, butter yellow Cape, with black shutters and a cheerful red door. Potted ferns flanked the entranceway, the flowerbeds were bursting with drought-resistant annuals, and an American flag flying from a bracket to the left of the door frame completed the charming picture. As Olivia pulled into the driveway, she could see that the family spent most of their time in the back of the house. With a fenced-in yard, the entire expanse of lawn was littered with toy trucks, a sandbox, a plastic swimming pool, playhouses, and a mammoth swing set.

Olivia left Haviland in the car, strode up a flagstone path, and reached out for the doorbell. Before her finger had the chance to make contact with the illuminated button, however, Laurel cracked opened the door, slipped outside, and hastily shut it behind her. She was wearing a pink short-sleeved sweater set, an apron covered with designs of cupcakes, and a look of panic.

"My in-laws came over to watch the twins," she whispered in warning. Grabbing Olivia's hand, she pulled her toward the Range Rover. "Just get us out of here as quickly as you can. I'll give you directions once we're clear."

Obeying Laurel's request with amusement, Olivia reversed the SUV. As she glanced in the rearview mirror, she noted that her friend was busy removing her apron. "You're even wearing a disguise," she teased. "Does this mean you need to be dropped off later on bearing a soufflé or beef Wellington?"

"Oh, I don't think it needs to be anything *that* fancy," Laurel answered seriously. "Maybe something left over from your lunch menu? I told them this was a course focusing on fundamentals. No one in the world will believe that I made a soufflé on my first day of cooking class. They'll be impressed if I figure out how to cook scrambled eggs without adding little bits of shell!"

Olivia laughed. "I'll see what I can do. Where to?"

Laurel fastened her honey blond hair into a neat French twist. "Turn right onto Mulberry Way."

"Is every street named after a berry?" Olivia quickly made a mental list of how many berry plants she knew.

"Yes. Isn't it quaint?" Laurel smiled with pride. "But I am *so* glad we don't live on Gooseberry Way. Doesn't that sound kind of goofy?"

Olivia declined to point out that Laurel's street, Cranberry Court, was equally inane. Instead, she asked to be given a bit of background on the neighbor they were about to interview.

"Christina Quimby is a stay-at-home mom, president of the Oyster Bay Elementary PTA, and treasurer of our homeowner's association. She plays tennis in a year-round league and *always* has perfect nails and makeup." Laurel paused to consider what else she should add. "Her husband, Robert, is in sales and goes out of town all the time. They have two kids, Bobby Junior and Zoe. Bobby is ten and Zoe is eight."

"Where was the family when the burglary occurred?"

"I asked her that question when we set up this interview." Laurel consulted a notebook. "Let's see. They went to a football game in Chapel Hill over the weekend and discovered they'd been robbed after returning home. That was the last Sunday in August." She tapped on her window. "That's their house up ahead on the right."

Olivia parked in front of a spacious brick Georgian and told Haviland he'd have to wait in the Range Rover. The poodle began to whimper but perked up when his mistress poured a small pile of treats into the cup holder in the center console.

"Your water dish is in the back," she told him, double-checking to ensure that all the windows were down. "Have plenty to drink. I don't know how long we'll be inside."

Haviland grunted in assent.

Laurel checked her image in the side mirror and then squared her shoulders. "Here we go!"

Christina Quimby was a tall, athletic blond with the tan and premature wrinkles indicative of someone who either spent a great deal of time outdoors or paid regular visits to a tanning salon. She was dressed in a white tennis skirt, lime green shirt, and a matching visor embroidered with the Nike swoosh. After offering them iced coffee, she led them to a living room redolent with the scents of furniture polish and Windex.

Laurel politely declined refreshments and sat on the edge of a floral wing chair, her expression all business. "I know you've discussed the robbery at length with the police, but could you tell us what happened? Starting from the moment you and your family entered the house?"

Christina pointed toward the kitchen. "We came inside through the garage like we always do. No one noticed anything unusual right away, but as the kids headed to their rooms with their overnight bags, I saw the butter dish sitting out next to the kitchen sink."

"And you're certain someone in your family didn't

forget to put it back in the fridge before you left?" Laurel asked, clearly surprised by how Christina was starting her narrative.

"Absolutely sure. I was the last one out the door and I always leave everything in order. Plants watered, bills paid, everything," Christina stated firmly and Olivia didn't doubt it for a moment. Every object within sight had been arranged with scientific precision. None of the many glass-topped tables bore a single smudge, and the brass picture frames were polished to a high luster. "The butter had melted all over and there were ants everywhere!" Christina continued, shuddering slightly in distaste. "Besides, no one in my family would use a carving knife to cut butter. Can you imagine?"

Laurel and Olivia exchanged glances and then the new reporter focused on the questions written in her notebook. "What missing possessions did you notice first?"

"The television in our bedroom." Christina rose, walked across the room, and opened a pair of cabinet doors in the center of the built-in bookcases, revealing an enormous flat-screen TV. "This one was more expensive, but we always close these doors after we're done watching a show, so we didn't realize this TV was gone until later. We haven't received the insurance check yet, but my husband couldn't wait to replace the set. It's football season and if he's actually around on a Saturday, he plants himself on the sofa from noon 'til midnight. Go Heels!"

Her cheer was less than enthusiastic, but Laurel let the comment slide. She asked her neighbor for a complete inventory of stolen items and Christina easily ticked the items off from memory. Olivia listened with interest, noting that the thieves had been very discriminating. The only jewelry they took was genuine gold or bore real gemstones.

Olivia couldn't help but inquire. "Where did you keep your jewelry?"

"In a wooden jewelry box. It had a lock, but the thieves just stuck a screwdriver under the lid and snapped the whole mechanism off." Christina's lips tightened into a thin line. "I hardly expected to need a wall safe in this neighborhood."

"So they didn't just dump the contents into a sack?" Olivia continued.

"No, they were quite neat. The jewelry they didn't want was placed back into the box. It makes me think they had plenty of time to sit here and calmly sift through our stuff." Christina was growing angrier as the interview progressed. "I can replace the things they took, except for the artwork, so it's not the financial loss that upsets me. It's the thought of someone touching my things." She looked away. "At night, I swear I can feel their presence. It's as if they were still here. Having strangers in my house, picking and choosing, sitting on my bed, going through my closet . . . It's hard not to feel like my entire home has been tainted."

Laurel put her notebook aside and took Christina's hand. "How awful! Did you install a security system afterward?"

Christina nodded. "Top of the line. I would have gotten a pack of pit bulls if my children didn't have pet allergies." She smiled wryly. "Between you and me though, I don't believe lightning will strike twice. Those guys are long gone and our stuff is in some dingy pawnshop somewhere. End of story."

Sensing the interview was drawing to a close, Laurel made a few more queries about the stolen art and then gestured around the room. "Your home is spotless! Do you use a cleaning service?"

"We have a woman who comes in once a week." Christina's look of pride turned to an affronted frown. "But she had *nothing* to do with this. She's been with us for years and is absolutely trustworthy."

Laurel held up her hands, palms facing out. "Oh, I didn't mean to imply that she wasn't. I'm just trying to establish a connection between the two area robberies. From what I read in the paper, similar items were taken from their home, so I was wondering if your two families shared a cleaning or lawn service or whether you'd recently hired the same electrician or plumber or another type of workman."

Olivia felt like giving her friend a thumbs-up. Laurel was digging deeper by searching for a common denominator. At that moment, she seemed every inch the investigative reporter.

Christina was impressed by the question as well. "I can e-mail you a list," she said. "There has to be some way the thieves knew the house would be empty that weekend. It's worth a look. Thank you, Laurel." She rose and began to walk toward the front door.

"I'd like to photograph that carving knife, if you don't mind." Olivia did her best to sound subservient. She knew that the *Gazette* readers would be interested in the description of the melted butter but suspected Christina wasn't keen on having that detail publicized. Quickly, she added, "And a shot of you too. I want to capture your resilience and show people how this episode made you angry, but not fearful."

Nodding, Christina led her guests to the kitchen and removed the knife from a drawer. She took the covered glass butter dish from the refrigerator and set it on the counter. Removing the lid, she eased the knife into the middle of the stick of butter. "I figure they set it up like this and then when the butter melted the knife fell to the side." She turned to Laurel as Olivia focused her camera on the tableau. "They were so tidy elsewhere. They even cleaned up the glass from where they broke the pane in the back door."

"Fastidious and particular," Olivia mumbled.

Laurel walked to the picture window and peered out. "Were your neighbors home that weekend?"

Christina shrugged. "Yes, on both sides, but no one saw anything unusual."

The women fell silent. The pewter-hued sky hung low, creating a sense that it was much later in the day. The mood had shifted and it was apparent each of the women longed to be alone with her thoughts.

Laurel wisely thanked Christina for her time, assuring her neighbor that she'd be in touch and to trust in the doggedness of the Oyster Bay Police Department's chief.

Back in the Range Rover, Haviland carried on as though Olivia had been gone for hours. Once he finally settled down and Olivia was able to speak over his petulant yipping, she eyed Laurel keenly.

"You seem to have a plan."

"I do. I'm going to interview the other robbery victims and look for connections. If *I* help solve the case, the *Gazette* will take me on as a staff writer for sure!"

Olivia considered the possibility of the former cheerleader cracking the investigation wide open and tried not to grin. After all, she could be witnessing the birth of a gritty and determined Laurel, and Olivia would do anything in her power to help her friend emerge from her suburban cocoon and soar into the open sky.

Driving to The Boot Top, the women exchanged thoughts and theories about the robbery. Olivia raised the possibility of comparing their findings with those in the Oyster Bay police file. "After we interview the other victim that is," she added.

Laurel raised her brows. "I thought this was a one-time deal."

Olivia shrugged. "I've decided to extend my offer."

Pulling into the restaurant's parking lot, she reached across the passenger seat and grabbed the gift bag from the floor. "But you're going to need this for when you truly strike out on your own."

Her light blue eyes sparkling with delight, Laurel peeled back layers of tissue paper, exposing the digital camera Olivia had purchased from Best Buy.

"Oh! This makes me feel so official!" She sniffed and Olivia gave her a suspicious glance. She hated it when Laurel got overly physical. "You are a treasure! I really mean that!" Laurel cried. "Your joining the Bayside Book Writers has changed my life."

Embarrassed by the compliment, Olivia slid out of the car. "You haven't achieved job security yet, remember? Let's save the toasts of gratitude for that moment."

"I'm not talking about some silly job, Olivia. I'm talking about our friendship." Laurel followed Olivia, smiling warmly. "It's not easy to become friends with another woman who honestly wants the best for you. Usually, we women can't escape our need to compete with each other. To fight about who's prettier, richer, smarter. Who has cuter kids, a more devoted husband, the lower golf score . . ."

Olivia chuckled. "I'm disqualified from most of those categories, so don't give me too much credit."

Laurel put her hand on Olivia's arm. "No, you're not. You're the smartest, most beautiful, most interesting woman I've ever met and yet, you see something in me. *Me.* Stay-at-home mom, former cheerleader, and romance reader. You believe that I can be whatever I choose to be."

"I do," Olivia answered and then tugged her friend forward. "Now that we've exchanged vows, let's pick up a few apple sausage pies for you to take home. They heat up nicely and your husband will be delighted with the results of your first cooking class."

Looking doubtful, Laurel paused to scratch Haviland's neck. The poodle gave her a toothy grin in gratitude. "Apples and meat together? In a *pie*?"

Olivia sighed. "Oh dear, you *do* have lots to learn about food. Come into the kitchen. I think Michel will enjoy giving you a tutorial."

Leaving Laurel in her chef's capable hands, Olivia went through to her office and immediately checked her e-mail. There were no messages from Chief Rawlings. Her voice mail was also empty.

"Where the hell are you?" Olivia paced back and forth, trying to suppress her urge to call the station. Finally, she grabbed her cell phone and punched in the main number. When the switchboard operator told Olivia that the chief was off duty, Olivia pressed her for his whereabouts. "It's important. I have information about one of his open robbery cases," she said, stretching the truth.

The operator offered to take her number. "This is Olivia Limoges. I'm actually a friend of the chief's. He's got my number, but he's not returning my calls."

Hesitating, the woman lowered her voice. "Honey, he won't be talkin' to anybody today 'cause it's the anniversary of his wife's death. He'll visit her grave and then sit for a long spell in the church. Oyster Bay could be attacked by aliens and the chief isn't gonna notice. He's in his own world right now."

Olivia thanked her and hung up, her mood sour. She tried to tell herself that she was cross because the evening writer's meeting would now be purely social because they were without Rawlings' chapter and that it was rude of him not to at least call to say that he wouldn't attend, but an inner voice said something different. *You're jealous of his dead wife. Sawyer Rawlings may drive a station wagon, wear tacky shirts, and be thick around the middle, but you feel something for him. You feel something and yet he still grieves the loss of his wife—enough to spend an entire day lost in the memories he shared with her.*

"No," she said aloud. "It would be too complicated. I can't . . ."

Rushing from the office, she strode through the kitchen, told one of the sous-chefs to drive Laurel home, and left through the back door, a befuddled poodle on her heels.

She sped home, stopped the Range Rover in a cloud of sand and dust, and rushed down to the beach. Kicking off her shoes, she ran to the water and waded in to her shins. The wind whipped her short hair and sprayed her limbs with sharp droplets of saltwater.

Olivia had successfully returned to a place of complete solitude, but neither the increasing wind, nor the darkening sky, nor the swelling of an ocean stirred by an offshore hurricane could silence the voice in her head.

You feel something for Sawyer Rawlings.

As the first raindrops began to fall, she lifted her face skyward and surrendered to the truth.

Chapter 7

The meeting of the Bayside Book Writers never occurred. Laurel was the first to telephone and give her excuses. With the storm making its presence known in the form of rain and a persistent wind, the young mother felt she'd better say at home and tend to her children and nervous in-laws.

"I'll be honest with you," she said in a hushed tone. "Steve also gave me a major guilt-trip over leaving the twins with him and his folks twice in one day."

Olivia couldn't suppress a harrumph. "Oh, *please*. You brought home a gourmet meal, didn't you?"

"Yes, but I haven't served it yet." Laurel sounded much meeker than she had during the interview with Christina Quimby. "Maybe after they taste Michel's food they'll start pushing me out the door in the future."

"Don't count on it," Olivia grumbled. "And what about your interview with the other robbery victim? Are you still going to pursue that or are you going to wait for your husband's permission?"

Stung, Laurel became defensive. "Actually, I'm going next Thursday, once Ophelia's moved through. It isn't easy, you know. Lying to my husband." She paused. "Or trying to keep everyone happy. It's really very hard."

Olivia was in no mood to enter into a conversation concerning the problems faced by today's mothers, so she promised to join her friend on Thursday's interview and then got off the phone. She knew she had treated Laurel callously, but couldn't help feeling annoyed by her friend's vacillating will. Now thoroughly out of sorts, Olivia was relieved when Millay was the next to call and cancel.

"I need to make some money before the bar blows away, so I'm not going to waste time eating mini quiches and sipping vino with you all," she stated with her usual frankness. "I'd come if there was work to be done, but the chief dropped the ball big-time this week."

For a moment, Olivia almost explained why the chief had failed to send the group his chapter, but then thought better of it. Let Rawlings keep the anniversary of his wife's death to himself. He would have to explain his involuntary sabotage of tonight's meeting to the writer's group in person. "May your tip jar overflow," Olivia told Millay.

It didn't take long for Harris to call and bow out too.

"You don't need to explain," Olivia said as soon as she heard his voice. "Everyone else is jumping ship. Honestly, I doubt Rawlings will be ready for next week's meeting either. With the storm's arrival and the clean up afterward, he won't have a second to catch a breath, so we're going to skip his turn and let Millay go next. She assured me her chapter was almost ready and she'd e-mail an attachment to the group late Sunday evening."

Harris grunted. "She'd better send it in the morning. I've got a Facebook friend who works for the National

Oceanic and Atmospheric Administration and he says that Ophelia's going to double in width over the next twenty-four hours. We'll lose power by dinnertime." Pleased to share the insider information, Harris went on to tell Olivia the other natural disasters his cyber-friend had accurately predicted. "I'm glad I live in an apartment away from the water. No need to worry about flooding or downed trees. The power outages will be a drag, but I'm charging two laptops in preparation. After they die, it'll just be me, a case of Slim Jims, some not-so-cold brewskies, and a fierce game of Risk between me and the guys in 4C."

It was impossible to be gruff in the face of Harris's boyish enthusiasm. "Good luck in your pursuit of world domination," Olivia said. "And don't underestimate the value of Australia."

"Never!" Harris agreed. "I will capture the continent in your honor, fair maiden." He paused. "On a serious note, be careful. If the road from the Point to town floods, you could be stranded for days."

Touched by his concern, Olivia resisted the urge to lecture him on her high level of self-sufficiency. "Never fear, my friend. I have food, a generator, excellent company, and a five-thousand-piece jigsaw puzzle of the Sistine Chapel to work. If Michelangelo hid any codes on that ceiling," she joked, "I'll have plenty of time to find them."

"Man, you are so cool," Harris declared before hanging up.

Olivia wasn't ready to hunker down until conditions notably worsened, so she and Haviland drove to The Boot Top. Normally, she'd mill about the restaurant greeting diners and offering wine recommendations. Tonight, however, the hostess had called in sick and Olivia didn't have enough wait staff to spare.

"I'll have to be Madeleine for tonight," she told Haviland apologetically. "And no getting underfoot in the kitchen.

Health code violations and all that. You stay in the office if you want to be fed."

Haviland seemed to focus on the latter phrase. Licking his lips, he trotted into the office and sat on his haunches, gazing with expectant adoration at Michel.

"Madeleine isn't ill," Gabe, the barkeep, said to Olivia as he stepped out of the walk-in fridge carrying a tray of lemons, limes, and oranges. "But she's scared. She has family in Wilson and wanted to drive west before the rain got heavier."

"It's a reasonable excuse, but an irritation all the same," Olivia answered, following Gabe to the bar. "Now I'll have to man the podium and I don't possess an ounce of Madeleine's charm."

Gabe slid a tumbler filled with Chivas Regal across the polished wood bar. "This might help." He smiled and Olivia accepted the glass with gratitude. Gabe, who was in his late twenties and looked every inch the sandy-haired surfer that he was, had attracted a loyal following the moment The Boot Top opened its doors. At first, the area's well-to-do women filled all the barstools, eager to flirt with the hunky barkeep. But soon enough their husbands came too, enjoying Gabe's affability as much as their wives.

Because much of the restaurant's profits were dependent on the sale of liquor and wine, Olivia paid Gabe well above the going rate. As a result, he took great pride in his job, viewing the bar area with its leather chairs, padded barstools, and tasteful nautical décor as his treasured domain. No one's snack mix bowl ever stayed empty and no one's drinks ever ran dry. And though Gabe could have his pick of the majority of The Boot Top's female staff and clientele, he never allowed the line between his professional and personal life to blur.

Of all Olivia's employees, Michel was the most likely to

get entangled in an ill-fated romance. He'd been involved with a married woman before, and though it had wreaked havoc on his emotions, it seemed as though he was ready to repeat the agonizing experience.

"I think I have a serious crush on your Laurel," he confessed, his face flushed from the heat of the kitchen.

One of the sous-chefs stopped chopping mushrooms and gestured at Michel with the tip of his knife. "His accent got much thicker when she was here. He actually sounded like a real Frenchman. *Très* debonair."

Michel glowered at his subordinate. His Parisian accent was nearly undetectable and only surfaced when he was angry, drunk, or flirting with a pretty woman.

Olivia put her hands on her hips. "Do you have amnesia? Your last affair with a married woman was ruinous! You went on a champagne bender and your cooking was way off. You used far too much salt and your meat was overdone. I don't think any of our customers will stand for that again."

Shaking a raw shrimp at her, Michel smiled. "But ah, the passion! It is worth all the pain."

"Forget about Laurel." Olivia's eyes flashed a darker blue. "She has enough to juggle without adding a crush to the mix. Set your sights on someone else. Join a gym. I'm sure you could cajole someone into committing adultery between spin and yoga classes."

Michel tossed the shrimp into a frying pan coated with sizzling butter and browned garlic. "Laurel is special. She has a pure heart and believes that love can overcome all things. She is a rare flower, an orchid in a greenhouse of daffodils."

"Spare me." Olivia crossed her arms. "I don't see how you arrived at this conclusion after spending thirty minutes with her."

"She was here longer than that, *chérie. You're* the one who flew from here as though your tail had just been seared." He tossed half a dozen sautéing shrimp into the air. Once, twice, three times. They landed neatly back into the frying pan. He gave the pan a final shake and then scooped the shrimp onto a small bed of linguine. Handing the plate to a waiter, Michel glanced at Olivia. "If I didn't know you better, I'd say you were having man trouble. I can't imagine any friction arising between you and your debonair bookstore owner. Actually, I *can* imagine friction, but the good kind. The kind two people produce on a summer night when they—"

"That's enough, Michel," Olivia retorted. "Why don't you focus your energy on cooking? I believe that is what I hired you to do."

Michel gave her a dreamy smile. "Tonight, my food will taste like nectar and ambrosia. Every drop will be filled with visions of Laurel, my muse. Beware, those who are brave enough to order my chocolate torte. It will be such exquisite torture!"

Olivia shook her head. "You're hopeless. I'm going out to seat our patrons. Try not to burn the place down while you wallow in inappropriate fantasies."

A party of four awaited her at the hostess podium and Olivia smiled at the mayor, his wife, and two children. "Sorry to keep you," she said and led them back to the mayor's favorite table.

The mayor glanced around the nearly empty dining room and frowned. "Do you think the out-of-towners are all gone?"

Olivia nodded. "They'll be back for the Cardboard Regatta. I'm booked for three nights from five until eleven at night." She swept an arm around the dining room. The flickering candlelight, the bud vases filled with sprays of wild chrysanthemum, and the pumpkin-colored napkin fans created an atmosphere of sophistication and warmth. "Your family and the couple enjoying the shrimp scampi linguini won't be dining alone this evening. We're expecting a decent crowd tonight, though some may cancel due to the inclement weather."

The mayor's wife laughed. "You're the only person in Oyster Bay who'd call a category three hurricane 'inclement weather.'"

"Ophelia's been upgraded?" Olivia tried to recall the wind gusts of a category three. She didn't need to tax her brain, however, as the mayor's son looked up from his menu, rubbed at his glasses with his napkin, and spoke in the fluctuating voice of one on the cusp of puberty.

"Wind gusts of one hundred eleven to one hundred thirty miles per hour," he recited with a distant look on his young face. "Likelihood of structural damage to wooden structures, loss of immature trees and a few big ones too, flooding to structures along the coast, and damage from floating debris to structures near storm surge or flooded rivers. Power outages are definite, lasting from three to nine days depending on level of isolation. Estimated total cost is four hundred million. Expect a tax hike this year." Upon finishing, he returned his gaze to the menu.

"You are *such* a dork," his sister said with a sneer. "Can I order my Coke now?"

While his wife argued with their daughter over the perils of caffeinated beverages on the developing teenage body, the mayor begged Olivia to get him a dirty martini. Relieved to escape the argument brewing between the females at the table, Olivia sent a waitress to collect the rest of the family's orders.

At the bar, Olivia asked Gabe for the mayor's drink. "He'll be wanting several of those by this time Monday night," a familiar voice said. Olivia turned and smiled at Flynn, remarkably pleased to see him. She knew that Flynn's charm could help her set aside all thoughts of Rawlings and the man's continued silence.

Flynn regularly stopped by The Boot Top for a drink after work and managed to visit Olivia's restaurant without ever behaving as though his presence bore the slightest connection to her. Olivia liked that about him. He could sit and chat with Gabe and the other patrons and then casually ask her to join him for a round. When she was too busy or not in the mood to comply, he was neither offended nor ruffled by the rejection. Yet he never failed to request her company and Olivia was flattered by his persistence.

Flynn took in her form-fitting black sheath dress and necklace made of amber and turquoise and toasted her with a frosted beer mug. "You're looking lovely this evening."

Olivia perched on the stool next to him. "Have your customers fled for the hills too?"

"I could only be so lucky." He took a sip of beer. "I had a hell of a time dealing with a woman channeling Mary Poppins today. She came into the shop with one of those frilly umbrellas and started singing. At first, the moms and kids loved it, but then it quickly became clear that this lady was no Julie Andrews. In fact, she was more like Cruella De Vil."

Olivia laughed. "You mean she didn't fly or dance around with a pair of cartoon penguins?"

Flynn shook his head. "Oh, she danced all right. If you can imagine a fisherman in foul weather gear with his shoelaces tied together, then you can picture this lady's moves." He pushed his hand through his wavy hair. "I think she did at least two hundred bucks of damage."

"Not to books, I hope." Olivia hated the thought of broken leather spines or rent pages.

Etching designs into the icy film on his glass, Flynn said, "Luckily, no. But I have some furniture to replace. I'm heading into Raleigh tomorrow to visit with an old friend, so I'll wait out the storm for a couple of days, pick up some new children's chairs, and hang my 'Open' sign again first thing Wednesday morning."

"She broke wooden chairs?" Olivia visualized a madwoman slamming pint-sized rockers against the floor like some frenzied heavy-metal rocker destroying his guitar.

Flynn nodded. "Yeah, she tried to mimic that *Flashdance* move in which the dancer drapes herself over the chair, pulls a chain, and is drenched with water. In this case, the chair broke with her imaginary chain pull and instead of water, she squirted herself with a sports bottle filled with I believe to be lemon-lime Gatorade." He grimaced. "At least, I'm *really* hoping it was Gatorade."

He chuckled and Olivia joined in.

The murmur in the dining room had increased, indicating that another party or two had been seated by a member of Olivia's selfless waitstaff while she lingered at the bar. "Duty calls," she told Flynn and then, while Gabe was occupied recommending cocktails to a pair of stylish young women at the other end of the bar, she added, "Maybe we could get together before Ophelia chases you out of town."

Grinning, Flynn saluted her with his glass. "You know where I live, darling. I'll leave the light on for you."

Olivia collected the mayor's drink and walked away.

The Boot Top stayed open late that night. The locals tarried at the bar until Gabe submitted to peer pressure and turned on the small television hung above a row of liquor bottles.

Men and women loitered over their whiskey and recalled other storms such as Donna, Hugo, Fran, Hazel, and Floyd.

Olivia's customers were reluctant to go home, knowing that after tomorrow morning's church services, the town would shut down. Oyster Bay still honored the traditional blue laws and only a few eateries remained open on Sunday. The Boot Top served a weekly brunch, Grumpy's provided breakfast and lunch, and Bagels 'n' Beans operated until noon, at which time Wheeler promptly turned off the lights, locked the door, and spent the remainder of the day fishing.

The hurricane specialist on The Weather Channel was in his element, gesticulating at the blue screen as he pointed at rain bands, the enlarged eye, and the overall width of the circulating mass. The other reporters shared his ecstasy, their faces gleaming like polished apples as they reviewed Ophelia's wind gusts, path, and predicted landfall.

Olivia and her Oyster Bay neighbors were hypnotized by the graphics and the commentary, but when the program switched gears and began to display footage from Floyd, Olivia told Gabe to lock up. Gathering Haviland from her office, she prepared to exit through the kitchen door.

"Do you think there's any point in coming in Tuesday?" Michel asked. Over steaming pots, cutting boards, and sinks of dirty dishes, the kitchen staff looked at Olivia expectantly.

"No," she answered without hesitation. "We won't reopen until the power is restored. When the lights come on in town, The Boot Top needs to be ready to serve dinner the same night. Tomorrow we'll offer brunch to the soggy church goers and then lock up until Ophelia's gone." Shouldering her purse, she gazed around the kitchen. "Be careful everyone. I don't want the inconvenience of having to hire a new staff because you surfer types were lost to a riptide or those of you with jacked-up pickups trucks decided it would be fun to drive through flooded streets."

One of the sous-chefs sniggered, but Michel silenced him with a glare.

"We will take care, Ms. Limoges," he said, issuing a formal bow. "Remember, if the waves get too high, you should climb to the top of the lighthouse."

More sniggering. "The generator will keep the freezer and walk-in fridge running, but if there's any perishable food beyond what's needed for tomorrow's brunch, feel free to take it home to your families."

The dishwasher thanked her in Spanish and then rushed forward to open the door for her. The floodlight above the door illuminated the persistent rainfall beyond the restaurant's walls.

Olivia and Haviland scurried to the Range Rover. The rain was deceptively gentle, like a steady and nourishing springtime drizzle. The only indication that the fury of nature was about to rend the town apart was the sickly yellow and puce tinge to the edge of the clouds.

The drive to Flynn's bungalow was eerie. The streets were nearly deserted and the wet pavement shimmered in the otherworldly light. Olivia passed only one car on Main Street and she could see that many of the shops had closed early. Even the streetlights lining the sidewalk seemed forlorn.

Flynn's Caribbean-style bungalow was a welcome sight. Every light was on and the house glowed with misty warmth, like a roaring fire viewed through an ice-crusted windowpane. Unfamiliar music drifted from the open front door. Olivia cocked her head. It sounded like Cuban jazz—a perfect mixture of vibrant rhythms blending with a seductive and smooth melody.

"Here's lookin' at you, kid." Flynn rose from his painted wooden rocking chair to greet her with a kiss.

Olivia returned the kiss with unusual tenderness. "It was sweet of you to wait up for me. Your place looks like a beacon in the night."

"I could hardly watch mindless television knowing you were on the way, so I decided to make it clear that I was anxiously awaiting your arrival." He dipped a wide-mouthed glass in salt and poured her a margarita from a nearby pitcher. Adding a lime wedge, he placed the glass on a rattan coaster and gestured at the other rocker.

Settling into the cobalt-colored chair, Olivia signaled for Haviland to find a discreet place behind the house to take care of business. Delighted to finally be allowed a measure of freedom after being cooped up in Olivia's office all evening, the poodle darted off the porch and disappeared into the rainy night.

Olivia and Flynn made predictions about the storm and listened to the rainfall. Haviland returned, detaching himself from the shadows, and sat on the front mat, clearly asking to be let inside. He was ready for bed, but Olivia was reticent to break the spell being woven out of night rain, tequila, and Flynn's jazz record.

"So who's this old friend you're going to visit?" Olivia asked, wanting to linger on the porch a little longer.

Flynn didn't answer. Instead, he got up, walked to her, and gently pulled her out of her chair. Pressing her against him, thigh against thigh and hip against hip, he cupped her face in his hands and whispered, "Hmm, a personal question. Are we taking our relationship to the next level?"

Olivia stiffened in his arms. "What does *that* mean?"

There was a smile in Flynn's voice as he murmured his reply in her ear. "It means that you'll stay for breakfast. Try it just once and see how it feels."

Relaxing, Olivia sought his lips. They were warm and inviting. "All right," she agreed, her voice low and deep with need. "But no stacks of pancakes or three-egg omelets. I prefer lighter fare."

"The best I could scrounge up would be bread and jelly," he said with a low laugh as he led Olivia inside.

The next morning, Olivia and Flynn ate toast with strawberry jam and drank coffee in front of the television. Ophelia had picked up speed overnight and was likely to make landfall just after dawn on Monday. As they watched, the program was interrupted by an emergency announcement. The screen turned cardinal red, and white letters appeared, alerting those throughout the county that the mayor was calling for voluntary evacuations.

"Wow," Flynn breathed, his coffee cup frozen midair. "This is serious."

Olivia carried her dishes to the kitchen. "You should get going. The roads will get crowded quickly."

Seeing that his mistress had no leftovers for him, Haviland moved to the door and waved his tail, obviously eager to leave.

"I need to go home and feed the Captain anyway. He's too much of a food snob to settle for toast." Olivia gave Flynn a little smile.

He put his mug down and walked her to the door. Taking her hand he said, "Are you sure it's safe to stay out on the Point?"

"Why? Do you want me to evacuate with you?" It had meant to be a jest, but Olivia saw a look of alarm dart across her lover's gray eyes. Fiddling with Haviland's collar, she turned away and gave Flynn time to decide whether he wanted to open up about his destination or keep the identity of his 'old friend' private.

Several seconds passed and she could sense a gulf widening between them. In that stretch of silence, they'd each taken a step away from one another.

Olivia was ready to go. She pasted on a carefree smile and said, "I'll be fine. See you soon." She watched Flynn relax and reach for an umbrella.

"Let me accompany you to your car. It's raining buckets. Geysers. Veritable tsunamis."

Waving off the umbrella, Olivia gave Flynn a peck on the cheek and left without looking back. Pulling the hood of her raincoat over her hair, she tried to avoid the deeper puddles polka-dotting the road, poignantly aware that whatever progress she and Flynn had made last night had been lost. The look on his face when she mentioned accompanying him to Raleigh told of secrets Flynn wanted to preserve. If he had truly wanted to let her in, he would have spoken up, but the moment had passed and he'd been returned to bearing the label of casual lover.

"It's better this way. Less complicated," Olivia told her rain-speckled reflection in the rearview mirror.

She vowed to never wake up in Flynn's bed again.

At home, Olivia fed Haviland and printed out Millay's chapter, intending to save the critique work as a means of entertainment during the inevitable power outage.

The rain had increased in tempo since Olivia's return. No longer the gentle and steady precipitation of last night, it fell in a disharmonious staccato. By early afternoon, the wind gained a voice, fluttering like heavy curtains in accompaniment to the rain. By four o'clock, however, it dominated the noise of the ocean and begun to rush around the sides of the house and over the roof like a low-flying airplane, growling and hissing. Soon, Olivia knew, it would sound less like an angry witch outsmarted by a fairy book child and more like the enraged howl of Jack's giant.

As the afternoon waned, Olivia's lights flickered several

times but did not go out. She kept near the television, watching in awestruck fascination as the storm hurtled toward the North Carolina coast. The recommendation to evacuate continued throughout the day and Olivia received several calls from her staff at The Boot Top as well as from members of the Bayside Book Writers asking after her welfare. The person she wanted to hear from most, however, did not call.

For dinner, Olivia ate beef stew and fresh bread slathered with butter, then returned to the sofa with a glass of red wine. She had to turn the volume of the television higher in order to compete with the clamor of the rain-laden wind. A sodden journalist reported live from the Outer Banks where widespread power outages had occurred minutes before their broadcast. Hearing the news, Olivia checked the placement of her battery-powered lamps.

"It won't be long now," she told an anxious Haviland.

She also had her raincoat, hat, and waders waiting by the front door in preparation to start the small generator hidden behind a wooden screen on the side of the house. It could only power the refrigerator and the kitchen lights, but Olivia planned to run an extension cord from the outlet behind the fridge to the countertop, ensuring the continued use of her coffee machine.

"Ophelia may huff and puff and try to blow the house down, but nothing will stop me from having coffee," Olivia had declared to Haviland earlier that weekend.

She also had a waterproof radio and TV unit to switch on once her main set went dark, but the little emergency television had a tiny screen and a flimsy antenna and Olivia doubted it would be of much good. Still, she turned it on and flipped between the three available stations until she was able to get a grainy picture of an anchorwoman's face. Shortly afterward, a powerful burst of wind shook the walls from roof to foundation and the house fell into a state of semi-darkness.

"I'll be right back," Olivia spoke soothingly to her agitated poodle. "I need to start the generator."

Outside, the sky had a surreal, white gray glow, as though Ophelia were exhaling wet smoke. Even dressed in her foul-weather gear, rain pelted Olivia's face and crept under her collar. The wind was nearly strong enough to knock her flat, and when she had to use both hands to grab the wooden screen surrounding the generator to regain her balance, a strong gust snatched her hat away.

"Damn!" Olivia tried to shout as she yanked on the generator's pull start, but her words were stolen before they could even leave her mouth. The generator roared into life and Olivia felt an exaggerated sense of triumph.

Her smugness was short-lived, however, for when she climbed into bed, she found it impossible to sleep. Ophelia pounded on every surface with fists of wind and water. It didn't help that the last report Olivia had seen on her tiny television in the kitchen had been of a missing fishing boat and the plight of its five-man crew.

Lying in the dark with Haviland burrowed under the covers at her feet, Olivia couldn't push away the memories of her final night with her father. She was tired of remembering his wild eyes and raised fist, of imagining him falling overboard and his body sinking to the cold depths where no sunlight penetrated, of wondering if the fog and sea had ruined her or rescued her. But the memories wouldn't leave her room.

Shortly after midnight, she decided that the only way she'd sleep was by downing a few fingers of Chivas Regal. She'd just poured a glass when someone knocked hard on the front door.

Olivia blinked but didn't move, a shiver rippling up the skin of her back.

"Who's there?" she shouted a challenge and was stunned

when Chief Rawlings bellowed in reply, "It's Sawyer! Open the door, Olivia!"

She immediately complied. "What are you—"

"Pack a bag," he ordered, stepping in out of the rain. Turning, he used both arms, locked at the elbows, to close the door behind him. "You can't stay here. The worst is yet to come."

Water dripped from the chief's regulation rain cape and boots. His face was pinched with anxiety and exhaustion and his presence filled up Olivia's spacious kitchen as though he were ten men, not one.

"But I'm fine," Olivia managed to protest. "Aren't there people who need you more than me? Those living near the shore or in trailers by the river? This house was built to withstand this type of storm. I've got—"

Rawlings reached her in two strides. Grabbing her arm, he gave her a rough shake. "Don't be a fool! I know you're capable and tough and independent, but this"—he pointed out the kitchen window— "is more than even *you* can handle! Now go upstairs and pack a bag. I'm taking you with me if I have to cuff your hand to my own wrist!"

Sawyer's eyes were blazing with filaments of jade green. He smelled of mud and coffee and wet rubber. Olivia raised her arm and touched the end of a soaked lock of his salt-and-pepper hair, catching a fresh drip between her fingertips. The chief's face softened instantly. Seizing her hand, she thought he might pin it behind her back and make good on his threat to place her in handcuffs. Instead, he lowered his chin and kissed her palm, like a knight receiving his lady's favor. "Please come with me. I can't do my job when half of my mind's on you."

Inexplicably, Olivia now remembered that she was angry at the chief. "And where would I stay?" she asked. "With you?"

"If you'd like. I have a guest room. It's nothing fancy, but I've got a generator."

She shook her head. "I bet your place is still filled with your wife's things. I . . . couldn't stay there."

Pain flashed into Rawlings' eyes. She'd hurt him by assuming that he surrounded himself with the relics of the past.

"Then go back to Flynn's," the chief said through gritted teeth. "You should have stayed put at his place a little longer."

Olivia drew back. "Have you been following me?"

Rawlings picked up his saturated cap from the counter. He wouldn't look at her. "Last chance. Are you coming with me?"

Even though every cell in her body crackled with desire and the soft flesh on the center of her palm where Rawlings had kissed her felt molten, Olivia knew she had ruined the opportunity to reach for the man she truly wanted.

Sawyer Rawlings had driven all the way to the Point to carry her to safety. He'd interrupted the haunted musings of her past to stand drenched and weary in her kitchen and she had responded by irrevocably spoiling his noble gesture.

Not knowing how to make amends, Olivia said nothing.

By the time she realized that an apology would have been a good place to begin, Rawlings had walked out the door and into Ophelia's aqueous embrace.

Chapter 8

*The little reed, bending to the force of the
wind, soon stood upright again when the
storm had passed over.*
—AESOP

By Monday night, Ophelia had spent her wrath. Her
winds were no longer roars, but whispers. The raindrops no longer slammed sideways against windows and
rooftops, but dropped reluctantly from the sky, as though
exhausted from the effort of having to detach from clouds
impatient to be on their way.

It was dark by the time the world finally fell silent.
Olivia stepped out onto the deck, feeling like she was in
the middle of starless space. The only illumination within
miles came from the lighthouse, whose beacon swept the
ocean and provided an illusion of normalcy.

She couldn't see how far up the beach the water had
come, but the hiss of incoming waves sounded closer than
usual. The sea was still swollen, and though it no longer
seemed boiling with violent surges, it was not yet at rest.

Olivia's house had weathered the storm, but she couldn't
stop wondering how others had fared. How were the rest of
the Bayside Book Writers? And what of Dixie, who lived
in a pair of doublewides haphazardly attached by a covered

breezeway? She refused to think how Rawlings had spent the past twenty-four hours, pushing away the image of him standing in her kitchen like a big, wet bear.

The night passed slowly. Olivia let Haviland out to stretch his legs, but she knew the terrain had become altered in the storm and it would be unwise for her to venture forth in the dark. She continued to work the mammoth jigsaw puzzle of the Sistine Chapel, the radio her only companion.

Ophelia still held the media captive. Reports were given every fifteen minutes on the effects the weakening hurricane was having over central North Carolina and southern Virginia. Around ten P.M., a sound bite provided by a representative from the Coast Guard told of their failure to locate the fishing trawler missing since Sunday morning. "At this point, it is unlikely that any of the five men aboard were able to survive," the man stated grimly.

Olivia looked down at the puzzle section she'd just completed. It was Michelangelo's rendition of God dividing the waters. She stared at it a long time, her thoughts fixed on the missing fishermen. She imagined the crew members being hurled into the water, fighting for air until their lungs burned and they surrendered their last breath to the ocean. She pictured their souls being pulled from their lifeless bodies by a pair of powerful yet tender hands, lifted up, up out of the cold and the wet, beyond the rain bands and the noise of the wind.

Running her fingers over the surface of the puzzle, Olivia touched the fine cracks where the pieces met and then switched the radio to a smooth jazz station, hoping to turn her thoughts to other things. But she found the music too upbeat, almost mocking in its vivaciousness, so she turned the radio off. She completed the section showing a portrait of Daniel and decided to call for Haviland and go to bed.

"Captain!" she shouted into the night air and waited for him on the deck. The poodle loped up the stairs, his fur slick with moisture and his tongue lolling in happiness. Envying him his freedom, Olivia took him into the kitchen, dried his coat with a towel, and kissed his damp nose.

"I'll have a major case of cabin fever if I spend another day inside," she told him later as she folded back the duvet cover on her bed. "Tomorrow we'll check out the cottage and then take a drive to see what's happened to our town."

Lying down, she curled around a spare pillow and looked out the window at the fathomless sky. "And to our friends."

Olivia was awake at first light. She dressed quickly, brewed coffee, and ate a cereal bar and banana for breakfast.

"One of Grumpy's Florentine omelets would sure hit the spot," she said, feeling energized by the rays of sun tentatively lighting the horizon. Pulling on her rain boots, Olivia and Haviland walked down a soggy path through the dunes. The tide was out and the ocean was a stretched canvas of Fourth of July sparklers.

"Glad to see you back, old friend." Olivia strode to the water's edge and inhaled a lungful of crisp air. When she entered the cottage, her delight quickly turned to dismay as she saw the brown stains around the baseboards. In every room, water had crept in and made itself at home. The carpet in the conference room and the hardwood flooring in the remaining three rooms were ruined. It was fixable, she knew, but there was something about the possibility of rot growing on the very bones of her childhood home that brought Olivia unhappiness. She'd hardly lived a Norman Rockwell life in her sad, little room facing the sea, but it was hers all the same.

Haviland sniffed every room and retreated outside in search of less distasteful smells, for the entire structure reeked of seaweed and brackish water. "We won't be meeting here this Saturday," Olivia said and left the front door wide open.

After leaving the cottage, Olivia drove straight to The Boot Top. She had to park in the street, for an enormous pine tree had fallen in a diagonal across the restaurant's paved lot.

"Could have been worse," she murmured with relief as she walked the perimeter of the building. Other than a few missing shingles on the roof and a pair of broken hurricane shutters, the eatery was unscathed. Olivia got back in the Range Rover and turned down Main Street. It was too early in the day to need air-conditioning, so she rode with all the windows down and raised a hand in greeting to the other residents and business owners who'd made their way into town at daybreak.

The most noticeable difference between the business district before and after the storm was the sheer amount of debris covering the streets and sidewalks. Branches, leaves, pieces of wood, cardboard, and paper were strewn about in clumps. The debris, the lack of electricity, and the shell-shocked looks on the faces of the few pedestrians she passed gave the town a foreign air, as though it belonged in a Third World country.

Slowing her pace even further, Olivia could see that dozens of storefront windows had been shattered, including the ones belonging to her favorite boutique, Palmetto's. Rain had drenched the display featuring a rainbow of knit shirts and had knocked the mannequins flat. Olivia glanced at the neighboring retailers and saw that many of their signs were crooked or had fallen to the sidewalk, splintering into nonsensical words.

It was apparent that several cars had been parked on Main Street during the storm and most had fresh spider-web cracks in the windshields or dents that still bore the imprint of a heavy bough. The morning's radio report included the news that federal aid for storm cleanup had been promised, but Olivia knew that Ophelia was going to empty the town's coffers. Oyster Bay had less than a week to reinstate itself as the picture of a seaside utopia in time for the kickoff of the Cardboard Regatta.

After making cursory inspections of her other properties, Olivia continued past the town limits and pulled in front of Dixie's trailer complex. She found her friend barking orders at a good-looking boy of about ten and a sullen teenage girl.

"Yours?" Olivia asked with a smile when the children stomped off.

Dixie nodded. "Yep. Those are two of the tall ones. There's two little ones 'round here somewhere, but Grumpy's probably got them doin' somethin' unpleasant. He's pretty ticked 'cause they snuck out to ride on a friend's ATV when the eye was passin' over and had us worried half to death." She put her hands on her hips and surveyed the wrecked laundry lines and dog kennel. "Thor's pooped in the house three times since the damned storm began. That dog is a wimp." Dixie reached out and touched Haviland's flank. "He doesn't have your fine manners either, Captain."

Haviland flashed her a toothy smile.

"Well, it looks like you and your clan are okay," Olivia said. "I'm sending Michel on a road trip to Costco. I thought I'd see if you were in need of supplies."

"Filet mignon, lobster tail, Vicodin," Dixie joked. "Actually, we're good. We had to bring home a ton of food from the diner 'cause it was gonna go bad." She raised an eyebrow. "My stars, you *have* gotten soft, 'Livia. I've known you for years, but you've never been to my place. Now, ten minutes after a hurricane's passed through, here you are." She dusted off her shirt. "You'd best say somethin' nasty or I'm gonna have to tell folks that you do have a heart."

Olivia scowled. "I'll just tell Michel to pick up some staples. Milk, eggs, bread, some birth control pills."

Dixie laughed until she sank down on the stoop. "I really don't have twelve kids, you know!" she shouted as Olivia drove off.

On the way to Michel's, Olivia was surprised to see several power trucks heading into town. When she passed a trio of tree-removal trucks, she suddenly realized that without power, none of the eateries or grocery stores would be open. Where were these workers going to get food? And there wouldn't be much of a community cleanup effort if those volunteering were distracted by hunger. Yet who could make hundreds of meals without electricity?

"Michel," she said aloud.

Her chef's ruddy features paled when she outlined her idea. "You're insane! I've always thought you might be, but now I'm certain of it!"

Olivia ignored his protests. "Call the rest of the staff. Two men can take care of the tree in our parking lot and you can organize the shopping trip. I'll round up some warm bodies to assemble sandwiches. Imagine being able to boss around all the people you've cooked for in the past. It's your fantasy come true. They'll finally see how hard you work and learn to appreciate your skill." She could see the idea appealed to her chef. "We can do this."

"For free?" Michel was astounded.

"Yes, for free. If you want to cook for a full house of paying customers this weekend, then we need to pitch in now." Seeing that Michel wasn't convinced, she added,

"Maybe Laurel will be available to help in the kitchen. I'm sure she could use a lesson in the fine art of sandwich construction."

Michel looked offended. "You jest, but there *is* an art to making sandwiches. One must begin with the right bread. A croissant or a crisp baguette—"

"Save it for Laurel," Olivia interrupted and handed Michel her corporate credit card. "Call me if you have any trouble."

Leaving Michel spluttering on his doorstep, Olivia headed to Blueberry Hill Estates next. Even though she knew that visiting Laurel meant having to apologize for her recent rudeness, Olivia suspected her harried friend might be in need of a few groceries.

Laurel's husband, Steve, answered Olivia's knock. They'd met before, but he didn't act as though he recognized her or the large black poodle nearly glued to her thigh. When Olivia explained that she'd come to see Laurel, Steve bellowed his wife's name and then removed a pair of work gloves from his jeans pocket.

"Excuse me." He brushed by Olivia, eyeing Haviland nervously. "I've got a hot date with a chainsaw."

Olivia stiffened as she heard her friend's light footsteps approach, but if she had expected Laurel to give her a cool reception, she was mistaken. Instead, the younger woman threw her arms around Olivia's neck.

"I am *so* glad you're okay!" she gushed. "I kept thinking about you—all alone in your house with the ocean lapping at your door. I must have dialed your cell phone number two hundred times!"

Olivia felt her face grow warm in the face of such caring. She studied Laurel's red nose and puffy eyes. Had Laurel been crying from worry for her friends? It was possible, but Olivia sensed something more serious had pinched the skin around Laurel's mouth. She touched her friend's elbow. "What's wrong?"

Sniffing, Laurel shook her head, as though frightened to give voice to what had upset her so. "I keep trying to pretend that if I don't talk about it, I might wake up tomorrow and find out that nothing happened. That it was all just a bad dream."

Leading Laurel into the kitchen, Olivia sat her down at the breakfast table and began to open cupboards in search of coffee.

"Please let me do that," Laurel begged. "It'll be easier to talk if my hands are busy." She began to fill the coffee-maker with water. "There's a woman I know from Dermot and Dallas's playgroup. Her daughter, Hannah, was born a few hours after my boys." She drew in a deep breath. "We met in the hospital and have traveled in the same circles ever since. She has two older children and is always on the move." Pausing to count out coffee scoops, Laurel set the machine to brew and then grabbed the edge of the sink, her shoulders hunched up to her ears.

"This woman, April, took her kids to a soccer tournament in Myrtle Beach over the weekend. She stayed there Monday night to avoid the storm, and when she came home this morning she found her husband . . ." She covered her eyes with her hands and Olivia waited to hear a sordid tale of infidelity. "He's in a coma," Laurel surprised her by saying.

Olivia watched as Laurel turned toward the coffeepot and struggled to collect herself. "Was he injured during the storm?"

"Yes, but the hurricane didn't club Felix on the back of the head with a seven iron." Laurel's eyes flashed with anger. "The person robbing his house did."

Stunned, it took Olivia a couple of minutes to notice

that Laurel served her coffee in a mug emblazoned with red hearts and a "World's Best Mom" slogan. Laurel drank from a white mug bearing the text, "I Perform Cavity Searches." When she put the cup down on the counter in order to add another splash of milk, Olivia could read the script on the backside of the mug. It said, "Don't Worry, I'm a Dentist."

Olivia was momentarily distracted from the subject at hand. Not for the first time, she wondered what kind of man Laurel's husband was. Did that mug reflect his sense of humor? He wasn't especially friendly when he'd opened the door. Olivia recognized that he was clearly busy, but she detected a lack of interest as well, as though anything to do with Laurel was likely to be insignificant. Stirring a bit of milk into her own coffee, Olivia vowed to do everything in her power to help Laurel become a household name in Oyster Bay. In time, Steve would view his wife with new eyes, but for now, Olivia's role was to listen.

"If this just happened this morning, how did you find out so quickly?" she asked her friend gently.

Laurel shrugged. "Female phone tree. Christina Quimby, the woman we interviewed last week, heard the news from a woman on her tennis team. That woman, Tina, is April's neighbor. Tina saw the ambulance and the cop cars arrive and ran next door. I bet she had the story out to twenty people before April's husband, Felix, made it to the hospital." Laurel gave Olivia a sad grin. "Tina might be a gossip, but at least she rushed April's kids over to her house so they didn't have to see their daddy being wheeled out on a stretcher or watch their mama fall apart."

"Another robbery," was all Olivia could think to say.

Joining her at the table, Laurel let out a long sigh. "I guess this is when I figure out if I've got what it takes to be a real reporter."

"What are you planning to do?"

"Drop the kids off at my in-laws and then go to the hospital," Laurel answered resolutely. "I'll say the boys have been worried sick about Grandpa and Grandma and wanted to see them as soon as it was safe. My mother-in-law will just eat that up. I'll pretend to drive off in search of diapers, even if it means I have to sit through one of her lectures on how I need to learn to plan ahead." She reached for Olivia's hand. "I don't know how much we can find out, but I'd love to have you with me."

Olivia gave Laurel's hand a maternal pat. "Not only will I go with you, but I'll make sure you have a giant box of diapers so you can keep your cover intact."

For the first time since Olivia had walked through the door, Laurel smiled. "Just once, I'd like to be around when you wave your magic wand. I've never actually seen one before."

Standing, Olivia pulled her wallet from her purse and waved it in the air. "Sure you have. It's called a Visa card. Bibbidi, bobbidi, boo!"

It took thirty minutes to get Dallas and Dermot dressed for the short drive to their grandparents' condo. Befuddled by how complicated the act of leaving the house was for Laurel, Olivia watched as her friend loaded Cheerios into small baggies, filled sippy cups with organic apple juice, and stuffed spare outfits, bibs, and diapers into an over-sized sack.

"Is this your typical exit routine?" Olivia asked, aghast.

Laurel scooped one of the boys onto her left hip and held on to the second with her right hand. "Are you kidding? This was fast! Look, I'll meet you at the hospital. Maybe you'll bump into Rawlings. He's sure to know something by now."

Olivia was torn over the idea. She would like to worm information out of Rawlings, but she was uncertain whether he'd be willing to speak with her about an ongoing case or anything else for that matter.

Back in the Range Rover, Olivia checked her cell phone and was pleased to note that her service had been restored. She put the phone on speaker mode and called Michel with an additional grocery list. He let loose several expletives in French, causing Haviland to bark excitedly in reply. She'd just pulled into the hospital parking garage when she received a call from Will Hamilton, the private investigator.

"Did Ophelia put you folks through the wringer?" he inquired. "We barely had a twig down in these parts, but the news footage has shown pictures of your area since daybreak and things look messy."

"We don't have power, but Oyster Bay will be up and running in no time," Olivia replied breezily. "What do you have for me?"

Hamilton cleared his throat. "Ms. Limoges, I have been watching Rod Burkhart 'round the clock. From what I've seen, he lives a pretty straightforward life. He works, tosses around a football with his two sons, mows the lawn, goes to church, and runs errands."

"And he seems financially secure?"

"Yes, ma'am. He drives a late-model truck, and his wife's minivan is only a year old. The house is tidy and well maintained. The Burkharts aren't rich, but they're solid. An average, upper-middle-class family. The guy's got a nice-looking wife and kids, a yellow Lab, and a dozen fishing poles. He went lake fishing Monday afternoon with another buddy. They drank a few beers and picked up Chinese takeout on the way home." He paused. "I could keep on him and you could go on paying me to look for dirt on

Burkhart, but I don't feel right taking more of your money. This guy is a regular Joe. He's got no record and the worst he's done is get a moving violation for a case of lead foot a few months back. No bodies in the basement or mistresses on the side. That's my professional opinion, ma'am."

Olivia let Haviland out so he could sniff the bushes lining the parking lot. "Okay, drop the tail for now, but we're not done yet. I'm going to send Mr. Burkhart one thousand dollars in cash. It will be in a neon pink mailer and will go to his box at The UPS Store. If I mail it today, it should be there on Thursday. I want you to follow that mailer. See what Burkhart does with it."

"Will do," Hamilton said.

"You don't need to contact me until Burkhart opens that envelope. When he does, I want to know everything that follows. Who he talks to, if he goes to the bank, if he buys a big-ticket item, et cetera. Every detail."

The investigator promised to be on alert for the arrival of the colorful package. Olivia got out of the Range Rover and looked around for Haviland. She found him sitting on the grass next to a wooden bench. A broad, masculine hand stroked the fur on the poodle's head and neck, and Haviland winked his caramel brown eyes in happiness.

"Hello." Olivia approached the pair with stealth. She didn't want to disturb Rawlings' train of thought, knowing that he often searched for a quiet place in order to reflect on the details of a case while they were still fresh.

The chief removed his cap and rose to his feet. "Hello, Ms. Limoges. I'm relieved to see you in one piece."

"We're fine, but the lighthouse keeper's cottage has suffered some flood damage," she said, feeling oddly shy. "We'll have to relocate for our next Bayside Book Writers meeting. Do you think you can make this one?"

He studied her face and, finding no judgment there, shook

his head. "I don't know. The department will be tied up with the town's cleanup detail for weeks and now we've got another robbery case to run down." He looked away. "Perhaps I shouldn't have approached you about joining the group in the first place. My work isn't ready and my time is rarely my own."

Panic welled in Olivia. She didn't want Rawlings to quit the Bayside Book Writers. She wanted the chance to read his work in hopes of discovering more about him. Most importantly, she wanted to be able to respond differently should he ever cross a room and pull her to him again.

"We would have understood why you didn't send us your chapter if you'd explained your reasons," she said softly and sat down on the bench alongside him. "We're a fairly easygoing group. Well, most of us are anyway." She tried to smile, but her mouth wouldn't respond. "And I'd like to believe even I have enough sensitivity to give you a pass because it was the anniversary of your wife's death."

Rawlings gave her a sharp glance. "That would be a handy excuse, but it wouldn't be the truth. What would you think if I told you that I brought my laptop to the cemetery? That I'd been trying to fix the damned chapter since Friday night, but every time I'd read it over, I knew what I'd written was crap. It's still crap. And then the day was gone and I had nothing to share with you all. I'm sorry."

Olivia was silent for a moment. "What's your book about, Sawyer?"

"Pirates."

She couldn't help it. She laughed. "I'm not making fun of you, I swear! I just had this image of you as Johnny Depp in *Pirates of the Caribbean*. Not that you wouldn't make a dashing buccaneer, but picturing you with dreadlocks and a sword threw me off guard."

The chief's eyes crinkled at the corners. "Dashing, huh?"

His amusement faded almost as quickly as it had surfaced. "I imagined writing a thriller in which a retired police chief hunts down a bunch of villainous treasure hunters. In the end, he finds Blackbeard's secret stash and turns it over to a museum."

"Sounds like a decent plotline," Olivia said.

Rawlings snorted. "It wasn't honest though. I created such a two-dimensional character that I could have slipped him through a mail slot. I need to start over."

Olivia pivoted her shoulders. Her fingertips reached for his, sliding over the cool metal of the bench. "I don't think it's ever too late to fix a mistake. To begin again."

Her heart was tripping over itself. For once in her life, she wanted nothing more than to make a connection with the man beside her, but the moment she made contact with the rough skin of his hand, her fingers caressing the ridges and valleys of his knuckles, the radio clipped to his shirt pocket crackled. She jumped back involuntarily.

Rawlings answered the call while trying to convey an apology with his eyes. He and an officer exchanged information in a series of terse codes. The chief's final words were that he'd meet his subordinate in the hospital lobby. As he stood and smoothed the wrinkles in his uniform pants, he gave Haviland one last pat. "Are you visiting someone here? Is everything all right?" he asked, gesturing at the boxlike building across the parking lot.

"Laurel is friends with April, the wife of the man assaulted during the latest robbery. She wanted me to come along for moral support though she should know by now that that's not one of my strong points." Seeing the chief doubted her explanation, Olivia hurriedly continued. "What is Felix's condition?"

Rawlings pulled his belt upward and made a slight adjustment to his holster. "I'm afraid it's quite grave. He has brain injuries, and from what I've been told, a dangerous amount of intracranial swelling. I don't know what hope his wife can hold out for, but for her sake, and the sake of that man's children, I truly pray there is hope to be had." He began to walk and Olivia fell into step beside him.

She peppered him with questions about the robbery, but his information was limited. The officers at the crime scene hadn't finished investigating and Rawlings had gotten all he could from April. In the end, he had ceased trying to get answers from the woman and, instead, held her while she cried. In the stiff, plastic chairs of the hospital waiting room, he had put aside his title as police chief and took on the role of big brother. He had handed April tissues and got her coffee and slowly, she told him what she could about what she'd found upon returning home from Myrtle Beach.

"Originally, Felix was supposed to go with them to the soccer tournament, but he had some presentation to do for work," Rawlings said to Olivia. "April told me her husband is an ad man and that his company threatened to let him go if he didn't come up with a dazzling campaign for a prospective client. Felix stayed home, fearing he could lose everything if he didn't."

Olivia glanced at Rawlings. "And now his family stands to lose more than they ever imagined." She grabbed his arm. "Will you promise me something?"

Startled, Rawlings stopped walking. "Go on."

"If this robbery bears similarities to the Quimby case and your department doesn't have the culprits behind bars by Thursday night, will you come to the restaurant and talk things over with me? Laurel and I might be able to help, but we haven't finished gathering information yet."

A glint entered Rawlings' eyes. "I don't know what you're

up to, Olivia Limoges, but I'm willing to find out." Sensing movement to his right, the chief put more distance between himself and Olivia. "Here comes Laurel now."

Laurel ran toward them, but as she grew nearer, she seemed to lose steam and almost tripped over the curb. Her face was ashen.

Rawlings reached for her and she sagged against his chest. Olivia put her hand under her friend's elbow, steadying her.

"I can't handle this, Olivia!" she cried, her fingers clawing at Rawlings' shirt, roughly creasing the blue material on either side of the buttons. Looking up she fixed an agonized gaze on Olivia. "This isn't a story about theft anymore. Now it's about murder! Oh, poor April! And those poor *children*! Felix Howard . . . husband, father . . . dead. *Dead*!"

Chapter 9

*We cannot live only for ourselves. A
thousand fibers connect us with our
fellow men.*
—HERMAN MELVILLE

Laurel was too upset to pick up the twins, so Olivia convinced her to drive home and calm down before venturing out again. Rawlings went back inside the hospital, promising to call Olivia that evening.

Not knowing what else to do, Olivia took Haviland to The Boot Top and was pleased to discover several members of her staff stacking pieces of the pine tree that had fallen across the parking lot onto the bed of a pickup. When she thanked them, one of the dishwashers replied, "We gotta get ready to open. None of us can afford to go without a paycheck."

"Your weekly check will look exactly the same," Olivia assured her employees. "I'm hardly going to dock your wages because an act of nature shut us down." She gestured at the building. "And you will work this week, even without power. We're going to make box lunches and deliver them to anyone who's out there trying to restore electricity, clearing away debris, or performing any other task that will help *us* return to business as usual."

Another member of the kitchen staff tossed a limb into the truck and then dusted off his hands. "We have a lot of fruit in the big fridge. I can start cutting that up. Maybe make a fruit salad."

"Too messy," one of the waiters argued. "These guys need sandwiches with a lot of meat, chips, and Gatorade."

"That's precisely what we're giving them," Olivia said. "Michel will be here shortly so let's get this parking lot cleared, and be ready to unload the van. I have a feeling he bought a few pallet's worth of supplies."

Olivia told Haviland he'd have to wait for his lunch and then joined in the cleanup effort around the restaurant. Once the tree had been removed, one of her waiters cleared the asphalt with a leaf blower and the crew set about picking up branches and litter from the flowerbeds surrounding the building. By the time they'd finished, Michel had arrived and thrown open the rear doors of the van with a flourish, revealing cases of bottled water, Gatorade, cold cuts, bread, condiments, fruit, nuts, granola bars, milk, ground coffee, and two jumbo-sized boxes of diapers.

Olivia was proud of her employees. Without hesitating, they immediately surged forward to unload the van. There was enough daylight in the kitchen to create a functional assembly line and Michel barked orders until the room hummed with the same brisk efficiency it did during the preparation of five-star meals. Everyone seemed happy to have something useful to do and it warmed Olivia's heart to see that her staff made sandwiches and arranged apple slices and pretzels into cardboard lunch boxes with the same measure of pride with which they created rose blossoms out of strawberries or drizzled remoulade over a shrimp and avocado salad.

Well before noon, the owner and employees of The Boot Top donned white aprons and piled into Michel's white van. By now, the streets were stirring to life. Industrious business owners and locals looking to help with Oyster Bay's restoration had replaced the curiosity-seekers of early morning. The town was suddenly alive, like a hermit crab creeping out from the safety of its shell. And like a colony of busy ants, people scattered over the sidewalks and streets bagging trash, picking up sticks, sweeping, and chatting.

The presence of the utility trucks seemed to add an extra dose of energy to the mix. People knew, despite the damage Oyster Bay had received, that they would recover from the storm. Lights would go back on, shattered windows would be replaced, roofs would be patched. There would be an endless string of phone calls to insurance companies and repairmen, but Olivia was confident that the town would sparkle by the Cardboard Regatta's opening day.

She and her staff wasted no time in handing out lunches. From anxious shopkeepers to sanitation workers, the simple meal was received with sincere gratitude. Olivia began to feel like Ebenezer Scrooge delivering a fat goose to Tiny Tim's family on Christmas Day. Her heart was swollen with affection for the town of her childhood and she felt drunk on the grateful smiles of her neighbors.

Her exultation ebbed when she noticed Flynn perched on the top of a ladder at the end of the block. He held a crooked street sign straight while a second man drilled the green- and white-lettered rectangle back into place.

Olivia paused for a moment, realizing that she hadn't thought of Flynn once during the storm. Had he wondered about her? The fact that he hadn't called to ascertain how she had weathered the tempest reinforced her conviction that the bookstore owner harbored no deep feelings for her.

"Not that I care," she muttered to herself. Still, it took no small effort to paste on a smile and airily called out,

"Top of the morning to you, gentlemen! Care for a roast beef and Swiss or a ham and cheddar sandwich?"

Flynn glanced down from the ladder and grinned. "Are you the new president of the Red Cross?" Waiting for the other man to give him a thumbs-up, Flynn nimbly climbed to the ground and accepted two box lunches. "You're better looking than Clara Burton."

"And my purse is deeper," was her breezy reply. "How's your store?"

"Untouched." Flynn made a wide gesture, encompassing all of Main Street. "I could probably open for business today. The windows of that old fish warehouse are huge and the shop has plenty of light, but I couldn't run my credit card machine and people carry around less cash then they used to." He shrugged: "So I thought I'd take the day off and lend a hand. I'm not much of a handyman, but I take orders well."

"Folks won't be lookin' to buy books today anyhow, more like milk and bread," the other man said. He scratched his graying beard pensively. "It's the same after every storm. People focus on the simple things. Me, I think it's a blessing when all our gadgets and computers get shut down against our will. Folks gotta play cards and tell stories like they did in the old days. It slows us down, reminds us who our neighbors are and how damned fine it feels to take a hot shower."

Olivia had to agree. Somehow, the lack of noise from car engines and booming radios allowed people to converse with greater ease. The town was filled with a different form of music; voices wove into a melody and the sound of people at work formed a steady rhythm. Every now and then, the high pitch of a gull's hungry cries overshadowed the human symphony.

Wishing the two men luck with their task, Olivia spent

another hour distributing food. She then waited for one of the men from the power company to take a much-needed break. Sitting alongside him on the curb, she asked how widespread the outages were.

"I need to get something in the mail today," she added, keeping an eye on Haviland, who had wandered off to sniff the base of a streetlamp. "So if you could point me to the nearest functioning township, I'd be grateful."

"Cedar Point," the man answered promptly while unwrapping his sandwich. "My cousin lives there. Only part of the town has power, but the business district is movin' along steady as a freight train."

Olivia thanked him. She and Haviland trotted back to the Range Rover and made their way to Cedar Point. There weren't many people on the road and the landscape was littered with hundreds of downed trees. It was as if one of the Titans of Greek mythology had swept a colossal arm across the entire region, flattening pines, oaks, and magnolias in a fit of rage.

The UPS Store was open, but hardly doing a brisk business. A bored clerk reluctantly shoved aside her *Star* magazine and examined Olivia's neon pink parcel. "You just missed the truck. We can send this overnight but it won't get there 'til Thursday morning at the earliest."

"Perfect," Olivia answered and paid for the service. In the Rover, she sagged against the leather seat. "Now there's nothing to do but wait," she told Haviland, picturing Rodney Burkhart retrieving the pink package from his mailbox while Will Hamilton followed his every move through a camera lens.

Haviland nudged her elbow, indicating he was ready for her to begin driving so he could stick his head out the window and partake of an hour of ecstasy delivered by the rush of wind through his nostrils.

As the afternoon passed into evening Oyster Bay remained dark. Olivia sat at The Boot Top's bar, surveying the mast lights on the boats in the harbor as she sipped a glass of Chivas Regal.

"Nothing to do but wait," she said to the empty restaurant.

By Thursday, people spoke of Ophelia as though she were a distant relative who'd come in for a holiday weekend, behaved poorly, and then mercifully departed, leaving the house in disarray.

When power was restored to the business district Thursday morning, the townsfolk milled about the shops and eateries comparing their hurricane woes. Many were still without electricity but had gratefully returned to their jobs and daily routines.

Hoping Steve was busy filling a cavity, Olivia called Laurel at home.

"Are we on for today?" she asked her friend and then realized she shouldn't have opened the conversation with that line. If she'd been more sensitive, she would have asked if Laurel had recovered from the shock she'd received over being present when a woman of similar age and circumstance suddenly, tragically, became a widow.

Laurel didn't answer immediately. "I've been thinking about the whole reporter thing, Olivia. I've been acting like my life is missing something, but I have this beautiful house and a husband who provides for me. Seeing April at that hospital . . ." She struggled to find the right words. "I should learn to count my blessings, not complain about them."

"Who says those should be limited?" Olivia demanded. "I understand your being upset. Afraid even. But, Laurel, do you want other women to go through this or do you want to help the police catch these bastards and put a stop to future murders?"

One of the twins whined in the background. "I'm sorry, but I need to take care of Dermot." Laurel clearly wanted to get off the phone. "You do the interview if you want. I'll e-mail you the address. Meanwhile, *I* am going to cook a delicious dinner for my family, even if it takes me all day to do it!" The sound of whining escalated into a full-blown howl and a second high-pitched voice joined in.

Haviland's ears lifted in alert.

"I gotta go!" Laurel shouted and hung up.

Olivia scowled at the phone. "Well, how do you like that?" She drummed her long fingers on the kitchen counter and recalled the chief's promise to compare notes with her that evening. If she didn't interview the other burglary victim, she might not have any useful information to impart and she very much wanted to be able to provide Sawyer Rawlings with a solid lead at the most and a few possible theories or relevant clues at the very least.

Picking up the phone, Olivia made another call. "Did I wake you?" she inquired genially when a very groggy Millay grunted out a hello. It didn't take long to fill the young woman in on the role Olivia wanted her to play. "You're sharp and you can read people, which is a surprising attribute for someone in their mid-twenties."

"I'm a bartender," Millay reminded her irritably, still half asleep. "If I didn't have that skill, I couldn't pay my rent."

"So you'll come with me?"

Millay produced a muffled grunt. "It's either that or do laundry. I'll be your wing man."

Pleased, Olivia had a final thought. "And I hate to say this, being that I admire most expressions of individuality, but could you strive to dress more conservatively for today's interview?"

Snorting, Millay replied, "Just for you, I'll take out one or two eyebrow rings."

"That would be a start," Olivia answered and rang off.

An hour later, Olivia pulled in front of Millay's apartment complex. When her young friend waved in greeting, Olivia almost failed to recognize her. Millay was wearing a simple black skirt, sandals with a wedge heel, and a short-sleeved white blouse beneath an argyle vest. Her hair was pulled under a beige cap and, instead of her customary black eyeliner, deep purple eye shadow, and crimson lipstick, she wore very little makeup. Olivia was struck afresh by the girl's beauty.

"Not bad," she said as Millay hopped into the car and reached around to pet Haviland.

"I only do this in the name of Truth and Justice," Millay answered. "And I'm not going anywhere without coffee, so swing into the Exxon on our way out of town."

Olivia was horrified. "You're going to drink *gas station* coffee?"

"Yeah, and I might eat a pink hot dog and a bag of pork rinds too," Millay taunted.

"Cover your ears with your paws, Captain," Olivia suggested. "This girl speaks of food whose existence is best forgotten."

Haviland spent most of the ride to Beaufort County sniffing the air in the Range Rover's cabin. True to her word, Millay had bought a large coffee at the Exxon station, but in lieu of a chemically enhanced hot dog, she'd purchased a custard-filled donut. She polished off the pastry before Haviland could even beg for a bite.

"No sugar for you, Captain," Olivia remonstrated. "You can have a nice organic Buffalo knuckle bone while we're inside the . . ." She gestured for Millay to read the paper resting on the dash. "What's Sue's last name?"

Licking the fingers of her right hand, Millay examined the sheet. "Ridgemont." She read the address aloud. "Sandpiper Shores. Jesus, who names these developments? The same people who write Hallmark cards and listen to Christmas music all year long?"

Olivia laughed. "Everything has to have a theme. Her house is on Blue Heron Circle, right? So, in this case, we have a shorebird theme. How original."

"Hey, not everyone has our vivid imaginations," Millay replied. "Personally, I'd like to see a bunch of streets named after food. I could live on Steak Street, you'd be on Pickle Place, and all the people we didn't get along with would be stuck on Cauliflower Court."

"I take it you don't enjoy the nutty flavor of the cruciferous vegetable," Olivia remarked. "Do you like other members of the cabbage family? Broccoli or Brussels sprouts."

"Ick, ick, and ick," was Millay's only response as they pulled into the driveway of a Dutch colonial.

"You're missing out," Olivia said, turning off the engine. "Michel makes the most unbelievable broccoli dish. He tosses market-fresh broccoli with olive oil, garlic, and pine nuts. Adds a little salt and viola! Perfection."

Millay frowned. "I get my fiber by eating edamame. Enough about food. I can only stand this preppy girl outfit for so long."

The Ridgemonts obviously had children, for their pricey SUVs were plastered with gold bear paw-print decals, the mascot of one of the area's prestigious and very expensive private schools. In addition, decals in support of various sports' teams, from lacrosse to swimming to tennis, declared that athletics played a major role in the Ridgemonts' lives.

Unlike Christina Quimby's house, this home lacked curb appeal. The lawn had been mowed and the bushes trimmed, but there wasn't a flower in sight and the potted ferns on the stoop were brown and wilted. Several newspapers littered the welcome mat, and the door's brass kick plate and knocker were being eaten away by rust.

Sue Ridgemont answered the bell wearing paint-splattered jeans and an equally colorful T-shirt.

"Oh, dear! I forgot you all were coming today. Sorry! Come on in." She gestured at her clothes. "I'm in the middle of a do-it-yourself project in the guest room." Leading them into the kitchen, she pushed a pile of books, newspapers, unread mail, two pairs of balled-up socks, and a Nerf football to the other end of the table.

"Thank you for agreeing to see us," Olivia said, trying not to frown at the dirty dishes in the sink or the brown bananas on the countertop. "I'm sure you're busy."

Sue blinked. "You mean because of the hurricane?" She laughed merrily. "I have two teenage boys. My whole *life* is a hurricane!"

Olivia smiled, quickly warming to Sue Ridgemont.

"So tell us about the robbery. Just start at the beginning and try to give us as much detail as possible." Olivia waved a hand at Millay. "My assistant will take notes as we talk."

Millay did better than that. She produced a mini recorder from her bag, pressed a few buttons, and placed it on the table near the pile of unopened mail. She then settled a notebook on her lap and grinned at Sue. "Just pretend the recorder's not there. I only brought it to ensure accuracy on our part." She then uncapped a pen and looked at Sue expectantly.

Sue's story was remarkably similar to Christina's except the Ridgemont family hadn't gone out of town. They'd spent the better part of a Saturday at a Little League All-Star game in Fayetteville.

"When we got home, we didn't think anything was wrong." She gestured at the kitchen. "It's pretty tough to tell if something's missing in this chaos, but it didn't take long for the boys to notice the big holes where their TVs, computers, and stereos had been. The thieves took my good jewelry, my husband's Rolex, and our emergency cash. We kept it in a lockbox under the bed. I guess we should have been more creative, but there you have it."

Olivia was struck by the fact that both the Quimbys and the Ridgemonts had been attending athletic events during the robberies. She asked Sue if they knew the Quimbys.

"Afraid not," she said. "I wondered about that when I read about their robbery case in the paper, but I think her kids go to Neuse River Academy. We're at The Bellhaven School. Goooo Bears!"

As Millay took down a list of stolen items, Olivia tried to deduce who would have knowledge of the family's weekend schedule. She waited for Sue to finish speaking and then asked, "How did the thieves get in?"

Sue got up and pointed at the cat door carved into the wall next to the door leading to the garage. "We have two cats and an aversion to litter boxes. When we're going to be out all day we leave the garage door cracked a bit. That way Lucifer and Beelzebub can come and go as they please."

Millay giggled. "Nice names. Very Old Testament."

"Like I said, I've got two teenage boys. God forbid they call our cats something sweet like Checkers or Mittens. The cats were strays three years ago but now they totally rule our lives. You'd of thought they were honorary members of the royal family the way they're treated around here." Sue walked over to the door leading to the garage. "We usually lock this, but I think we were in such a hurry to get to the game on time that we forgot. I guess we made it easy for the bad guys. They just slipped in under the crack in the garage door—we hadn't made it small enough—and walked into the house. I doubt they spent more than thirty minutes taking what they wanted."

Olivia nodded. "I'm sorry. It's a shame someone took advantage of you when you were merely trying to be considerate of your pets." She rubbed her chin. "Can you think of anything else we should know? Did the thieves leave anything odd around the house?"

Sue picked up a slingshot from the next chair and brandished the weapon. "You'll have to be more specific!"

In response, Olivia told Sue about the melted butter and knife left on the Quimby's countertop.

"Actually, I would have never thought about this if you hadn't asked, but there was a deck of cards on this table. Two hands had been dealt, like the boys had just finished playing a game of poker or something." She shrugged. "The weird thing was I hadn't seen them get the cards out before we left. I never thought to ask them either. I just shoved them into a stack and put a rubber band around them." Picking up the crumpled newspaper, she began to search for the cards.

"Can you ask your sons about the cards?" Olivia asked. "If the deck doesn't belong to them, it might have been placed there by the thieves. They may have even left their prints on them."

Her eyes widening, Sue nodded. "They're at a friend's house clearing downed trees, but I can send them a text." She felt her pockets. "Now where did I leave my phone?"

The three women began a fruitless search for Sue's cell phone until Millay had the smarts to suggest Sue simply dial the number and listen for its ring.

"Before I do, I want you to know that my sons programmed the phone to play the song 'Bootylicious' whenever someone calls me. It's completely embarrassing but I don't know how to change it." She picked up the kitchen phone and dialed. Millay followed the sounds of Destiny's Child into the front hall and pulled a phone in a magenta case from the soil of a fake potted Ficus tree.

"How on earth?" Sue shook her head in wonderment. She fumbled over the keys, trying to recall how to send a text message until Millay offered to complete the task for her. That being done, she also changed the ringtone so that Sue would now hear Handel's "Water Music" instead of "Bootylicious." "Thanks. That reminds me of my wedding, before my life wasn't in a complete state of chaos!" She sighed happily. "But I wouldn't change a thing."

"You don't seem to be too upset over the robbery," Millay remarked. "I'd be furious."

Sue put a hand over Millay's. "My family was unharmed. What was taken can be replaced. They can't. Let those guys have our stuff, as long as they never return. That's why I agreed to talk to you. Anything I can do to help catch them means that they won't come back."

Her phone blipped and she examined the screen. "The cards are theirs, but they haven't played with them since the vacation we took in June." She glanced at Olivia with excitement. "Wouldn't it be something if the thieves get caught over a deck of cards?" She put a finger on her lips and tapped. "The question is . . . where did I put them?"

"Did you return them to one of your son's bedrooms?" Olivia hazarded a guess.

Sue smirked. "That would be the logical place to start, but I'm easily distracted, so even if I meant to put them away, it doesn't mean I succeeded. Let's see. I put a rubber band around them and stuck them in a pocket while I was still standing in the kitchen." She touched her pants. "But it was a deep pocket, like you'd find on a coat."

"It's too hot for a coat, unless it was a rain jacket," Olivia pointed out.

Throwing open a hall closet, Sue shoved coats around but came up empty-handed.

"An apron?" Millay asked.

"I don't cook. I heat things up or order takeout." Sue began tapping her lips again. "Oh! I remember! I was painting the day after we'd been robbed. I was hoping it would settle me down, but I ended up covering up the whole thing with primer and starting all over again. Didn't like the color. Still, the cards must be in my smock."

She dashed from the room and quickly returned, holding the cards by the edge. They were loosely wrapped in a tissue. "Let me stick these in a plastic bag."

Once the cards were safely sealed in plastic, Olivia reached out for them. "I'm meeting with the chief of police in about two hours. I'll see that he gets these." When Sue looked perplexed by the declaration, Olivia colored. "It's okay. He's a friend of mine." With the deck of cards safely in her purse, Olivia shook hands with Sue and thanked her effusively for an interesting afternoon.

Back in the Range Rover, Haviland looked up from his bone and sniffed the air, his warm brown eyes alight with curiosity.

"Dirty socks and rotten bananas. That's all, Captain," Olivia told him.

Millay scratched the poodle behind the ears and then chucked Olivia on the arm. "Smooth move back there, by the way."

"Which one?" Olivia asked in jest.

"You told Sue you'd deliver the cards to the chief of police, but you neglected to mention that the chief you'd be seeing rules over the Oyster Bay fuzz, *not* Beaufort's men in blue."

Olivia's laughter filled the car's cabin and then floated out Haviland's open window. "I didn't want to burden Sue with such a trivial detail. She's got enough going on, wouldn't you agree?"

Millay shrugged. "I am *so* not doing the married with kids thing." She paused. "At least not until I'm forty. By then, I'll be too old to care."

"Watch it," Olivia growled. "I'm forty."

"I'm just kidding. I really want to be you when I grow up," Millay continued wryly. "I'd especially like to have your bank account." She sighed. "I'm going to have to dress in a *very* provocative way tonight to make up for two nights of lost tips. We're talking hoochie mama gear. Like Old Mother Hubbard, my cupboard is freaking bare!"

Later, Olivia pulled up in front of Millay's apartment complex and wagged a finger in mock warning. "You've been compensated for this afternoon's work, so there's no need to dress like a prostitute. I appreciated having you along today."

Millay frowned in confusion.

"Check your bag," Olivia directed with a smile. "See you Saturday."

She was pleased to see Millay's mouth drop open in surprise as she removed a gift card to the Piggly Wiggly from her bag. She flipped it over, noted the amount of the card, and widened her eyes in delighted surprise.

"Haviland." Olivia ruffled the black curls on her poodle's head. "Our work here is done."

Chapter 10

*Nothing would be more tiresome than
eating and drinking if God had not
made them a pleasure as well as a
necessity.*

—VOLTAIRE

Olivia's laptop was open on one of the small café tables at Bagels 'n' Beans. Aside from her coffee mug, every inch of the table's worn, wooden surface was covered with her copies of Laurel's notes from the interview with Christina Quimby and Millay's from their meeting with Sue Ridgemont earlier that day. Olivia piled newspaper clippings on area robberies on the spare chair under which Haviland dozed.

The laptop was less than a month old and Olivia wasn't familiar with the nuances of the new program bundle. She'd bought the lightweight machine online and had had no problem figuring out how to write and save documents, send and receive e-mails, or print, but she didn't know how to create a chart showing comparisons between the robberies. If she weren't so impatient, she would have invested time in reading the program's Help section. Instead, she called Harris.

"Where are you, my resident IT genius?" she asked.

Harris shouted over the loud hip-hop music playing in the background. "In the car! I just got off work! I'm rolling with the windows down and, uh, hold on a sec . . ." Abruptly, the music ceased. "Sorry, I can hear you now."

"Can you change into your superhero costume, come down to Bagels 'n' Beans, and rescue me? I need to make a spreadsheet on my computer."

Clearing his throat, Harris responded in a lower octave. "I won't let you down, ma'am. Let me pick up my cape and Lycra tights and I'll be right there. But I *will* exact a price for my services. The Firewall Avenger only operates after an eight-hour day when fueled by an Asiago bagel with cream cheese and a large mocha latte."

"A small sacrifice in exchange for wearing tights. Your request shall be granted."

Once Harris had polished off his snack and was busy creating Olivia's chart, she pivoted in her seat and sent several withering looks in the direction of a group of high school girls at the other end of the narrow room. Within seconds of Harris's arrival, they'd been attempting to gain his attention by giggling, shrieking, and taking photos of him with their cell phones.

"Harris. Would it bother you if I scattered that collective of hormone-crazed Hannah Montanas over there? I'm sure it's nice to have a throng of pretty admirers, but I cannot concentrate in the face of all that hair flipping and squealing. It would be quieter in a slaughterhouse."

Glancing over his shoulder, Harris met the laughing gazes of four pairs of eyes and immediately turned back to Olivia. "They're probably just making jokes about my skin. I'm used to it. I ignored girls like them all through high school. It really doesn't bother me anymore."

Touching his hand, Olivia forced him to look up from the screen. "Harris, your rosacea has gotten remarkably less noticeable. A few more treatments and you'll be as unblemished as a Hollywood starlet. Those girls are staring at you because they think you're cute. Fine. Hot. I'm not familiar with teenage lingo. Most of them speak Text Message—all abbreviations and code. LOL, BFF, WTF."

Smiling, Harris ventured another glance at the girls, causing them to redouble their giggling. "How are you going to get rid of them?"

"I'll pretend we're an item," Olivia said with a wry grin. "Just act like you're attracted to older women."

Harris produced a feline growl, causing Haviland to jerk his head off the floor. "Oh, I do like the cougars." He put a placating hand on the poodle's neck. "I am totally kidding, my friend. Please don't bite any digits off. I need every one of my lightning-fast keyboard fingers."

Once Olivia had shooed away the gaggle of girls, the two friends concentrated on their task. Harris created a spreadsheet that included the thieves' method of entry, the items taken from each house, the day of the week in which the robbery occurred, and a complete list of services each family used.

"The houses were entered through the garage or the back door," Olivia noted when he was done. "And in each case, the thieves were neat and particular about what they wanted."

"They prefer jewelry and electronics," Harris agreed. "But I'd imagine bling and hi-tech toys are easiest to unload to a pawn broker or some other shady third party." He pointed at the screen. "I'd try to track the art. Those paintings are unique, and if these guys are looking for quick, fast cash, then they're not traveling too far to sell the pilfered stuff."

Olivia was impressed. "That'll be the first point I raise to the chief, if he hasn't thought of it already." She searched the chart eagerly for connections. "I really thought we'd plug in all the data and voila! There'd be a cleaning service or a housepainter or a pet walker they all had in common. Instead, the only dots connecting these families is that they have kids and those kids play sports, taking the families away from home for a large chunk of time during the weekend."

"And then there's the whole weird butter-dish thing." He eyed Olivia's purse. "Do you have the cards with you?"

Nodding, she produced the deck in its protective plastic bag.

Sue Ridgemont had removed the tissue encasing the deck after dropping it into the bag. Harris peered through the plastic and then, without asking permission, used his long, agile fingers to push the rubber band off the deck without opening the bag.

"Whoa," Harris murmured in admiration over the illustrations of scantily clad warrior women. "These are all Boris Vallejo images. His fantasy art is amazing. I've got one of his Conan the Barbarian prints. When you look at it, you feel like you could bounce a quarter off the guy's pecs." He fanned the cards out as much as he could without removing them from the bag. "Cool. The centaurs are the jacks and these mermaids are the queens. Man, they are smoking hot." Blushing, he continued to inch the cards apart. "Ah, here's a quartet of barbarian kings." He frowned. "Wait a sec. Did I miss one?"

Olivia, who wasn't as fascinated by the artistry of the cards as Harris, picked up their cups, walked to the counter, and handed them to Wheeler. "Two refills please." She paid for the espresso drinks and then returned to the table, eager to study their chart in search of inspiration before heading to The Boot Top to meet Chief Rawlings.

"There's a queen missing," Harris pointed out as she sat down. "Not that I'd blame one of the robbers for taking one of these gorgeous matriarchs, but now the Ridgemont boys have no hopes of ever playing with a full deck."

He handed the cards to Olivia, but she didn't move a muscle. "Not playing with a full deck." Her blood quickened. Words clicked into place in her mind and she tapped excitedly on the computer screen. "Like a knife through butter!"

Harris followed her train of thought. "Clichés? The thieves are leaving behind clichés?"

"Two might not be enough to prove a theory, but if the third robbery—the one that turned violent—had some bizarre tableau in the kitchen, then these guys have a signature."

Harris dropped the cards on the table. "Even if they do, would that help the cops catch them?"

Olivia shrugged. "I think Rawlings apprehends guilty parties by getting to know them, by discovering their story, so to speak. This modus operandi of the robbers is a message. It's part of their story."

"Whatever you say." Harris looked doubtful. "I just hope theirs has an unhappy ending."

Rawlings was comfortably established at The Boot Top's bar by the time Olivia arrived. He and Gabe chatted amicably despite the din created by a party of four devouring a bowl of snack mix at one of the nearby tables. Olivia led Haviland into her office, said hello to the kitchen staff, and hurried to the restroom before Rawlings could spot her.

Olivia checked her reflection in the mirror, smoothing tiny wrinkles from her belted scoop-neck dress. The garment's simple cut and deep blue shade was accentuated by a triple-strand necklace of red coral beads. In the low light of the ladies' room, she brushed her hair until it shone like moonlight and then spritzed the skin of her neck and wrists with Shalimar.

As though the perfume announced her presence, Rawlings raised his chin and pivoted in his seat, watching intently as she closed the distance between them.

He rose, and though his face remained stiff and formal, his eyes smiled. "When I was a boy, I was fascinated by mythology, yet I never understood why a sailor would willingly jump into the ocean because he heard a woman's song. But I believe that if saw a siren looking like you do tonight, I would leap overboard at the sound of her first note."

Rawlings may have delivered the words in a breezy voice, but Olivia had never been given such a unique and lovely compliment. Suddenly, she felt as though everyone in the bar could tell that the air around their bodies was electrically charged, like lightning before the strike.

Gesturing at an open table, Olivia led the chief to one of the leather club chairs and made eye contact with Gabe. Though he was busy mixing a martini, he glanced over at her and nodded. Within minutes, he was at their table with a tumbler of Chivas Regal and one of the restaurant's microbrews in a frosted glass.

Rawlings and Olivia clinked glasses, sipped from their drinks, and then the chief arched his brows in curiosity as Olivia placed her laptop on the table.

"Did you bring your file on the latest robbery?" she asked.

Glancing at the images surfacing on Olivia's computer screen, Rawlings patted a worn leather-handled satchel at his feet. The bag called to mind an aging professor or laboratory scientist, but somehow suited the police chief as well. "This is a murder case now, Olivia. I'm not going to simply hand it over for your perusal."

She bristled. "I hadn't expected that, but could you take a look at the chart Harris created? It shows a thorough comparison of the other robberies, including the one that occurred in Beaufort County."

The chief's brow rose higher. "This is Laurel's work?"

"In part," Olivia answered cryptically and pointed out the athleticism of all the victim's children. "None of them play the same sport or belong to the same country clubs, but these families send their kids to private schools. What of the third?"

Now Rawlings removed the case file from his satchel. "Let's see. The Howard children attend The Neuse River Academy." He examined the computer screen. "As do the Quimby children, I see."

Olivia fell silent and let Rawlings think. His gaze grew distant as he turned his face toward the window and fixed his eyes on the twinkling lights out in the harbor. She followed suit, wondering if a tutor or teacher or bus driver linked the families, but dismissed each possibility as it surfaced in her mind.

"Is it plausible that there's some sort of coach working at both schools?" she ruminated aloud. "Perhaps an assistant coach? Or a referee? Someone knew *exactly* when these families would be away from their homes."

Rawlings removed a sheet of paper from his file. "These are the names of all the teachers, coaches, close friends, and carpool drivers who come into regular contact with the children." He placed another piece of paper on top of the first. "Here are the cleaning, garbage, and lawn services used by each family as well as doctors, beauticians, barbers, dentists, veterinarians, accountants, et cetera. Notice anything interesting?"

He waited for Olivia to read through the names. When she came across the one he'd also recognized, she jabbed at the paper with her finger. "Steve Hobbs! These families all go to Laurel's husband to have their teeth cleaned?" She released the paper as though it had singed her fingertips. "Pure coincidence."

"I'm certain it is as well, but nonetheless, I'll have to establish his whereabouts on the days the robberies occurred." Rawlings looked miserable over the prospect.

Olivia took a generous swallow from her glass. "Can you talk to him during office hours? I'd rather Laurel not have to worry when this turns out to be nothing."

Rawlings smiled. "Of course." He looked up as a waiter hovered over them, clearly unsure how to ask his boss to move her laptop to make room for the hors d'oeuvres Michel had prepared especially for Olivia and her guest. "Allow me," the chief told the waiter and put the computer on a nearby chair.

"Chef Michel sends his compliments," the waiter said to Rawlings. "He's made several items not listed on this evening's menu in your honor. First, we have Boursin and spinach bouchée. Next, duck canapés and beef teriyaki brochette. And finally, crab cakes with a Cajun remoulade and mushroom crescents drizzled with a creamed sherry sauce. Enjoy."

Rawlings rubbed his chin and stared at the gourmet fare. "Boursin? Bouchée? Brochette? What are we eating?"

Olivia smiled. "Boursin is a cheese that comes from Normandy. Bouchée is a pastry. Brochette simply means food cooked and oftentimes served on skewers." She served him a sample from each of the dishes.

"Do all of your patrons speak gastronomy?"

"Hardly. That's one of The Boot Top's charms. We sound fancy, but the trick is blending the correct fresh ingredients together. We awaken the senses through a single mouthful of tender duck or a sip of fine burgundy." She gestured at the food on their table. "None of this would be possible without Michel. He could work anywhere, but he chose to be here."

Rawlings tasted a crab cake and moaned. "Mother of God! There are so many flavors in this one bite! Sweet and salty, creamy and crispy—all going off like a perfectly timed fireworks display. Michel is a maestro."

Pleased, Olivia enjoyed some of her meal before Gabe appeared with two glasses of pinot noir. "While the food has you in such an agreeable state, would you tell me whether any unusual objects were left in the kitchen of the Howard household after the robbery?"

The chief finished chewing and took a swallow of wine. He dabbed his mouth with a napkin and then slowly sipped from his wineglass a second time, obviously appreciating the Pinot's cherry bouquet. "How on earth did you know that?"

She took the deck of playing cards out of her purse. "These were left on the Ridgemonts' kitchen table, set up as though two people had been playing poker." After describing the butter dish and knife found on the Quimby's countertop, she explained how she and Harris had both recognized that the tableaus represented well-known clichés.

Rawlings didn't need to check the Howard file. He leaned forward, the sumptuous fare on his plate forgotten. "The culprits set out three wooden blocks—taken from a old set that Mrs. Howard's had since childhood. She kept them in a box in her bedroom closet. The thieves picked out three blocks and turned them so that the numbers faced outward. The numbers were one, two, and three."

Olivia ran her fingertip along the base of her wineglass. "As easy as one, two, three?"

"That'd be my guess." Rawlings agreed. "But why? What are they trying to say? Who is their audience? The victims? Law enforcement?"

"It implies a level of intelligence." Olivia said, knowing Rawlings wasn't directing his questions at her. "I doubt your average thief could define 'cliché,' let alone create scenes using such a specific literary device."

The pair fell silent. Olivia leaned back in her chair, listening to the familiar sounds of subdued laughter from the patrons at the bar and the rise and fall of quiet conversation from the diners in the next room. The noises floated around her and she found comfort in the blend of murmurs, of cutlery being laid against an empty plate, of the tinkle of crystal as a couple toasted one another with flutes of champagne.

"Perhaps there are only two of them," she said after a few minutes. "That's why two hands were dealt in their mock poker game."

Rawlings nodded. "It would certainly take two strong individuals to tote some of those flat-screen televisions. I know they're not as heavy as they once were, but they're still unwieldy. And it would be extremely time consuming to maneuver the goods without a partner, so yes, I believe we're talking about a pair or a team working together."

A waiter materialized behind Olivia's shoulder. Seeing that his boss and her guest were no longer eating, he asked for permission and then, after receiving an absent nod from Olivia, removed their plates. He returned shortly to serve them a platter of bite-sized pastries and then poured steaming cups of coffee for the pair. When he started to walk off, Rawlings reached out a hand to stop him.

"Excuse me, good sir," the chief halted his retreat. "Could you rustle up a glass of chocolate milk for me?"

If the waiter was surprised by the request, he didn't show it. "Certainly. I'll be back in a moment."

Olivia waved at the selection of éclairs, Napoleons, cappuccino mousse, and hazelnut dacquoise cakes. "Not enough sugar for you here?"

"It's how I get my daily supply of dairy," Rawlings answered, unruffled by Olivia's teasing.

Lacking a taste for sweets, Olivia sat back and enjoyed her coffee. She was eager for the waiter to clear away the food so she could input the information from Rawlings' file onto her spreadsheet. She knew he wouldn't reveal the entirety of its contents and she didn't want to see the medical examiner's report or catch a glimpse of the crime scene photos in any case. What she hungered for were the facts. Indisputable, concise, comprehensible data. She didn't want to think about the grief-stricken, shell-shocked family or wonder how April Howard would survive without her husband's income.

Olivia Limoges had always run from loss. Now was no different. She sought to escape from focusing on another woman's terrible sorrow by training every thought on times and dates, school names and sports teams.

The chief's chocolate milk was delivered and he drank it pensively, his eyes locked on the dessert platter, unseeing. Finally, Olivia raised her hand and the waiter materialized as silently as a specter and removed their dishes. The noise from the bar area increased as more patrons arrived well ahead of their reservations in order to socialize before enjoying a delicious meal.

Olivia and Rawlings remained wrapped in their cocoon of silence. As always, they were able to enjoy one another's company without filling the space between them with unnecessary prattle.

When Rawlings spoke, his eyes reflecting the light from the votive on their table, it was apparent that he'd decided to put aside the topic of burglaries for the moment. "I like being here with you, Olivia. It seems like a contradiction, but you are the only person who can infuriate me beyond rational thought and yet are also able to bring me the deepest sense of calm. You are much like the ocean." He indicated the harbor beyond the window, which was just a dark smudge beneath an indigo sky. "It must be why your eyes remind me of the open sea."

Olivia smiled at him. The smile was so wide and warm that it felt unfamiliar to the muscles of her mouth. "Sawyer—" she began.

"Hello!" The chipper visage of Flynn McNulty abruptly appeared before them. "Is this a meeting of future Hemingways and Dickensons, or might a simple shopkeeper pull up a chair?"

Rawlings stood and shook Flynn's hand. "I think you're giving us too much credit. At least in regards to my writing. Ms. Limoges possesses the only genuine talent at this table."

Flynn set his tumbler of whiskey down and settled into a chair, crossing an ankle over the opposite knee in a posture of utter relaxation. For the first time, Olivia was irritated by Flynn's easy confidence. Rawlings queried the bookstore owner about new fiction arrivals and the two men began to toss about author names as though they were playing a game of catch. Olivia heard Michael Connelly, Nick Hornby, Stieg Larsson, and Daniel Silva before she tuned out.

Eventually, Flynn needed a refill and, wanting to chat with Gabe, went up to the bar instead of signaling a waiter. Rawlings had drained his drink and had a speck of chocolate milk on his chin. Olivia reached over with her napkin to wipe it away, but Rawlings caught her by the wrist before she had the chance and placed her palm flat against his chest. She could feel his heart beating as though she held it in her hand.

"I'd better be going," he said, his voice heavy with regret. He gently released her and swiped at his chin with his napkin. "I have two unsolved murder cases now, and though I doubt they're related—" He stopped abruptly and his mouth went slack. His gaze was fixed on the framed reproduction of Vincent Van Gogh's *Beach at Scheveningen in Stormy Weather*, that hung on the wood-paneled wall behind their table. "But they *are* related," he breathed into Van Gogh's muted browns and grays and the small splotches of black that formed the villagers waiting at the water's edge as a lone fishing boat returned to shore.

Olivia rose and moved to the chief's side, standing shoulder-to-shoulder with him.

Rawlings raised one of his large hands, uncurled a finger, and pointed it at a solitary male figure on the right side of the painting. With a few simple brushstrokes, Van Gogh had managed to convey a sense of urgency as the man hurried across the sand. His featureless face betrayed no emotion, but his body pressed forward, legs bent, shoulders lurching forward, hands raised above the waist. Even the wind seemed to be against him, blowing the grass growing over the dunes nearly flat.

"John Doe's death scene is a cliché," Rawlings whispered and then gathered his satchel. "Thank you, Olivia. For the meal, the company, and your ability to help me see clearly. I—"

Again, they were interrupted by Flynn who had returned to the table with two tumblers of whiskey. He gave Rawlings a look of apology. "I didn't know whether you'd be interested in chasing your milk with whiskey."

Mumbling a hasty good-bye, Rawlings departed.

Olivia took the whiskey from Flynn's hand with a brief thank-you and drank it down, her eyes never leaving the painting on the wall. "What cliché? What did you see?"

"Olivia." Flynn waved his hands in an attempt to gain her attention. "Are you free to stay awhile?"

She turned to him, her deep blue eyes nearly black in the dim light. "Not tonight. I need to go home and think."

And with that, she strolled out of the bar and through the swinging door into the kitchen. The door had a small, rounded window and was marked by a sign that said "Staff Only, Please." Olivia knew Flynn wouldn't follow her into the restaurant's inner sanctum.

It would be like chasing a dragon into its cave.

Chapter 11

On life's vast ocean diversely we sail,
Reason the card, but passion is the gale.
—ALEXANDER POPE

Olivia carried the Bounty Hunter on her shoulder as though she were a lumberjack heading into the forest for a day's work. Haviland bounded out in front, splashing in the surf, his brown eyes burnished gold by the early-morning light.

It wasn't difficult to find the spot where the body had been buried in the sand. There were still multiple sets of tracks leading up to the dunes left by either the police or, judging from a scattering of empty beer cans, curious locals. Olivia switched on the metal detector and frowned.

"I know it's pure hubris to believe I could find a buried clue when a dozen cops, not to mention one of the area's finest K-9 units, could not," she confessed to Haviland. "But I hate standing idly by."

Slowly, deliberately, she began to sway the metal detector's disc over the sand. She started where she believed the body had been and moved up the beach toward the dunes. Her machine was unusually silent and failed to signal the presence of useless pieces of metal like soda can tabs or bottle caps. The display screen was also lifeless.

Olivia completed a wide semicircle and began to repeat the process in the opposite direction, heading toward the water's edge. Again, the Bounty Hunter had nothing to offer and she set it aside, keenly disappointed. Kicking off her shoes, she sat down, curling her toes in the moist sand just shy of the ocean's watery fingers.

"You sent me signs last time someone I cared for was hurt," she whispered, reaching out to touch the frothy ridge of a wave. "This man was a stranger to me, but someone must be missing him. Someone will want him to be at peace. You were the only witness. What secrets do you carry?"

The water gently bubbled and hissed and then Haviland was at her side, nudging Olivia with his nose before racing off again to chase a gull. Though the poodle was a threat, the bird flew just out of Haviland's reach, as if enjoying a game with the canine.

When Olivia looked back down at the sand, she noticed that it was pocked with fiddler crab holes. Recalling a trick from childhood, Olivia pierced the sand next to one of the holes with a twig and the crab darted out of the burrow. Olivia followed the creature's progress, which was made slightly awkward due to the one large and fiddle-shaped claw. The crab scuttled several yards away from the water line and immediately began to dig a new hole. Olivia had watched the crabs do this hundreds of times before, but she still loved to sit and wait as the tireless creatures produced a tidy ball of sand in the process of creating a new home.

"Not a very exciting existence," she mused aloud. "You dig yourself a hole—" She stopped and glanced up the beach. "Dig yourself into a hole. *That's* the cliché Rawlings figured out at The Boot Top." She stood, brushed sand from her pants, and whistled for Haviland. "Felix Howard wasn't the first person to suffer violence at the robbers' hands. They've killed before. They committed premeditated murder right *here!*"

Reclaiming the metal detector, Olivia switched it on, ignoring Haviland's plaintive look. "I know you've had enough, but I can't quit yet. Just pick a spot and start digging. I'm going to sweep this entire perimeter once again. There must be *something* here."

There wasn't.

Tired, hot, and frustrated, the pair set off for home.

Olivia spent the afternoon critiquing Millay's chapter. Her phone rang once, but she was so engrossed in Millay's fantastical world that she allowed the answering machine to pick up. It was Flynn, asking that she return his call as soon as possible. "Otherwise I'm going to have to turn to *another* smart, no-nonsense woman to help me out," he teased. "She's not *quite* as attractive, but I'm out of my league here. Call me, please?"

The sound of Flynn's voice seemed incongruent with Millay's narrative. Her heroine, Tessa, was about to embark on her first battle, and Olivia felt anxious for the fictional girl. In the previous chapter, the Bayside Book Writers had learned that Tessa could not learn the secret name of her Gryphon until they were victorious in three battles against terrifying foes. Only by calling the Gryphon by his true name would the young warrior girl and her mount be truly united. This union would awaken Tessa's magical abilities, giving her the necessary prowess to face the enemy of her people: the Dark Witches and their mounts, the Wyverns.

Taking a sip of iced tea flavored with lime, Olivia returned her attention to Tessa.

Learning to fly had been hard enough. Tessa had to sit at the base of the Gryphon's neck, her legs folded and her hands buried in the thick, downy feathers behind his head. Her thighs ached from having to squeeze the Gryphon's shoulders where his feathers gave way to fur. In the beginning, she had fallen again and again, but now that she was more skilled, the Gryphon soared higher into the sky, above the shimmering green seas and lush fields of her homeland. On the morrow, they would leave the secluded valley behind and travel to the edge of the Sea of Bones.

Three girls had gone before her.

Three Gryphons had returned without their riders.

Tessa spent the night in her Gryphon's cave. The other girls chose to sleep in the communal lodge. Though the lodge's linen covered pallets were far more comfortable than as pile of straw, Tessa found she could not wander too far from her beast without feeling an ache to be near him again.

At dawn, one of the priests blew a shell horn into the mist. The deep, lonely call resonated inside the cave, waking Tessa immediately. She dressed in her warrior's garb of deer hide breeches and a flowing white tunic and shouldered a quiver made of dark green leather. The image of a Gryphon's haughty profile had been stitched on both sides in white thread. Tessa's arrows also had white shafts with moss green fletches. The weight of the quiver on her back was a comfort, and she prayed her aim would be true.

As they flew toward the Sea of Bones, she feared that her prayers would not be enough.

Before saying good-bye to the other girls, Tessa had strapped a lance to each leg, and now, as the Gryphon stretched out his neck and cried with the voice of one thousand eagles, she untied a lance and gripped it tightly in her fist.

She'd heard tales of the monsters living in the black water of the Sea of Bones since she could walk. With the face and torso of a giantess, two pairs of finlike arms as pliable and slithery as eels, and a dozen coiled tails like those of a sea serpent, this breed of water witch was especially feared.

For years, the Gryphon warriors had whittled down their numbers, but the water witches were far from extinct, and those that survived had become very strong. They fought with their arms and tails, spewed mouthfuls of seawater powerful enough to knock their enemies off their mounts, and wielded serrated swords fashioned from the spines of sea dragons.

The Gryphon released a second battle cry and the head of a sea witch burst through the surface of the water directly beneath them. Tessa nearly lost her seat as her mount abruptly pivoted to the left to avoid the sweep of a barbed serpent's tail.

Aiming at the witch's eye, Tessa released her lance. The witch batted it aside with a slick arm and laughed. It was a horrible sound, a wet gurgle of insatiable hunger and timeless evil. Most warriors would have been filled with dread, but the noise only served to anger Tessa. She hadn't worn herself out with training for the past few weeks to fail here.

She threw her second lance, again aiming for an eye. The witch lifted her chin and Tessa's weapon cut her lower lip. Howling, the monster wiped at a trail of black blood and snarled. Suddenly, four bone swords sliced through the air. The Gryphon dove out of reach, but Tessa was unable to fire any arrows because she was forced to cling to her mount's neck or be flung into the churning waves below.

Olivia finished reading the chapter without pausing to make notes. She needed to know that Tessa had succeeded in vanquishing the sea witch before jotting comments on word choice or passages in which she wanted more detail. At times, Olivia felt that Millay's writing was too fast paced and wished her friend would learn to ease back on the narrative throttle. Tessa was a fascinating character, but it was difficult to get to know her because she was always on the move.

Let us in, Olivia wrote at the end of the chapter. *What is Tessa feeling? Even when she defeats the sea witch, she just flies off into the sunset. I know she's exhausted from the experience, but you're keeping the reader at a distance by not sharing what's going on in Tessa's mind.*

The phone rang again, but by this time Olivia was ready for a break. When she saw Will Hamilton's number on her caller ID box, she snatched the receiver from the cradle.

"I hope you have news for me, Mr. Hamilton," she said.

The private investigator cleared his throat, which Olivia sensed was a sign that he was about to impart bad news.

"Mr. Burkhart picked up the package in question at quarter past eleven on Thursday morning. While still inside The UPS Store, he examined your return address carefully, and then tossed the envelope on the passenger seat of his truck. It's been there ever since."

"That's it?" Olivia didn't bother to hide her irritation.

"He made a phone call as soon as he got in the truck but the package has remained unopened."

This surprised Olivia. "Are you certain?"

"Yes, ma'am." Hamilton paused. "And seeing as that

envelope contains a thousand bucks in cash, I'd say Mr. Burkhart isn't exactly hurting for money. Either that or he's holding the envelope for a third party."

Olivia considered the latter theory. "You may be on to something there." She sighed. "I haven't been completely forthcoming with you, Mr. Hamilton, but it's high time I was. When I first hired you, I was afraid that I was being made a fool of, but now I'm so confused that I don't know what to think. I have no interest in entering into a business arrangement with Rodney Burkhart. That was an untruth." Having confessed as much, she told the private investigator about the letter she'd received concerning her father.

"I've handled dozens of missing persons cases, ma'am," Will answered solemnly when she was done. "They rarely have happy endings."

"I want to know who sent me this damned letter! And I want to know *why*! Is this only about money or is there some possibility that my father is alive?" Olivia felt her cheeks flush in indignation. "After all this time, to have this wound reopened . . ." She struggled to steady her voice. "Mr. Hamilton, I need closure. Once and for all. Keep watching Mr. Burkhart. I can wait a little longer to see where that envelope ends up and it's well worth the cost of your services if you can identify the bastard who's ruined any chance I have of a sound night's sleep!"

The private investigator heard her anguish. "I won't let you down, ma'am. On my honor, I'll find out who's behind this."

Satisfied, Olivia hung up and went upstairs to change into a silver-hued sheath dress and a necklace of large turquoise stones. The Boot Top would soon be packed with tourists in town for the Cardboard Regatta and she wanted to be present to ensure that her restaurant sparkled like Oyster Bay's crown jewel.

She'd barely had time to settle Haviland in her office

before patrons began streaming into the bar. Most of the Cardboard Regatta participants attended the race year after year and had come to know one another on a first-name basis. In general, they were an extremely friendly and fun-loving group and the locals were glad to have them.

Gabe was hugged and kissed like a long-lost relative and Olivia received her fair share of hearty handshakes and embraces as well. Wine, beer, and cocktails were consumed in hedonistic amounts and the noise in The Boot Top's dining room escalated beyond its traditional murmurs and soft laughter. As the evening progressed, the competitors exchanged boisterous boasts and taunts while the wait staff scurried about, frantically trying to keep glasses filled and to set course after course of Michel's exquisite fare in front of the diners.

Saturday promised to be even more hectic. The Bayside Book Writers were planning to watch the races and then gather for a midafternoon critique session. Millay had to be at Fish Nets earlier than usual and Olivia wanted to be at The Boot Top by six, so their time together was limited.

The regatta was Oyster Bay's last tourist-driven revenue generator until spring returned, and by nine o'clock Saturday morning, there wasn't a parking space to be found within miles of the harbor.

The downtown merchants had dressed their store windows with the deft touch of Fifth Avenue designers. The flower planters lining the streets were bursting with a vibrant mix of gold lantana and red geranium, and canvas flags celebrating the Cardboard Regatta hung from every signpost. The streets closest to the docks had been closed to automobile traffic and local vendors were selling a variety of wares, from beaded necklaces to handmade ceramics to funnel cakes, at a rapid rate.

Olivia and Haviland strolled among the tourists, enjoying

the September sunshine and a strong sense of community pride. One would never know that Ophelia had done her best to cripple the town. Every piece of broken glass or tattered shingle had been replaced. New coats of paint freshened front doors and shutters, and the sidewalks had been swept until they glimmered in the late morning light.

Unable to resist buying roasted corn on a stick, Olivia chewed on the salty, buttery snack until her attention was caught by a display of oil paintings. She recognized Sawyer's work immediately.

"Gorgeous day, isn't it?" a woman asked, looking up from a book of crossword puzzles. Her gaze was friendly and warm, but sharpened slightly as she recognized the tall woman with the white blond hair. "Ms. Limoges. I don't believe we've ever met. I'm Jeannie, Sawyer's sister."

Olivia reached out to shake Jeannie's hand. She was a handsome woman closing in on fifty, with a trim figure and soft waves of auburn hair.

"I was hoping you'd stop by," Jeannie said. "Sawyer put me in charge of giving something to you." She lifted the skirt of the cobalt tablecloth and peered around. "Now where did I put that thing?"

While she hunted, Olivia examined the paintings. Much smaller than the chief's usual works, they were all simplistic beach scenes. Though skillfully executed, they lacked the central object or figure Sawyer traditionally placed in his large-scale paintings. However, the tourists thronged around the booth, looking over this work with keen interest. A husband and wife grabbed a painting each and entered into a good-natured debate over whether to purchase a landscape of the beach at sunset or a painting of three children flying kites along the water's edge.

"What the hell, let's get them both!" the man declared and was rewarded with a kiss from his spouse.

Meanwhile, Jeannie had found what she'd been looking for. "Give me a sec to take care of these lovebirds first. I don't want to miss your reaction to this," she added with a wink.

Turning away to toss out her corncob, Olivia felt an inexplicable impulse to walk away. She could disappear within seconds and simply allow the throng to carry her off like a powerful current. What had Sawyer entrusted to his sister? Olivia doubted he wanted to pass along information regarding the robbery cases and it was unlikely that his chapter had been rewritten and was now ready for her perusal, so what *was* Jeannie about to deliver? Olivia thought of how Sawyer had placed her hand on his chest and her face grew warm. If only she could be alone with him again, to figure out why he possessed the ability to stir her feelings as no one else had before.

"Here we are!" She carefully reached over a group of paintings displayed on wooden easels in order to place a rectangular package in Olivia's hands. "Go on, open it, honey."

Olivia obeyed, peeling away the brown butcher paper enveloping a canvas. When she saw the image, she cried out in surprised delight. "Haviland!" She put her fingertips on the layers of dried paint Rawlings had used to form her poodle's black curls. There were Haviland's intelligent, smiling eyes, the color of golden caramel, and his toothy grin. His seated posture was somehow as dignified as a king's and as jaunty as a rogue's.

"It's amazing!" Olivia exclaimed, her throat tight with emotion. When she spoke again, her voice was a mere breath, barely audible above the multitude of tourists. "It's the most wonderful thing I've ever seen, let alone been given."

Jeannie's eyes, which were the same shape as her brother's but more green than hazel, sparkled with pleasure. "He'll be glad to hear that."

Tenderly rewrapping the small painting in its protective layer of butcher paper, Olivia moved closer to Jeannie. "Why didn't he give this to me himself?"

"Oh, some stuff and nonsense over having to be on duty right up until the start of your writer's meeting and that wasn't the time or the place to give it to you anyhow and blah, blah, blah." Jeannie shook her head in exasperation. "The man cares for you. It's plain as day, but he's afraid of having feelings for anyone after what he went through with his wife."

"If he doesn't feel, he won't get hurt." Olivia understood his rationale.

Jeannie nodded. "I suspect you know a bit about that fool notion."

She began to tape the corners of the butcher paper together and then slid the painting into a grocery bag. She set the bag gently on the table and smoothed the paper as though she were petting a cat.

"I was a teenager when your daddy went missing. I remember seeing your grandmother's fancy car motoring through town. I figured she must be a movie star to have her own driver." Jeannie smiled at the memory. "Do you know what? I was actually jealous of you. You rode off in that big, black car and it seemed so glamorous to me, like you were going to live a real life while the rest of us stayed here and rotted." She reached out and touched Olivia's arm. "I was a silly girl then. But after you came back, I wish I'd had the guts to walk up and tell you that I'd wondered about you over the years, that I'd always prayed you were okay."

Embarrassed by the other woman's sincerity, Olivia looked away. "I did lead a glamorous existence to some extent. I ate croissants at a sidewalk café near the Eiffel Tower, climbed on the pyramids at Giza, felt the spray of

Victoria Falls on my face . . ." She trailed off. "But I would have traded it all for another day with my mother or to have had a brother or sister. Someone to share a bedroom with, to whisper to when we were supposed to be asleep."

The loneliness of her childhood—all those years spent with only imaginary playmates as she drifted from room to room or wandered the grounds of one of her grandmother's several mansions—came back in force. Jeannie must have recognized the sadness flit over Olivia's features and immediately sought to dispel the gloom.

"Well, you're back where you belong now," she declared brightly. "And I hear you bought the old cotton mill." Jeannie gestured vaguely in the direction of Olivia's new property.

Grateful for the change of subject, Olivia nodded. "Yes. My offer was accepted yesterday. I plan to open a crab house this spring."

"That's good. More jobs for the locals and another of the town's landmarks that won't slide into the sea." Jeannie's attention was caught by a girl dancing to a bluegrass tune coming from the radio at the next booth. "Are you going to have music?"

Olivia smiled. "Oh, yes! Live bands, a cappella groups, jazz ensembles, all kinds of music."

Jeannie scrawled something on a piece of scrap paper. "You call me when you're ready to book bands. My son's been doing church gigs for the past two years and he's pretty good. His band can play anything from The Rolling Stones to Jimmy Buffet to Dave Matthews. Cody's a high school sophomore but has been putting away money for college since he was in the third grade." Her eyes shone with pride. "Me and his father had two years of junior college and that was enough for us, but Cody wants to be like his uncle Sawyer."

"Not a bad role model," Olivia answered and then stepped away to allow a new wave of customers to view the chief's paintings. "It'll take months to get the place ready, but I promise to put your son's name on the top of the audition list. What's his band called?"

"Excelsior," Jeannie said and then shrugged. "Whatever *that* is."

A man in overalls seemed frightened to approach the table where Haviland stood so Olivia put a hand on the poodle's collar, drawing him closer to her side. "Excelsior means 'ever higher.' I wonder if Cody's read the Longfellow poem with that title."

"I wouldn't be surprised. My brother is always buying that boy books and CDs and sports gear. Spoils him rotten." Olivia wasn't fooled by Jeannie's pretense of disapproval. "Sawyer would have made a fine daddy, but I guess that just wasn't part of the Lord's plan." She met Olivia's eyes. "But I hope *you* are." And with that, she turned to assist an eager customer.

Clutching her painting, Olivia wandered toward the harbor and the launching area of the cardboard boats. Her mind was full of thoughts of Sawyer. What did she really know of his private life? Of his childhood? Had he lain in his bed reading Longfellow? Somehow, she could picture him doing just that, for the poem was a tribute to the courage and perseverance of a young man. Did Rawlings see himself as that boy, trudging onward and upward through the frigid night, his throbbing arms refusing to lay down the banner of Excelsior?

Before her grandmother shipped her off to an exclusive all-girl boarding school, Olivia had had to memorize the poem for one of her many tutors. The words tiptoed back into her memory.

The shades of night were falling fast,
As through an Alpine village passed,
A youth, who bore, 'mid snow and ice,
A banner with the strange device,
Excelsior!
His brow was sad; his eye beneath,
Flashed like a falchion from its sheath,
And like a silver clarion rung
The accents of that unknown tongue,
Excelsior!

Haviland barked, drawing Olivia back to the present and the thick knot of people gathered to witness the start of the first race.

"You're right, Captain. That's a poem for a cold winter's day." Seeing Laurel waving to her from the dock while keeping a tight hold on her double stroller, the lighthearted mood Olivia had felt when she first arrived downtown returned.

Laurel gave Olivia a shy smile. "You seemed kind of lost in thought."

"I was mumbling poetry. Haviland is particularly fond of verse," Olivia answered and rubbed the fur on the poodle's neck. She then apologized to Laurel for being so abrupt the last time's they'd spoken.

"Sure. It's already forgotten," Laurel said as she handed each of the twins a soft pretzel. "Harris told me about the cliché clues. Do you have any idea what they mean?"

Olivia shook her head and wondered whether Steve had told his wife about being questioned by the police. From the serene look of Laurel's face, she doubted it. "So far, the only common denominator is that all the families have kids that play sports and attend area private schools."

"And the messages the thieves leave behind. What are they trying to tell the people they've stolen from?" Laurel asked and then sighed. "I miss the feeling that I had something to contribute to the *Gazette*, to this town." She gave a self-effacing laugh. "My cooking attempts have certainly been a disaster! Steve has begged me to go back to culinary school more than once. If only he realized there isn't one!"

"Is he working today?" Olivia looked around for Laurel's spouse.

"No. He's racing." She pointed at a small motorboat anchored off to the right of the end of the dock. "That's his team from the office. Their boat is that giant toothbrush."

Shielding her eyes from the glare of the sun, Olivia watched as Steve and two other men eased their cardboard boat into the water. Carefully, a man wearing a baseball hat climbed into the bow while Steve took up the captain's position in the stern. "They've entered the Oars Only category, I see. Harris is in the Sail-Powered Race, but I have yet to spot his boat. I figured he'd have made a *Star Trek* ship or a floating robot."

Laurel also began scanning the harbor. "He'd better get here soon. The judges need to examine his boat before the race. Poor Millay's been pacing the docks since I got here, sending Harris text after text. I've never seen her this anxious."

The two women secured a place to watch the first race. The twins, whose bellies were full of soft pretzels, apple juice, and cheese crackers, had fallen asleep in the stroller.

Olivia dug a pair of binoculars out of her purse and watched the contestants line up the bows of their boats until they touched a rope slung between two buoys. She'd never seen such an assortment of cardboard vessels. There were pirate ships, canoes, catamarans, and submarines, but there were also floating hot dogs, crocodiles, smoking cigars, sea serpents, sharks, dolphins, and rubber ducks.

A horn blasted and the contestants surged forward, their oars creating swirls and white froth in the water. Steve's toothbrush boat took an early lead, but it became clear that the vessel was too long to make quick turns around the course's buoys and they began to lose their advantage.

"Oh, dear." Laurel watched her husband through a pair of hot pink binoculars. "His partner said they should have made the boat shorter, but Steve insisted on adding more bristles to the brush."

A bright blue boat resembling a congenial killer whale passed by Steve's toothbrush and a snarling shark to capture first place. Steve's boat came in third, but he and his first mate were too busy shouting at one another to notice. Watching Laurel's red-faced spouse, Olivia wondered if he had serious anger issues.

As though reading her thoughts, Laurel spoke hastily. "He'll shake it off. This is supposed to be just for fun, right?"

Olivia ignored the question. "Laurel, what did you tell the editor of the *Gazette*?"

"That I needed more time to finish a major story," Laurel answered after a long pause. Lowering her binoculars, she met Olivia's stare. "I said that I had to interview April Howard before I could write a complete piece about the robberies." She looked back out at the harbor. "Several papers have sent crime reporters to speak to April, but she's refused to talk. I've been thinking about calling her. I feel like it's my duty to do what I can to stop these crimes, that it's my responsibility, just like caring for my kids or keeping the house clean. Does that sound ridiculously self-inflated?"

Shaking her head, Olivia said, "No, it doesn't. You'd like to wear more than one hat. You want a rich home life and a fulfilling career too. That doesn't make you a self-centered person. It simply means you wish to share your gifts with a wider audience."

Laurel blinked away tears. "Why do you have so much faith in me? No one else does. I told Steve that I wanted his parents to watch the twins so I could be a reporter and *not* Paula Deen and he just laughed."

"Look at those boats," Olivia replied soothingly. "They're made of cardboard, tape, and glue. They don't look like they'd float, let alone speed through the water, but with a little ingenuity and determination, there they are."

"Who would have thought being compared to a piece of corrugated cardboard could be so flattering?" Laurel managed a grin.

At that moment, Millay dashed through the crowd toward Olivia and Laurel, her face glowing with excitement. "Harris is here! And you will not *believe* his boat! It's the most beautiful thing I've ever seen!"

"Where is it?" Olivia asked, raising her binoculars.

"I see him! He's tacking toward the starting line!" Laurel shouted. "Oh, Millay! It's breathtaking!"

Irritated to be the last to know what her friends found so amazing, Olivia took a step forward and adjusted the focus on her binoculars. She found Harris's glimmering boat.

The bow was a gracefully curved griffin's head with a sunflower yellow beak and shining black eyes. A pair of lion's legs formed the stern and the vessel's rudder was in the shape of a tail. The entire boat had been painted gold, and Harris had added rhinestones to the griffin's feathered neck and had made a set of sails out of an iridescent fabric.

"I sewed the wings," Millay whispered. "I didn't even know what I was making. Harris gave me the material and a bunch of instructions. I thought he'd totally lost it using that filmy-looking stuff, but now . . ."

"He painted *Tessa* on the stern!" Laurel bounced up and down on the dock. "What a *lovely* tribute to your character."

Grinning, Olivia watched the wind catch the griffin's sails. The golden boat soared through the water as if it could truly take flight. "I know I've said this before, Millay, but I'm going to say it again. That boy has got it bad."

Millay rolled her eyes. "I know, I know. But guess what? If he was trying to get my attention, then he's got it. For once in my life, I am seriously impressed by a man."

Chapter 12

Widow: that great, vacant estate!
The voice of God is full of draftiness,
Promising simply the hard stars,
the space
Of immortal blankness between stars
And no bodies, singing like arrows up to
heaven.
—Sylvia Plath

Millay sulked through the length of their Bayside Book Writers' meeting, and Olivia sensed her foul mood had less to do with the minor criticisms she received and more to with her response to seeing Harris receive the adulation of his pretty coworker.

Harris's griffin boat had crossed the finish line yards ahead of the competition. During the awards ceremony, he was handed not one, but two cash prizes. He'd won the Sail-Powered Race and had secured a runner-up position in the Most Beautiful Boat category. Ironically, it was another bird that beat his craft: a peacock. The colorful vessel hadn't been designed for speed, but its graceful lines and showy tail had earned its builders a tidy sum. Still, Harris was the event's cash king. Olivia figured he'd earned several thousand dollars that morning.

Olivia, Millay, and Laurel had watched in surprise as Harris accepted his winnings and then was promptly mauled by a young woman wearing a Harry Potter Team Gryffindor T-shirt and a pair of denim cut-offs. She pushed her way through the crowd and threw her arms around Harris. Her display of affection nearly knocked him right off his feet, but he reacted with a look of amused bewilderment.

"This is Estelle. We work together," Harris told the other writers and stood by uneasily as Millay and Estelle sized one another up.

"I don't think Harris has ever mentioned you," Millay said coldly, veiling her dislike with a plastic smile.

Estelle was unfazed by the cool reception. "That's probably because I haven't been at the company too long and Harris and I aren't in the same division. See, *he's* an artist!" She stared at Harris as though he might walk on water at any moment. "I'm just a receptionist. I got hired because of my phone voice and because I can stay calm no matter how upset others might get. I help keep our customers happy."

"What an exceptional talent," Millay remarked but Laurel quickly stepped in and began to chat with Estelle about her favorite Harry Potter characters.

Harris thanked Estelle for being such an exuberant cheerleader and then made his excuses to his coworker explaining that he needed to get going to his book writer's meeting.

"Oh, Harris!" Estelle clung to his arm. "You're a writer too? There are *so* many sides to you! What *else* are you good at, I wonder?"

Harris blushed and gently disentangled himself from the pretty woman's grasp. "See you Monday, Estelle."

"Not if I see *you* first!" she shouted after him.

Millay remained silent about Estelle until the other writers had finished critiquing her chapter. Olivia shared her observations first and then listened intently as Rawlings pointed out examples of well-crafted prose followed by two sections of writing requiring further work.

"The battle scene was very well done," he told Millay. "I had no difficulty imagining the sea witch rising out of the black waters. I agree with Olivia about closing the distance between reader and character. Tessa is fascinating but often strikes me as too collected for someone of her age and situation." He studied his notes. "I realize the traditions of her culture prepared her to be a warrior, but I wonder if it's wise to keep her so solitary. She has no confidante, no one to show her affection or even share a joke with. The loneliness must be affecting her, but I'm not sensing any desire to make a connection on Tessa's part."

Millay sent a withering glare in Harris's direction. "Not everybody needs to be fawned over."

Rawlings, who hadn't been present for the Regatta's awards ceremony, sent Olivia a questioning look. She gave a little shake of the head as if to say, "Leave it be."

"Enough of Tessa," Millay declared regally. "I need something to eat. Harris, you got anything in that bachelor fridge of yours?"

Harris sprang up from the plaid sofa in his living room and crossed the industrial beige carpet to the laminate floor of his kitchen. The entire apartment had been decorated in shades of light brown. Whether khaki or tan or an unattractive taupe, the walls, floors, and furniture was utterly lackluster. As though he were still living in a college dorm room, Harris had tacked a variety of posters to the walls. Most were of science-fiction movies and had seen better days. Water stains and small tears gave them a bedraggled appearance, making them the perfect accompaniment to the mismatched chairs in his kitchen, the sagging sofa in the living room, and the tattered shades on every lamp.

"What are you going to do with your winnings?" Olivia asked Harris as he dug around inside his refrigerator.

He emerged, examined the expiration date on a hunk of cheese, and tossed it in the trash. "I'm going to buy a house." He picked up the phone. "But first I'm going to order pizza. Anyone object to mushroom and pepperoni?"

No one did. While they waited, Laurel peppered Harris with questions about where he planned to look for houses and what style he favored. As Harris didn't know the difference between a Cape and a ranch, Laurel used the homes featured in television shows as examples.

"I think the house from *The Brady Bunch* is the most famous ranch-style house in the world," she said.

"Okay!" Harris understood immediately. "So the house from *Six Feet Under* is Victorian, right?"

The two continued to name famous television houses until the pizza arrived.

The delivery boy from Pizza Bay had barely left when Rawlings' cell phone rang. Excusing himself, he took the call on the tiny balcony overlooking the apartment's parking lot.

Olivia accepted a slice of pizza, informed Haviland that under no circumstances was he allowed to partake of the junk food, and watched Rawlings through the glass of the sliding door.

Initially, the chief's face registered surprise, but the wide-eyed expression was quickly replaced by one of consternation. Millay, who had raised her slice toward her mouth, was observing the chief as well. With remarkable stealth, she stuck out her bare foot and used her toes to pry the door open by several inches.

Rawlings' voice floated inside. ". . . Yes, it sounds like the same perps. I hadn't expected them to strike again. It seems they're willing to take more risks. Did this family have kids?" He listened to the answer and nodded. "Same as the Howards. But the homeowners were away, right? No one was hurt?" His mouth turned down in a deep frown. "Dolls?" A shake of the head. "This is the first time they've deliberately destroyed the homeowner's belongings. Up to this point, they've taken what they wanted and cleared out. With the exception of the assault on Felix Howard, which I certainly don't mean to belittle by what I'm about to say, these have been the most respectful and delicate thieves I've ever seen."

Millay and Olivia exchanged curious glances. By the time they turned their focus back to Rawlings, he was staring directly at them. "See you in twenty minutes." He studied the phone for a moment and then released a heavy sigh. Olivia wondered what emotion had been released into the air through the chief's exhalation.

"There's been another robbery," he announced as he stepped back into the room. "I've got to drive to Beaufort County and meet their officers at the scene."

Laurel swallowed and covered her mouth with her hand. "There wasn't another—"

"No. The family entered a boat in the Cardboard Regatta so they were here in town all day. They only returned home about forty-five minutes ago."

Millay picked a piece of pepperoni from her pizza and folded it in half between her fingers. "What's with the dolls?"

Collecting his car keys and a can of Coke from the kitchen table, Rawlings paused. "This isn't to be discussed beyond this room, but this family had an antique doll collection. The thieves smashed in the faces, probably using a hammer. One was left intact, but the mouth was drilled wider and a silver spoon was inserted into the opening."

Everyone immediately fixated on the reference to the silver spoon. Millay and Olivia began to speak, but Harris shouted louder than both women. "Born with a silver spoon in one's mouth!" He grimaced. "Man, that is a creepy thing to do. To the dolls, I mean. Leaving clichés are one thing, but the dolls are like little people."

"They *killed* a person," Laurel reminded Harris in a small voice. "They obviously don't place much value on a human life."

The chief put his hands on his hips and stared down at the writers. "I'm only mentioning this detail because I want you to think about the significance of these messages. My men and I have been researching the clichés and what connections are shared among the families, but nothing these folks have in common has led us to a suspect yet."

Millay responded quickly. "We'll do what we can, Chief. I'll introduce the subject of the thefts at work and listen as the gossip spreads around the bar. If the Fish Nets crew repeats anything useful, I'll let you know."

"Can the rest of us do anything specific?" Harris inquired.

Rawlings shrugged and reached out for the doorknob. "I really don't know. I've had men calling pawnshops and auction galleries up and down the East Coast looking for the missing artwork and we've had no luck. Unless you know of a black market for electronics, I'm not sure what you can do."

"We can focus on the clichés," Olivia answered. "These families have been chosen for a reason. They're well off so they're profitable targets, but I think there's something personal about these crimes too."

Laurel cocked her head and considered what Olivia had said. "I agree, but I'm not sure why. I think what they did to the dolls shows that they're angry."

"Perhaps the four of you could write down some

theories. I value your opinions. I need to go." Rawlings gestured at a manila folder on the table. "That's my first chapter, not just ten copies of page one. If you're willing to give me another chance, I'd welcome your critiques at our next meeting."

"Of course we are!" Laurel smiled at him tenderly. "Chief, I'm going to interview April Howard tomorrow. If she thinks of anything she forgot to mention, I'll be sure to pass it along to you."

Rawlings thanked her and then left. Millay followed shortly afterward, saying that she had a few errands to run before her shift. Laurel and Olivia congratulated Harris again on his victory and headed out as well, both more somber than they had been upon first entering the apartment. Even Haviland exited the apartment without a spring to his step.

"I'm coming with you tomorrow," Olivia told Laurel as she let Haviland into the Range Rover.

"Good," Laurel answered and drove away.

Olivia felt restless, but didn't want to spend the afternoon wandering up and down the beach near her house. She felt compelled to sit amid a group of strangers, to listen to their murmurs without being a part of the conversation and to silently observe their mannerisms as if the smallest action or expression might reveal the motives of the thieves.

Without thinking much about it, Olivia found herself searching for a parking spot in front of Through the Wardrobe. The store was packed. Flynn was working the floor while Jenna, his attractive assistant, rang up a line of patient customers with a warm smile.

Flynn kept a close eye on the comings and goings of his customers and it wasn't long before he appeared at Olivia's side. "Can I tell you how much I love the Cardboard

Regatta?" He spoke in a hushed voice. "I was all ready to settle down for months of tedium and an empty bank account. I had visions of six months of meals consisting of raw spaghetti and water."

Laughing, Olivia gestured at the dozen people waiting to pay for books. "You could probably treat yourself to at least one steak this winter." She led him to a relatively private nook between two massive wardrobes.

Flynn took her elbow and growled. "What are we doing back here? Something naughty, I hope."

Olivia scowled. "You called and asked for my help. Here I am."

"I managed on my own, thank you very much, but I *would* like to show you what all the fuss was about." He glanced behind him. "Where's Haviland?"

"In the car. I decided there'd be too many tourists with little kids in here. Haviland doesn't appreciate too much uninvited petting."

Flynn pretended to be appalled. "Well, who would? Come into the storeroom. I can attempt some uninvited touching with you in private."

Ignoring his playful leer, Olivia followed Flynn through the noisy children's section and into the back room where extra books were stored. Flynn opened the door with caution, hurried Olivia through, and then shut it quickly behind him.

"Let's see if they're in bed," he said sotto voce.

Olivia immediately detected an animal scent. There was a faint odor of urine and canned food that hadn't been present in the storeroom before.

Flynn took her hand and tiptoed to a small basket filled with shredded newspaper and a cotton dishtowel. Two kittens were arranged in a tight circle of fur inside the basket. Both were sleeping soundly.

"Where did they come from?" Olivia whispered.

Flynn touched the orange kitten gently, caressing the soft fur behind the ears. The kitten shifted in its sleep and began to purr but did not open its eyes. "They showed up at my house after the hurricane, wet, shivering, and starving. I had no idea what to do. I tried giving them milk from a bowl and finally from an eyedropper. Nothing worked. I thought they were goners."

"Did you call the vet?"

Flynn nodded. "In the middle of the damned night! I told myself that these little guys were just worn out and would eat when they felt like it, but they became listless as the hours passed. I didn't want to wake you, so I called the emergency number and Diane got right back to me."

"She's an excellent veterinarian," Olivia said, feeling a pang of guilt that she hadn't responded to Flynn's call.

"I have no experience with animals and I had no idea vets made house calls. Diane came to my place after midnight, examined the kittens, and took them to her office. She said they were severely dehydrated." He rubbed his brow, his anxiety over the tiny animals evident in his eyes. "I picked them up the next day. I checked on them every five minutes like some crazed new mother and even fed them organic baby food. Do you have any idea how foul lamb is when rendered into a gray, pudding-like substance?"

Olivia laughed. "No, thank God. So now two cats own you. And what are their names?"

"They have none as of this point. I thought I'd run a contest for my younger customers. Let them come up with a pair of creative names."

"Just don't pick something too cutesy. Eventually these two will grow into dignified felines and their names need to mature along with them," Olivia stated seriously.

Flynn feigned offense. "I wasn't going to call them Mopsy and Wubzy. Give me a little credit, lady." He placed a proprietary hand on the gray kitten's back. "I invited Diane to dinner as a apology for dragging her out of bed. I wanted to tell you, just in case you read it in the Oyster Bay gossip column and became wildly jealous."

Olivia touched the orange kitten on the fur above his pink nose. "You don't belong to me, Flynn. And Diane is a lovely woman." She glanced at him quizzically. "Did you want me to be jealous?"

After a pause, Flynn answered. "I guess I did. If only a tiny bit."

It's time, Olivia thought. *Tell him that it's not working out between the two of you.*

"Flynn—" The voice of Flynn's assistant came through the intercom mounted on the wall. "I need a hand out here. I can't leave the register and some folks are having trouble locating the books they want."

"In other words, get my ass out on the floor?" Flynn asked after pressing the reply button.

Jenna giggled but obviously didn't have time to engage in further conversation.

"Your public awaits," Olivia said and pushed open the stock room door. Flynn put a hand on her arm as she held the door for him. "That's supposed to be my job," he scolded. "And don't think you've escaped so easily. You've been as slippery as a piece of seaweed since the storm." When Olivia didn't respond, he dropped his hand and smiled. "All I'm saying is don't be a stranger."

Olivia watched him walk past the puppet theater, where he paused to pick up a *Cat in the Hat* puppet and return it to a young girl with pigtails. Her final thought before leaving Through the Wardrobe was that even though she and Flynn had been physically intimate, they were still strangers to one another. And now she no longer desired for them to become anything else.

The next day, Olivia parked the Range Rover in front of a spacious transitional brick home located in a subdivision called The Marshes. Laurel was waiting for her, pacing in the driveway with a cell phone pressed to her ear.

"I can't come home just yet," she said and rolled her eyes for Olivia's benefit. "Just put Dallas on his bed and tell him he has to stay there until he apologizes to his brother. Oh, you'll forgive me when I bring you something incredible for dinner. Bye!" She sighed and gave Olivia a plaintive look. "Do you have something incredible for me to take home?"

Olivia indicated they should proceed up the flagstone walk. "I'm sure Michel can produce something to satisfy your husband. Pastry-wrapped tenderloin in red wine sauce is always a crowd-pleaser." She noticed that Laurel's fingers were shaking as her friend pressed lightly on the doorbell.

A haggard-faced woman with a small boy clinging to her thigh answered the door. "Laurel? Come in. Excuse the mess. I just . . ." She touched her child on the head, easing him away from her and giving him a gentle shove toward the stairs. As he began to climb, she finished her thought. "I just don't give a damn anymore. Why make the bed? Why dirty a dozen dishes making a beautiful dinner? Why water the plants? If they die, it's one less thing to deal with."

April spoke in a flat monotone as though she had cried and raged so much already that there was no emotion left. In Olivia's opinion, April had entered the worst phase of grief. She would have to wake every morning and face the emptiness within. One hundred times each day, she'd feel the vacuum that her husband's death had created. It would suck all color, all taste, all the light from her world. The past was out of reach and the future was a frightening, black void.

Laurel murmured the customary words of condolence, but Olivia reached out and touched April on the elbow. The widow flinched, her eyes flying open as though the slight human contact had burned her flesh. Instead of removing her hand, Olivia curled her fingers around April's forearm. "It will seem endless. They say time helps but some wounds don't heal completely. You just go on. You drive to the grocery store and watch television and read books you'll never remember. You'll cry in unexpected places, eat the same foods over and over, and avoid your friends because they remind you too much of the woman you were before." She removed her hand. "But you'll make it. You will make it through this."

April nodded. "Thank you. I don't feel like I exist with everyone tiptoeing around me, like *I'm* the one who died." She looked away. "Though in a sense, I did. We all did."

Laurel turned her head, wiped her eyes with a tissue, and whispered, "Can we sit down for a moment?"

"Sure." April absently led them to the dining room. The room had been decorated in muted greens and golds with dark walnut furniture. "We never use this room," she remarked, looking around as though seeing the space for the first time. "I think I'll sell all this stuff. The whole house. Everything. I can't sleep in my room anymore."

For a moment, Laurel seemed in danger of rising to her feet and fleeing from April's grief. It filled the air like smoke, robbing the room of oxygen and replacing it with the family's stifling loss. But Laurel rallied, took out her notebook, and uncapped her pen. "April, will you tell us everything? From the beginning?"

April did. She began with Felix. She shared the image of him lying on the kitchen floor with a puddle of red blood spread out beneath his head across the bright white tiles. "It was like a crazy dream. I thought I could just close my eyes and when I opened them, everything would be normal. Even when I started screaming, I felt like the sound was coming out of someone else's mouth."

It took some time before April could speak again. The thieves had taken the usual items: computers, sterling silver, jewelry, and a few other electronics. The Howards didn't keep any cash in the house and they owned no original art, so their haul was less substantial than previous takes.

Laurel wrote down the name of the children's school, learned that the family had no pets, and then asked April for the names of their household services.

April shook her head. "Felix had been worried about losing his job all summer long, so we'd been tightening our belts for months. I've been doing the cooking, cleaning, and gardening. Felix was in charge of lawn and car maintenance. The only service we still used was the dry cleaner's and I didn't drop off clothes unless I had a coupon."

"I keep all mine in a special wallet," Laurel said in an effort to commiserate. "I really like it when those big value packs come in the mail. And we use the Pizza Bay coupons religiously."

This earned her a small smile. "We do too," April said and then frowned. "You know, I forgot to tell the police something. When they asked me about what we'd done over the course of the week leading up to . . . the robbery, I tried to remember all the little details. I made this huge list, labeling each day and every activity. It gave me something to do—a way to help the cops bring justice to my husband. But, of course, it didn't help or they'd have caught the bastards by now." Her eyes filled with tears, but she shook her head and blinked them away. "But I forgot something. Hold on, I'll show you."

Olivia and Laurel waited quietly as April sorted through a pile of papers in a kitchen drawer. She pulled out a green flyer and handed it to Laurel. "We took these guys up on their offer a few days before the kids and I left. I did it to lighten Felix's load a bit and give him the chance to fully concentrate on his upcoming presentation."

Laurel studied the flyer and something flashed in her eyes. She engaged April in another line of questioning while sliding the paper over the polished table to Olivia. As soon as Olivia began to read, she felt her breath quicken. This had to be a tangible clue. She reread the advertisement.

Tired of Mowing, Fertilizing, and Mulching?
Let Us Handle All of Your Lawn-care Needs!
We Want Your Business So Badly That We'll Do a
Complete Yard Cleanup Package for FREE!
Just Mention This Ad When You Call.
GREEN AS GRASS
LAWN SERVICE:
We Strive to Make Your Life Easier!

Olivia could barely sit still through the remainder of the interview. That is until April made a comment about how difficult it would be for her to find employment as an interior designer. "I haven't worked for years and my last job involved a huge office complex."

Diverted by thoughts of her Bayside Crab House project,

Olivia said, "April, I'd love to see photographs of your work. I happen to know someone in need of your skills. There's no rush," she added gently and handed April a business card.

April stared at the card in confusion. "I thought you were Laurel's photographer."

"I am," Olivia agreed. "But I left my camera in the car. I assumed you wouldn't welcome photos today."

"I do want a picture of Felix in the paper," April insisted firmly. "I want those sons-of-bitches to see the face of the man they killed. And I'm ready to show my portfolio to anyone, anytime. *I* may want to spend the next year in bed but I can't. I have three kids to feed."

Olivia promised to phone again in a few days, and she and Laurel walked to the door. Laurel, who had reclaimed the lawn service flyer, held it up to April. "Can I keep this?"

"I guess. You can only use it once anyway." Now that the interview was over, April seemed to deflate. Holding herself together for over an hour had taken its toll. She leaned heavily against the door frame and rubbed her eyes.

Laurel squeezed the widow's hand in farewell and then she and Olivia walked down the front path to their cars. "It's a cliché, Olivia!" Laurel whispered as they drew alongside the Range Rover. "Do you think it's simply coincidence?"

"No," Olivia answered. "And neither will Rawlings. Bring the flyer to him, Laurel. This is your discovery. I believe you were born to do this job."

Flushing with pleasure, Laurel tucked the paper into her purse. "I won't be needing any of Michel's food tonight. I came clean to Steve over the phone and I don't care if he doesn't believe I'll even get the job, I'm submitting every article I've written about these robberies to the *Gazette*'s editor tomorrow. If he hires me, I'm going to give this career one hundred percent." She glanced back at the Howard house. "After all, you can never tell what the future's going to bring and I want to say that I did more with mine than change diapers and iron my husband's shirts."

Laurel thanked Olivia and got into her car.

Olivia watched her friend drive away. "Brava, Laurel," she murmured as the minivan disappeared around a bend.

Chapter 13

It doesn't matter who my father was; it
matters who I remember he was.
—ANNE SEXTON

Her room was still filled with shadows when the ringing of the phone jolted Olivia awake. A few weak
rays of sunshine crept through the windows, striping Haviland's black fur so that he looked like an exotic species of
antelope or zebra.

Olivia grabbed the receiver and managed a raspy hello.

"Sorry to wake you, Ms. Limoges." Olivia recognized
the voice of Will Hamilton. "For days I had nothing to
report, but I have something now." He paused for effect.
"Your pink envelope was passed on. Rodney Burkhart drove
down to the port here and handed it off to the crew member
of a fishing boat. I couldn't exactly leap aboard, but I found
out the vessel was bound for Okracoke Island."

"Okracoke?" Olivia flung off her covers and headed
downstairs.

Will explained that he'd immediately set about hiring a charter boat, but was warned that the trawler, the
Ritaestelle, might not return directly to its home port. As
he talked, Olivia opened a coffee table book on coastal

North Carolina and rapidly turned the pages to the section containing a group of maps.

"The charter boat captain told me to save my money. For a few bucks, he'd make some calls on his radio to determine the ship's destination. Sure enough, the *Ritaestelle* was headed back out to sea. The captain said to expect it to dock in Okracoke in three days' time."

Olivia traced an imaginary line from Oyster Bay over the Pamlico Sound to the shores of Okracoke Island. The distance was approximately fifty miles.

Even in a storm, half out of his mind and choking down whiskey, my father could have navigated that distance.

"Are you going to be there when she docks?" Olivia asked Will.

Will's next words were a surprise. "I'm actually calling you from the island. If the envelope is on its way then your father might actually be here. I thought I'd find out for myself, but the locals are a tight-lipped group. I'm going to pose as a vacationer and keep my ears open until the *Ritaestelle* returns."

Olivia was pleased with Will's doggedness and told him as much, but after she'd hung up the phone, anxiety began to surge through her body. As she stared at the skinny green smudge that was Okracoke on her map, she had a powerful feeling that her father was there, that he'd been there all along.

"So close," she murmured, experiencing a fresh bout of grief and resentment. "If you've been this close all these years . . ." The possibility was too painful to acknowledge and Olivia slammed the book closed.

Haviland joined her in the living room, but he ignored his mistress and headed straight for the door leading to the deck. Olivia followed him outside. She sat in one of the deck chairs and let the burgeoning light wash over her, wishing that it held the power to burn all her memories away.

As she sat there, breathing in the salt-tinged oxygen and releasing her anger with every exhalation, her thoughts eventually turned to yesterday's writers' meeting. She went inside, poured herself some coffee, and returned to the deck chair.

"The dolls," she said to the waves. "The thieves must have felt the dolls' eyes on them. Why would they care? Do they feel guilty about stealing? Over having committed murder?"

The water rushed to the shore.

"No." Olivia shook her head as though the ocean had disagreed with her. "They killed a man and buried him on the beach, leaving him naked to the elements. It's not a moral dilemma, so why did the glass-eyed stares of the dolls bother them?"

As she ruminated, Haviland trotted up the dune path, his black fur covered in wet sand. He politely shook himself off at the bottom of the stairs, but his long nose and forehead were still caked with sand. Olivia grabbed a dishtowel from inside and brushed him off, smiling at how odd he looked with his mask of gritty white. The poodle stayed quite still until she was finished and then jerked away in order to take up an eager stance by his dinner dish.

When Olivia didn't come back indoors, Haviland barked to signal that he was ready for breakfast, but his mistress was staring down the beach toward the area of the Point where they'd discovered the buried body.

"It's something physical, I'm sure of it," she said, rushing back into the house and picking up the phone. "They don't like to be on the receiving end of stares, but why?"

Rawlings answered his cell phone immediately and listened as Olivia presented her theory. "Something like a birthmark or burn scars?" he asked rhetorically. "It might explain the connection between the victims. Perhaps the children ridiculed our thieves at an athletic event. I'll have to find out if anyone who came in regular contact with the families had some kind of physical deformity."

"Did Laurel bring you the lawn-service flyer from the Howard residence?"

"Yes, and we moved on the information immediately," Rawlings assured her. "Each victim received a similar flyer over the course of the summer. However, the name of the lawn service and the overall appearance of the flyer were altered. Every family had been given a unique flyer."

Olivia considered the implications of this statement as she put Haviland's breakfast in the microwave. "The thieves put in some serious effort to get to these families. What were the other names of these lawn service companies?"

"Green Thumb Lawn Care, Down the Garden Path Landscaping Service, and Neat as a Pin Yard Care," Rawlings said.

"Such obvious clichés! How did I miss them?" She tried to recall the names of the lawn services Harris had typed onto their spreadsheet.

"You didn't." Rawlings soothed. "In every case, the families took advantage of the free yard cleanup offered on the flyer, but none of the homeowners were impressed enough by the work to hire the men again. The Ridgemonts were the only ones who tried to call and set up another job, but after no one replied to their voice mail messages, they forgot all about the subject."

Olivia chuckled. "That certainly sounds like Sue Ridgemont. Lovely, but a bit absentminded." She grew serious again quickly. "So this was how the thieves were able to break into the homes in broad daylight. They posed as yard men and parked their truck in the driveway. One of them broke into the house while another crew member mowed the lawn. The neighbors wouldn't hear a thing over the noise of a mower or weed whacker."

"Precisely," Rawlings agreed. "And the free service included a tune-up of the irrigation system. Therefore, in nearly every case, the homeowners willingly left their garage doors open. In these subdivisions, the sight of a landscaping truck and unfamiliar men testing the sprinklers would be totally commonplace. Though they were working in plain sight, they were nearly invisible."

Olivia had to admire the forethought of the burglars. "They could carry stuff from the garage to their truck without anyone batting an eyelash. What a clever scam."

Rawlings grunted. "They should have stuck with pilfering TVs. Killing Felix Howard has made them number one on the department's hit list. We're going to interview every existing lawn-care company in the county. Anyone who's registered a trailer within fifty miles of Oyster Bay will be visited by a man or woman in blue."

"I know you will. At least Laurel's husband is in the clear. What was he like during questioning?"

"Um," Rawlings stalled. "Let's say that he was rather indignant over having to provide us with details about his comings and goings and leave it at that. I wish he'd never been on our radar in the first place. We're going to get these guys, Olivia, I promise you that."

"Make sure to give Laurel an exclusive on the story. She's going to be a hell of a reporter." Olivia removed the casserole dish from the microwave and gave its contents a stir while Haviland danced back and forth in anticipation. Waving a potholder over the steaming casserole made of lean ground lamb, brown rice, and cheese, Olivia shook her head at Haviland, indicating that he'd have to wait a minute for it to cool.

"And I hear you make a superb photographer. Perhaps you'll have your own booth at the next Cardboard Regatta," Rawlings quipped.

Horrified, Olivia realized that she had yet to thank the

chief for the painting he'd made for her. She hurried to do so and then told him that it hung in a prominent place in her kitchen. "It's on the wall behind the coffeemaker and is one of the first things I see every morning. Now I can actually crack a smile before I've had a single sip of coffee."

"That *is* a compliment." Rawlings paused. "Olivia, when this case is over, you and I . . ."

A silence followed and Olivia knew he was searching for the words to acknowledge the attraction between them. She too wanted to address the feelings he'd awakened in her, but not over the phone. She wanted to be alone with Rawlings, perhaps on a blanket on the beach with only the stars and the sea bearing witness as she made herself vulnerable to him. Most of all, she wanted Rawlings to be near enough to touch, and at the moment, he felt very far away.

Olivia broke the charged silence, changing the subject by telling the chief about Will Hamilton's call.

"Don't make a move until I wrap up this case," Rawlings directed. "I don't want to appear at our next writer's meeting to find that you've driven off to catch the ferry to Okracoke. You shouldn't go there alone, Olivia."

"And miss the chance to finally critique your chapter?" she said. "Never. I'm switching to my red pen just for you."

She heard the voice of another police officer in the background. Olivia caught the words "victims" and "Pampticoe High" and then Rawlings told her he had to go.

Olivia glanced at her watch. The chief was at work and probably had been for hours, but he had thieves and murderers to catch and it was probably too early to call Laurel. She wondered if Laurel had managed to turn in her articles to the *Gazette* editor before having to attend to the needs of her family.

"I'll call her later," Olivia told Haviland as she served him breakfast.

Feeling restless, Olivia waited for Haviland to finish eating and then the pair set off for a walk. On this occasion, the metal detector was left at home and Olivia carried nothing in her arms. She walked to the end of the Point where a narrow and irregular spit of sand jutted out into the ocean like an arthritic finger. While the sea stirring on both sides and the wind whipped her hair off her face, Olivia stared east across the water. East toward Okracoke.

It wouldn't take me long to get there, she thought, still a little surprised that she hadn't jumped in the car the moment Will Hamilton had finished speaking. Yet there was something preventing her from acting, an irrational fear that she would once again become the frightened, reclusive girl of her childhood should she come face-to-face with her father.

The morning sun soon gained in strength until Olivia had to turn away from its powerful rays. Back inside her cool house, she peeled a tangerine and sat at her desk, Rawlings' chapter before her. She took a bite of the ripe fruit and closed her eyes, reveling in its sweetness. Uncapping a pen, she hesitated. What would the chief's writing lay bare? Would his chapter reveal a flaw Olivia would be unable to accept or be filled with intimate memories of his late wife? Would there be a darkness she hadn't sensed before or, even worse, a lack of substance?

Casting aside such ridiculous thoughts, she began to read.

Grandfather spoke of treasure until his dying day.

It was what I remembered most about him. No matter how much he was told he was a foolish old man by his wife and, later, by his daughter and son-in-law, he believed in its existence.

"Pirates!" my mother scoffed in exaggerated disgust the day they moved my grandfather into a nursing

home. "He's wasted half of his life on these damned pirates. He's studied hundreds of books and letters and maps, and what's he got to show for it? Nothing! Absolutely nothing!"

I knew my mother wasn't really angry about my grandfather's obsession. She was upset because he'd taken early retirement to conduct research on two of North Carolina's most infamous buccaneers and in doing so had squandered every cent of his savings buying rare books and documents from auction houses across the country. My parents were thus forced into inviting him to move into our small house.

At first, they thought having Grandfather around could prove useful. He would be readily available to watch us kids while my folks worked extra shifts or went out on a rare dinner date, but after a few months it became clear that the old man couldn't look after himself, let alone three hellions.

Grandfather was eventually diagnosed with Alzheimer's and my parents' anger turned bitter. My father paid for my grandfather's nursing home, complaining about the cost each and every time the bill was pushed through our brass mail slot. My mother stopped visiting him altogether.

I was seventeen when he died.

I was alone with him in his sad room with its gray carpeting and faded butterfly wallpaper. The smell of mold and rot clung to every surface. But I was there—the only one to hear his final words.

I was seventeen and didn't pay much attention to what he said. I was heading off to college in a few weeks where I'd study a little, party a lot, and decide that I didn't want to be a doctor or a lawyer or any of the other respectable professions my parents hoped I'd *pursue. I wanted to be a cop. And after that, I wanted to figure out what my grandfather had been talking about when he muttered, "Look in . . . Ruth's . . . log . . ." and shuddered as though he felt a sudden chill.*

After that final quiver, he died.

I sat there for a while, staring not at his slack face or the line of spittle near the corner of his mouth but at the hundreds of tiny butterflies on the wallpaper, forever trapped in a field of dirty white.

Olivia hadn't expected to encounter Rawlings as a young man. She knew she was reading fiction, of course, but wondered which elements might have been pulled from the chief's actual childhood. Perhaps an aging relative had moved in with the family or Alzheimer's had afflicted one of his grandparents. Perhaps someone close to Rawlings had been consumed by an obsession. Olivia could easily picture him playing the role of confidante, even as a teenage boy. He was a gifted listener, patient and quiet, coaxing the speaker to continue with a soft word of encouragement.

With her green pen hovering over Rawlings' pages, Olivia finished her read-through. Rawlings had named his character Easton Craig and had set the story in what was clearly a fictionalized version of Oyster Bay. Choosing his hometown made sense when penning a tale about pirates, for Blackbeard had made his home in the area. In fact, there had been long-standing rumors among the locals that Edward Thatch had hidden plunder along the banks of the Neuse River and hosted wild parties for other notorious buccaneers such as Charles Vane.

Blackbeard's other refuge was Okracoke Island. Olivia sat back in her chair, considering the irony.

The infamous pirate met his death off the shores of Okracoke, run down by a lieutenant from the Royal Navy by order of Queen Anne. Blackbeard's sloop, the *Adventure,* was anchored offshore the island. Cutting anchor, he tried to outrun his pursuers, but the wind, which had been his ally for hundreds of raids, betrayed the pirate when he needed it most. Blackbeard's ship was boarded, and in a sword fight to the death, the pirate's head was severed from his neck in an act of genuine barbarity.

Pushing herself away from her desk, Olivia was once again drawn to the map of North Carolina within her coffee table book. She stared at Okracoke, her thoughts fluctuating between a murdered pirate and a missing father.

In an effort to prevent herself from becoming maudlin, Olivia called Laurel.

"I did it!" Laurel shouted into the phone. "I submitted my articles this morning and I just got an e-mail from my editor. He's putting them in tomorrow's paper! I'm officially hired!"

"Wonderful news," Olivia said with a proud smile. "And how did your conversation with Steve go? Do you have his support?"

Laurel hesitated. "I figured I would show him the articles first. You know, put the *Gazette* next to his bacon and eggs and let him see that someone is actually going to pay me to write."

Olivia could imagine Laurel on the other end of the line, clasping her hands over her heart, her lovely face rosy as she indulged in a fantasy of her husband suddenly seeing her in a new light. Olivia hated to burst her bubble, but she wanted Laurel to be prepared for an unfavorable reaction. "What will you do if Steve's unimpressed?"

"I'll cry, I suppose," Laurel answered honestly. "But I'm not going to back down. I've never felt so sure about myself as I did when I sent in that file. And I don't think I've thanked you for helping me realize my potential. I wish there was some way to express my gratitude."

"There is," Olivia said. "Don't give up. No matter what *anyone* says, don't give this up."

The next day, the lead-in to Laurel's article was featured prominently on a right-hand column on the front page. Olivia read it eagerly and was impressed by how Laurel had managed to infuse the facts with compassion for the victims. There was also a short piece on the robbery in Beaufort County and a quote from Chief Rawlings about the department's progress in the investigation. Laurel had indeed proved herself a capable reporter.

Over the course of the week the *Gazette* ran pieces on the burglaries. Laurel's name appeared in the byline below each article and Olivia assumed that she hadn't heard from her friend because she was too busy writing.

Olivia decided to be industrious as well. She and Michel designed an autumn menu featuring dishes like apple and Brie salad, veal cordon blue, chicken and pears in a gourmandise sauce, pork chops with roasted shallots and carrots, pumpkin bread pudding with candied ginger, and apple crisp with a dulce de leche drizzle. She also finished critiquing Rawlings' chapter and added five thousand words to her own manuscript.

On Thursday morning, there was a knock on her door. Peering through the kitchen window, Olivia recognized Will Hamilton's face from the photograph on his website.

"I'm sorry to just show up like this, but my cell phone went for a swim in the Pamlico Sound and I knew you'd want this as soon as possible." He handed her a padded mailing envelope.

At a loss for words, Olivia indicated the investigator should come inside. She stepped back to let him pass and then removed the contents of the envelope. It was a vial of blood.

"What the hell is this?" she asked, slightly repulsed.

Hamilton stood alongside the kitchen table and laced

his fingers together. "It's supposedly your father's blood." When Olivia didn't respond, he gestured at the nearest chair. "Could we sit?"

Nodding, Olivia sank down a chair. She couldn't take her eyes off the vial in her right hand. Was it possible? Had this blood recently flowed through her father's veins? "Tell me how you got this."

"I kept a constant eye out for the *Ritaestelle*. When it docked, I recognized the fisherman who'd taken possession of the pink mailer containing your cash. When he disembarked, the envelope was in his hand. It was still unopened too. Anyway, I followed him."

Olivia leaned forward. "Where did he go?"

"To a café near the harbor. He ordered a big breakfast and chatted with just about everybody in the place. He was clearly a local. I sat at the booth behind him and could easily listen in. Once his food came, he gave the envelope to the waitress, a worn-out-looking woman in her thirties. She looked at the postmark suspiciously and said, 'What's he up to?' I could tell she wasn't happy. She tossed the envelope on the table and walked away."

"And then?"

Hamilton sat back in his chair. "She disappeared into the kitchen and a man followed her back out to the fisherman's booth. He wore a dirty apron and looked at the envelope as if there was a snake hiding inside it. Still, he sat in an empty corner booth and sliced the envelope open with a knife from his apron pocket. Looked like he was gutting a fish," the PI added. "He peered inside, saw the cash, and stuffed it in his front pocket, like he wanted to hide it. Then the woman, who I discovered was his wife, demanded to know what was going on."

"Did you get these people's names?" Olivia demanded tersely. Anger was rising within her and she tried to push it back down. "What do they have to do with my father, or more importantly, my father's *blood*?"

"Their names are Kim and Hudson Salter. They own the café and a little bed and breakfast above the eatery. After I explained who I was and why I was there, Hudson told me that your father had rented rooms from them until he fell ill. Seem as though he's run out of money and is almost out of time too. Pancreatic cancer. The Salters have been taking care of him. "

"And no doubt they think I'll pay them a small fortune for their kindness toward their elderly tenant. I wonder exactly when they discovered that he's my father." Olivia didn't trust the couple at all.

Hamilton looked a little embarrassed. "Ma'am, I believe the family is in a hard way and don't have the funds to spare to cover the costs for his treatment. Mrs. Salter seemed pretty upset over the way this whole thing was handled. She didn't say a word, but I could see that she was ashamed."

"Did you see this dying man who's supposed to be my father?"

"No. Hudson wouldn't allow it. He was very protective of your father." The investigator hesitated. "Mr. Salter seems like a hard man, but from what I've been told by the locals, he's been really good to your father. They kept telling me that Hudson and your dad were *very* close. But they're a tight-lipped lot on that island. They don't like to talk about their own to a stranger."

Olivia curled her fingers into her palms, digging her nails into the flesh as rage coursed through her. "I don't care what the locals say. When I'm done with this man, he will regret his attempts to manipulate me."

"Ma'am, Hudson swears that he did not send you a letter. He told me that he could guess who'd written it. He left me there then and came back about twenty minutes later with the blood sample. His face was flushed and it seemed like he'd had words with the letter writer, but he refused to give me their name."

"I wonder why." Olivia frowned deeply. "I don't understand any of this! Why would these people take care of some elderly tenant? Why would they pay for his medical bills? Did they think *he* was some kind of cash cow? And who is the real blackmailer? Who are they protecting?"

Hamilton nodded in sympathy. "This certainly isn't a clear case, but I didn't want to push Hudson without talking to you first. He asked me to give the blood to you, in case you were interested in getting a DNA test." Hamilton kept his voice soft and even. It was obvious that none of his news had been easy for Olivia to take. "Hudson told me you were welcome, once you were convinced that the sick man is your father, to travel to Okracoke and see him before time runs out. He's keeping his best room reserved for you."

Exhaling loudly in frustration, Olivia cried, "This guy's claiming he didn't write the letter and yet he took the money! What kind of fool does Hudson Salter think I am?"

The private investigator shifted uncomfortably in his seat. "There's a lab in New Bern where you can get DNA results in twenty-four hours. Would you like the address?"

"Yes," Olivia answered in a tight voice. She stuffed the vial back into the envelope and then pulled her checkbook from her purse. "At this point your services are no longer required. You've done excellent work, Mr. Hamilton, going above and beyond the call of duty. I appreciate your dedication and would be glad to send you a written recommendation for your files." She scribbled out a check, pressing her signature deep into the paper.

Hamilton waved his hand for her to stop. "You don't

need to worry about payment now, Ms. Limoges. My secretary can send you a bill. This must be quite a shock for you."

"I'm sure this will more than cover your fee." Olivia put the check on the table and rose. She desperately wanted the man to leave, needing solitude at this moment more than ever before.

Blinking at the amount of Olivia's check, Hamilton folded it in half and slid in into his pocket. "This is very generous of you, ma'am, thank you." He moved to the door and then paused. "I hope you find the closure you were seeking, Ms. Limoges. One way or another."

And then he was gone.

Olivia sat motionless at the table and listened until she could no longer hear the rumble of Hamilton's car engine. When all was silent, she shoved her chair back so roughly that it toppled and clattered on the tile floor and she rushed out to the deck, Haviland bounding after her in expectation of a walk. Olivia didn't even notice as the poodle shot over the dunes ahead of her. Kicking off her sandals, she rushed into the waves, droplets of salt water stinging her eyes. She pumped her arms and legs, going deeper and deeper. When she could no longer touch the sandy bottom, she began to swim. Eyes closed, she struck out toward the cold, dark blue water well offshore.

Haviland yipped from the beach and then dove in after his mistress. An excellent swimmer, the poodle was beside her in a matter of minutes. When Olivia finally became aware of his presence, she stopped her forward progress and began to tread water. She turned toward the shore and watched her house bob up and down in the distance. Her gaze then shifted to the lighthouse keeper's cottage.

"Come on, Captain," she said breathlessly, and together, the sodden pair returned more leisurely to the beach.

Back on dry land, Olivia twisted water from her cotton

skirt and then walked slowly to the cottage, dripping as she walked. She'd hired her regular contractor to repair the building's flood damage and, stepping inside, she could see that he'd made decent progress. The carpet had been removed and the floors and baseboards were primed. Without the furniture, it was easy for Olivia to picture the rooms as they'd once been during her girlhood. She could picture her father seated in his favorite chair, whittling a pipe bowl. He often worked on pipes during winter evenings while Olivia and her mother worked a jigsaw puzzle or played card games for pennies.

"It's you, isn't it?" she asked the empty room, her voice bouncing off the bare walls. "I can feel it. You're alive on that island and you can't die because you're waiting for me." Her eyes filled with tears and her lips trembled. "I waited for *you* for thirty years!" She moved forward, accusing the space where her father's chair had been. "And all this time you were *so* close! Didn't you want to see me? Didn't you *care* how I was?"

Haviland whined, nosing Olivia's hand with his nose.

Olivia was crying freely now. "Why didn't you love me enough to come back for me?"

Her tears fell on the pristine white floor, mingling with the salt water pooling from her clothes.

She stood in that puddle of salt and water and felt as insignificant and alone as she had as a little girl, the healed scars within her heart pulling apart.

Chapter 14

The blood jet is poetry and there is no stopping it.
—Sylvia Plath

Olivia dropped her drenched clothes in the washing machine, showered, and dressed in black yoga pants and a loose, russet-colored cotton shirt. She escorted Haviland to the Range Rover, buckled him into his canine seat belt, and then sped inland toward New Bern.

At the first red light, Olivia examined the blue vein lying just beneath the skin in the crook of her right arm. Her eyes traveled over the freckles on her forearm to her long, graceful hands. They were her mother's hands. Though several inches taller than her mother, Olivia favored the Limoges line. The women were all naturally thin and graceful. Most had eyes the color of Delft blue pottery, but Olivia and her grandmother's were of a darker shade and tended to change hue like the shifting colors of the ocean. Olivia looked nothing like her father. The only attributes she'd inherited from him were a strong jaw and a forceful will.

She pondered her parentage on the drive to New Bern, which took far longer than usual. Obstacles seemed to appear from nowhere and Olivia was forced to plod forward below the speed limit for the majority of the trip. On the two-lane highway leading out of town, she got stuck behind a logging truck. When it finally turned off, a line of school buses from the neighboring county got onto the road in front of the Range Rover while Olivia sat helpless beneath the unyielding glare of a red traffic light. She cursed and struck the steering wheel.

Despite maintaining a distance of several car lengths behind the last bus in the row of electric yellow vehicles dispensing clouds of black smoke from their exhaust pipes, Olivia had nowhere else to look but at the children pulling faces at her through the rear windows. They poked out their tongues, stretched their eyes into slits, and wiggled their fingers behind their ears. Taking clear enjoyment in their antics, Haviland bobbed excitedly in his seat. He'd stick his head out of his window, his tongue flapping in the breeze as he smiled at the children, and then he'd come back inside and start the whole routine again.

This comical exchange reminded Olivia of the thieves and the possibility that something about their appearance marked them as being obviously different. She then recalled overhearing one of the chief's men mention the name Pampticoe High toward the end of her phone conversation with Rawlings yesterday.

Her mind began to churn. Had the victims attended Pampticoe High? Had the thieves? She pictured the school, a squat, worn brick building surrounded by scraggly bushes and sandy parking lots. Out front was a rusty flagpole flying Old Glory and the flag of North Carolina. There was also a set of park benches facing a magnificent bronze sculpture of a Pampticoe Indian paddling a dugout canoe. Olivia knew the county had been using the funds from its coffers—fuller than in the past as a result of several resoundingly successful tourist seasons—to improve roads, the business district, and the public beach areas, but the school was in dire need of attention.

"That building requires refurbishment," Olivia told Haviland. "It hasn't been updated at all while I was away. The town needs to look after its youth, create a sense of pride of place or they'll all move away." Making a mental note to raise the issue at the next Board of Education meeting, another thought occurred to her. Laurel had gone to Pampticoe High. She must have several yearbooks sitting around. Perhaps one of the thieves was even a classmate.

"Unlikely," she mused. "But it's worth a look."

Once in New Bern, Olivia drove to an off-leash dog area and allowed Haviland a few minutes of freedom. She tried not to be too impatient as he greeted other dogs and sniffed the base of every tree and garbage can. Finally, she called him to get back in the car and promised to return to the park as soon as she was through at the lab.

She pulled the Range Rover beneath the shade of a massive oak tree, put the windows down, and poured Haviland some water. Then, because she wasn't sure how long she'd be inside, she gave him a large bone.

"Be back soon, Captain," she promised, but the poodle was too interested in his treat to so much as glance up in acknowledgment.

Inside the lab's office, it was obvious that she wasn't going to be breezing in and out of the lab quickly. A dozen names were listed on the receptionist's clipboard. Once she'd added hers, Olivia asked the receptionist for an estimate on the wait time.

The woman shrugged. "'Bout thirty minutes." She handed Olivia another clipboard. "Please complete these forms and make sure to sign and date them at the bottom."

Retreating to an empty corner of the waiting room, Olivia raced through the paperwork and handed the pile back to the receptionist. The woman scooped up the forms, asked Olivia for payment in advance, and then called an elderly man forward and began to chide him for not having an updated insurance card. He searched through his wallet with trembling, age-spotted fingers but could not find anything to satisfy the receptionist.

Everyone in the room looked bored and miserable. A television mounted on the wall nearest the exit was turned to CNN, and an anchorman droned on about the state of the nation's economy. Rumpled magazines sat untouched on veneered end tables, and a plastic display case filled with health pamphlets covered a coffee table in the center of the gray- and mauve-speckled carpet. The patients waiting to be taken into the back looked like zombies. No one met anyone else's gaze, but each person took regular turns glancing at the large clock above the receptionist's desk.

Olivia had paid in cash, slipping two extra twenties into the receptionist's plump hand in hopes of being able to cajole the woman into seeing that Olivia was seen quickly. The attempt was unsuccessful. The woman counted out the bills and then called Olivia up to her window. Raising her pencil-drawn brows, she said, "You gave me too much money."

She spoke loud enough for the rest of the room to hear and her tone was replete with disapproval. Olivia had no choice but to apologize, take back her cash, and return to her seat. She could feel the receptionist's accusatory eyes on her back, but felt no shame. Haviland was waiting outside, so she had a valid reason to try to expedite her stay at the lab.

The minutes dragged on as one person after another passed into the next set of rooms. These patients moved deeper into the lab with slow and heavy steps. Olivia shared their feelings of reticence. She was not fond of

having blood drawn and tended to become dizzy and nau-
seated during the experience.

Finally, a woman wearing purple scrubs encasing wide
shoulders and a solid bulk resembling that of a NFL line-
backer called Olivia's name. "Olivia . . ." She frowned over
her clipboard. "Limodges?"

"Limoges," Olivia corrected. And then, because this
woman was about to stick a needle into her, tried to amend
her answer so that it sounded more conversational. "It's the
same name as the French porcelain."

The woman blinked at her and then smiled. "Oh, I've
seen that stuff on *Antiques Roadshow*. Pitchers and cups
and the like painted with flowers. That's not my style. Too
fancy. Me? I collect unicorns. All sorts of unicorns. I just
think they are *so* magical." She gestured for Olivia to enter
an empty exam room to the left and continued to list the
types of figurines or plush toys she'd bought or been given
over the years even though Olivia was paying her little
heed. She was too busy wondering whether to sit in the
reclining chair or lie flat on the cushioned exam table to
focus on crystal unicorns.

She opted for the table and sat on its edge. Pushing her
sleeve up her arm, she waited for the woman to get to work,
but she continued her recitation of her unique collection.

In order to stop the phlebotomist's prattle, Olivia abruptly
thrust the envelope containing her father's blood into the
woman's free hand. "You need this more than I do," she
said and eased back against the cushioned headrest of the
exam table.

Temporarily derailed, the woman checked her clipboard. "Paternity test, huh? You can sit in the chair, you
know. The table's for folks who don't do well when they
see the needle coming."

"It's not the needle, but I have a track record of wooziness when my blood is drawn," Olivia admitted reluctantly. "I'd feel more comfortable on this contemporary fainting couch."

"The what?" The woman asked but didn't pursue the subject. Humming softly, she tied a rubber tourniquet around Olivia's bicep and tapped on her skin a few inches below the tourniquet to make the vein swell.

Already feeling a bit clammy, Olivia looked away and tried to find an interesting focal point in the room but could only comfortably see a poster of the human circulatory system. She imagined the red and blue veins as highways on a road map. No matter which road one followed, the end would always be the metropolis of the heart.

Olivia did her best to study the body's most significant muscle as the phlebotomist stuck her twice before finally hitting the vein. "There we go!" The blood must have filled a vial quickly, for after a brief moment of silence, the woman placed a cotton pad over the needle hole and then applied pressure over the small wound for several seconds. She then slapped a Hello Kitty bandage over the cotton and straightened.

"You just stay still for a bit," the woman directed. "You've gone a bit pale."

Grunting once in assent, Olivia closed her eyes. That was a mistake. She immediately felt a wave of nausea wash over her. Jerking her eyes open, she searched out the red and blue heart on the poster again, taking in deep breaths through her mouth. By the time the phlebotomist returned, Olivia was able to sit up.

"When will I get my results?"

The woman tidied up her work area, dropping the spent syringe into a biohazard box and putting the bandage wrappings in the trashcan. "They'll probably take two days."

Olivia didn't care for this answer. "I thought results were

completed within twenty-four hours. You're talking about *twice* the expected wait time."

Unperturbed, the woman opened the door and indicated that Olivia was free to leave. "We're pretty backed up right now. Seems like everybody in the county has come down with shingles. You'll just have to be patient."

Pausing in the doorway, Olivia made it clear that she wasn't going to follow the woman to the checkout area. "I need these results immediately. If those blood results are positive, it means that my father, whom I believed drowned thirty years ago, is alive. But he's *barely* alive. He's got pancreatic cancer and is almost out of time. Do you think it's acceptable to ask me to be patient, to possibly miss the chance to see him before he dies, because this lab is backed up identifying cases of *shingles*!"

The woman didn't so much as flinch in the face of Olivia's indignation. "We'll do our best, ma'am," was all she would say before walking up the hall to the waiting room. "Ms. Limoges is ready to check out," she told the sour-faced receptionist, wished Olivia a good day, and called for the next patient.

Olivia received an instruction sheet on obtaining her lab results and marched out of the office, eager to vent her frustration. Seeing no nearby outlet, she returned Haviland's boisterous greeting by hugging him around the neck. She then drove to a nearby sandwich shop to pick up lunch for herself and several slices of roast chicken breast for Haviland.

Keeping her promise to Haviland, she returned to the leash-free park. After serving him the chicken, Olivia stuffed salt and vinegar potato chips into her mouth without the slightest regard for ladylike delicacy. While Haviland frolicked under the afternoon sun, she consumed the entire bag, a tuna fish sandwich on whole wheat, and a dill pickle spear. With her hunger satiated and her frustration marginally relieved, Olivia looked at her watch and wondered what diversions could prevent her from obsessing over the lab results.

She called Laurel's house but no one picked up. After leaving a brief message requesting that her friend get back to her as soon as possible, she threw out the empty potato chip bag and paper sandwich wrapper and dialed April Howard's number.

"Are you and your portfolio free this afternoon?" she asked when April answered. "Can you meet me at Bagels 'n' Beans in an hour?"

"Yes. I don't know if my appearance will look entirely professional, but I'll be there. I need at least an hour to find my one decent suit and iron three years of wrinkles out of it."

Listening to the fatigue in April's voice, Olivia sought to ease the widow's mind. "You're only meeting with me, and frankly, I don't care if you show up wearing pajamas. I'm serious, April. I'm your potential client and I don't give a damn whether you're in a suit and heels or sweats and sneakers. I just want to see your work and chat over a cup of coffee. Can someone look after your kids on such short notice?"

April issued a dry chuckle. "They'd love to get away from me for a few hours, trust me. I've been selfish to keep them close to me. When they're around me, they feel guilty about playing or laughing at things on TV. My kids are better at grief than I am. They're more resilient and more hopeful that they can be happy again one day."

"I think it's easier for them to put their feelings aside for periods of time," Olivia agreed. "But they experience grief as deeply as you do. They just might not be able to express how it's affecting them."

"One day you'll have to tell me how you know so much about this subject," April answered. "But I'll send the kids to Tina's. She's wanted them to come over for pizza for days and they could use a change of scenery. I'll see you in an hour."

Pleased, Olivia whistled for Haviland and set off for Bagels 'n' Beans. When she reached the café an hour later, Wheeler was in the process of handing over the reins to a pair of high school students.

When he saw Olivia, he stopped and pointed at her arm. "You givin' your blood away, 'cause I could use a fresh supply. Mine feels like it's movin' slower and slower through these droopy ol' veins."

Olivia dismissed the notion with a wave of her hand. "That's total nonsense. You'll outlive us all." She placed her drink order and then smiled at the feisty octogenarian. "Where are you off to now?"

Wheeler grinned. "I got a date. First one in a decade too. Her name's Esther. I met her on the computer."

Olivia couldn't mask her disbelief. "You're cyber-dating?"

"When it comes to women, I'm better at writin' than talkin'." He shrugged. "I just hope she looks like her picture. She's a dead ringer for Betty White." Wheeler stooped to pet Haviland and then strolled out the door, his jaunty step belonging to a man a quarter of his age.

"Betty White, huh?" Olivia laughed and settled back in her chair. Haviland curled up by her feet and closed his eyes, worn out from his exertions at the park.

Sipping her cappuccino, Olivia stared out the front window and felt a rush of affection for the town and its inhabitants. Somehow, just being back in Oyster Bay dissipated a fraction of her anxiety over the blood test results.

The bells hanging from the front door tinkled and April Howard walked in, a black portfolio case tucked under her arm. She spotted Olivia and made her way to the table, pausing to glance at the black-and-white photographs for sale on the wall above Olivia's head.

"These are new," she said. "Last time I was here there was a display of watercolor paintings."

"Wheeler told me he couldn't put up pieces of art fast enough during the Cardboard Regatta. Even with all the vendors selling comparable wares dockside, the tourists bought everything he had hanging on this wall." Olivia studied the photographs of downtown, which had been taken during the busy season. She liked the movement captured within each shot—how the people on the sidewalk and the cars on the street appeared to be in motion even though the camera had rendered them permanently immobile.

Directly over her cafe table was a head-on shot of Grumpy's façade. It showed a trio of teenage girls in shorts and bikini tops, a pair of children holding pinwheels, several women with shopping bags, and a cluster of locals chatting alongside the diner's door. It was a quintessential summer day in Oyster Bay—a glimpse of small-town Utopia.

April was also staring at the photograph. "My folks want me to move back to Ohio, but I could never leave this place. I fell in love with Oyster Bay on a day just like the one in that photo. Felix and I were here for a weekend getaway. On Sunday, while we were packing to go, I told him I wanted to move here and start a family. And we did."

"I grew up here, but I remember coming back to town after being away for a long time. I felt like I could breathe for the first time in ages." Olivia pointed at the portfolio. "May I?"

"Of course." April jerked her thumb toward the counter. "I'm going to order a complicated drink so you'll have time to look that over without me staring at you."

As the espresso machine gurgled and sputtered, Olivia examined April's designs and was satisfied by what she saw.

"Give her a takeout cup," she ordered the young barista.

Confused, April added a packet of sweetener to her drink and followed Olivia and Haviland outside.

"Let's show her our new acquisition, Captain."

The two women walked toward the harbor. A cool wisp of air drifted over them, carrying a hint of autumn. Olivia led April to the warehouse she'd own as soon as all the closing paperwork was finalized.

"This is it." She gestured at the building. "I want to change this wreckage into the Bayside Crab House. Delicious food, lively music, and a casual setting overlooking the water. What do you think?"

April was stunned. "You want *me* to do the designs? I've never worked on a structure this . . . old before."

Olivia laughed. "Don't be daunted by her age. This girl's about to have major cosmetic surgery. You'll be working with my contractor, Clyde. He's the best in the business. He can build anything I ask him to, but he needs design feedback."

"Do you have blueprints?" April asked and then, without waiting for an answer, began to slowly move around the perimeter of the building. Haviland followed behind, sniffing an invisible trail of human and animal odors as April began to talk to herself. "The kitchen should be on this side. There's decent access to the road for deliveries and garbage pickup. The front should be dominated by a large bar and I can see an expansive deck with plenty of room for tables . . ." She placed a hand on an exterior wall. "This place could become Oyster Bay's next hot spot."

Olivia smiled. She liked how April touched the building, acquainting herself with its bones of brick and wood.

"The job's yours if you want it. And before you give me an answer, I want you to know that there will be days you are simply not going to be able to work. No one expects you to act as though you haven't been knocked flat by loss."

"I'll do my best," April mumbled.

The clicking of Haviland's manicured claws over the planks of one of the lower docks caught Olivia's attention. She signaled for him to return and then focused on April again. "Right now I'd just like you to look over the schematics and do some preliminary drawings. Once the closing is done, I'll want you to meet with Clyde. When you're ready I'd then like you to present a final proposal to me." She raised her hand to stop April from speaking. "Take the night to think it over. The terms of your employment are outlined in this contract, and I trust they will help relieve some of your financial worries."

April was tactful enough not to peer inside. She thanked Olivia and walked away with her head held a little higher and Olivia knew she had judged the other woman correctly. April was a fighter. She'd hold herself and her family together despite the crushing blow they'd received. Eventually, perhaps years from now, she would emerge from her cocoon of grief. Olivia hoped that when that happened, a good man would appear and give April a second chance at happiness.

Evening fell and Olivia arrived home to the ringing of the phone. For a moment, she thought her lab results might have been completed early and dashed across the kitchen to grab the receiver from the cradle. She simultaneously noticed Laurel's number on the caller ID.

"I've been meaning to catch up with you," Laurel said hurriedly. "But there was a break in the case and I had to interview one of Rawlings' officers and then submit an article to my editor before Steve came home."

"What break?"

Laurel put her hand over the speaker and said something to one of her sons. She apologized for the interruption and then said, "The John Doe from the beach has been identified. When the cops were interviewing the area lawn-care companies, they found out one of the crew members of a large landscaping company stopped showing up for work around the time you found that man's body in the sand. Not only was he in the lawn-care business"—Laurel paused theatrically—"but the man was also a parolee. His name's Alan Dumfries."

Olivia glanced at the clock. It was earlier than her usual cocktail time, but she didn't care. Dropping a few ice cubes into a crystal tumbler, she opened a fresh bottle of Chivas Regal Reserve. "Let me guess. Alan served time for robbery."

"Bingo! However, he doesn't seem to have ties to anyone in town. No family, friends, nothing. Alan lived in Fayetteville before he got caught stealing in this county. Apparently, he preferred to break into cars, but I think it's safe to assume he graduated to home burglaries. He must have done a few jobs with the Cliché Burglars before they killed him." She paused thoughtfully. "Actually, they're more like the Cliché Killers, aren't they?"

"The Cliché Killers. Yes, that seems more accurate." Taking a sip of her scotch whiskey, Olivia murmured, "I guess Alan was the third wheel. If he had no connection to the families who were robbed, I'd bet this bottle of Chivas Regal that he was just a lackey."

"Maybe he was murdered because he broke a rule or something," Laurel theorized. "Or the thieves in charge couldn't trust him in the end."

"Plausible," Olivia agreed. "But it doesn't give Rawlings much of a lead. It's a step forward, something tangible for you to print in the paper, but knowing Alan Dumfries' name doesn't answer the who or the why in this case." She shook the ice cubes in her glass. "Do you have your high school yearbooks handy?"

Laurel hesitated. "I think they're in a box in the attic. Why?"

"I think our villain may have attended Pamplicoe High." Olivia described how she's overheard one of Rawlings' officers connecting the victims to the school. "We should look through them for anyone with a physical abnormality."

"That sounds so *mean*!" Laurel protested. "But I agree, though I can't do it now. I have to make *something* for dinner or Steve will say that I can't balance having a job with my responsibilities at home. Come over in the morning. The twins will be at preschool until twelve thirty. We can look through my yearbooks and then drive over to the high school if need be. The librarian, Ms. Glenda, has been there for ions. She has an uncanny memory for name and faces."

Olivia refilled her glass, trying not to think of how much she'd rather find out the results of her lab test and formulate a plan based on the results instead of going through page after page of Laurel's yearbooks. Her treasured tomes were undoubtedly filled with girlie signatures, hearts, *x*'s and *o*'s, smiley faces, and the usual gushing promises to remain best friends forever. Olivia had left her own yearbooks in her boarding school dorm room, having made no close friends. Even as a teenager, Olivia planned for an adulthood of solitude. All relics of her school days, whether they were report cards, art projects, or ribbons from horse shows, had been discarded at the end of every term. She didn't want to look back. It was simply too painful. The only way to survive was to move stubbornly forward, forging no human connections.

"I'll see you at nine," she told Laurel and hung up.

Glancing at Rawlings' painting of Haviland, Olivia raised her glass in salute. Here was evidence that she had become much more sociable since her school days. Repeating the Virginia Slims slogan, she declared, "You've come a long way, baby."

Chapter 15

We grow tired of everything but turning
others into ridicule, and congratulating
ourselves on their defects.
—WILLIAM HAZLITT

After consuming two liberally poured cocktails, Olivia decided it would be unwise to drive back into town just to spend the rest of the evening milling about her restaurant.

Instead, she ate a salad of endive, roast chicken breast, crumbled blue cheese, and apple slices on the deck. She then poured herself another drink and watched the sky darken. Haviland roamed the beach until the first stars came to life on the night's blue black canvas. Only when her arms grew chilled did Olivia collect her poodle and return indoors.

Though her body was tired, thoughts whirled around Olivia's mind with the disruptive force of a thunderstorm and she knew sleep would prove evasive. She moved from one activity to another—wondering if the police were closing in on the thieves, planning how she'd react should her blood test reveal that her father was alive and imagining what Rawlings was doing at the moment, whether he was at the station or at home, perhaps searching through case files again and again.

In an attempt to still her mind, Olivia tried to read. However, the book she'd begun earlier in the week was too frivolous for her current mood. Casting the paperback aside, she turned on the television and flipped from one reality show to another. Marveling that she couldn't find a single thing to capture her interest even though she had access to over three hundred channels, Olivia unwrapped a candy bar made of fine Belgian dark chocolate and gazed around her living room in search of a better distraction.

In the end, she pulled a DVD from the cabinet below her television and finally settled onto the sofa to watch the 1940 classic, *Rebecca*. Olivia knew every word of the film by heart but never grew tired of it. She viewed the movie at least once a year, usually when she was in a state of agitation. Somehow, the haunting presence of Rebecca de Winter and the scenes filmed at the base of the cliffs below Manderley captivated her every time.

Rebecca didn't let her down. When the movie was over, Olivia was finally able to fall asleep, though her dreams were punctuated with fragmented images of shipwrecks, dark and hungry waves, and a distorted, witch-like version of the phlebotomist from the lab in New Bern.

The next morning, Olivia and Haviland took an early walk on the beach and then headed into town for breakfast at Grumpy's before meeting Laurel. She'd barely sat down at her favorite window booth when Dixie skated over and served Olivia coffee.

"You look like a diminutive version of the tooth fairy," Olivia told her friend, gesturing at Dixie's purple top, ballet tutu, and striped tights.

Dixie curtsied. "Actually, I'm channeling the cartoon character Pinky Dinky Doo. She's my youngest girl's favorite. If I'd had more time, I woulda gone all out and dyed my hair pink too." She touched the ends of her high ponytail. "But I had to settle for glitter."

Oblivious that Dixie was dressed in eccentric costume, Haviland made it clear that he was very glad to see the small woman. Wagging his tail, he gave her a gentlemanly lick on the back of her hand. She beamed at him.

"Captain, you're a shameless flirt. Don't you fret, my darlin', Grumpy'll cook up something extra special for you on this fine mornin'." Glancing over her shoulder, she put the coffeepot down on Olivia's table. "I'm not bringin' *you* a thing until you tell me what in the world is goin' on with you and Flynn."

"Lately? Not a thing."

Dixie poked her on the shoulder. "Don't go all mysterious on *me*. I'll take this coffeepot to the kitchen and keep it there."

Olivia held up her hands in surrender. "Our relationship, and I use that term loosely, has run its course."

"My, my. Explains why I've been seein' him all over town with Diane the vet." Dixie studied her friend's face. "You hadn't heard that tidbit, had you now?"

"I knew they'd had dinner once, but if they've gotten serious already then frankly, I'm relieved. Saves me from having to recite my it's-time-to-move-on speech." Olivia pointed at the pad and pencil in Dixie's apron pocket. "I'd like something with eggs, herbs, and diced tomatoes. Perhaps half a grapefruit as well?"

Sensing that other customers required attention, Dixie frowned and skated off. Olivia turned her attention to the *Oyster Bay Gazette* and eagerly read Laurel's article about the identification of Alan Dumfries.

Sipping her coffee, Olivia studied the photograph of the man she'd found buried in the sand. There was little resemblance between the ruined flesh and sunken eyes of the face hidden beneath a green bucket and the defiant stare and chiseled features of the portrait in the paper. Death had robbed Alan Dumfries of his strong jaw, his proud nose, and the blend of anger and arrogance in his dark eyes.

"Why did they kill you?" Olivia asked the surly visage. "How did you screw up?"

"Talking to yourself?" a voice questioned.

Olivia glanced up from the paper and saw Flynn grinning over her shoulder. She tried not to be annoyed by how the man constantly appeared when she was otherwise occupied. Still, she now had the opportunity to make it clear that she was no longer interested in pursuing a relationship with him beyond that of casual friends. She indicated he should sit. "Care to join me for breakfast?"

"I would indeed," he answered, a smile in his gray eyes. Olivia felt a prick of doubt. Flynn was so lively, so capable of lightening even the gloomiest of her moods with his ready humor and affable manner. As she stared at him now, she had to admit that he was awfully easy on the eyes too.

Dixie skated from the *Cats* booth to take Flynn's order, betraying not the slightest surprise over finding him sitting across from Olivia moments after her friend had claimed that she and Flynn were finished. "Your tomato and mozzarella omelet will be out shortly, ma'am," Dixie said to Olivia and winked as she shot off toward the kitchen.

Olivia gazed at Flynn over the rim of her coffee cup. "The word around town is that you and Diane have become friendly."

"She's a fun gal," he replied nonchalantly. "Except when she's loading me down with endless amounts of reading material on raising kittens. Life as a single parent." He sighed theatrically. "It is *so* hard."

Olivia laughed. "Have your little felines been given names?"

"Oh, yes. Digory and Polly, after the children in C. S. Lewis's *The Magician's Nephew*." Dixie arrived in the middle of Flynn's sentence, carrying Olivia and Haviland's meals as well as a cup of coffee for Flynn.

"My kids entered your contest, but I think they wanted to name your cats after video game characters or pop stars." She fluffed the lowest ruffle of her tutu. "And my youngest boy was real set on you callin' one of them Chinese Takeout."

Flynn chuckled. "I should have given him an honorable mention for creativity, but you'll be happy to know that the winner is from a family facing hard times. When I told this kid that he'd won and could pick out fifty dollars worth of books, he grinned from ear to ear. One of the books he chose was a dictionary. He said his folks didn't see a need for one, but he'd been asking for this particular book since his sixth birthday. I sold him a leather-bound version at cost and he petted the thing like it was a puppy."

Dixie wiped a tear from her eye. "You've gone and made my mascara run. Shame on you, Flynn McNulty."

"Will you forgive me long enough to put in an order for Grumpy's apple pancakes?

"I suppose I might." Dixie sniffed and skated away.

Olivia cut into her eggs, allowing a vent of steam to escape from the molten mozzarella interior. "Returning to the subject of you and Diane . . . I wanted you to know that I am—"

"Madly jealous?" Flynn reached across the table and grabbed her hand. "She and I are friends. You're the only woman I want to make burnt toast for in the morning."

A movement close to the window drew Olivia's attention. She looked outside to see Rawlings, in uniform, carrying a cardboard beverage tray filled with coffee. He handed the tray to the officer in the passenger seat of a double-parked cruiser and then hustled around to the driver's side, sunlight winking off his mirrored shades.

"Damn it all!" Withdrawing her hand from Flynn's, Olivia took a bite of her food and chewed mechanically, her gaze fixed on the police car. When it turned out of sight, she sighed. What had Rawlings seen? She and Flynn holding hands like the lovers they'd been? After all, she was the only one who knew she no longer wished to have a physical relationship with Flynn, as she hadn't managed to break it off.

I'll make things clear to Flynn first and then I'll tell Rawlings he caught a glimpse of our final moment of intimacy.

Flynn was watching her curiously. "What's going on in that beautiful mind of yours? World domination, complex mathematical problems, physics formulas, the plot of a future bestseller?

Olivia put her fork down. "I asked about you and Diane because I wanted you to know you are free to pursue a relationship with her. Not that you needed my permission, because you and I never set parameters as to what we were to one another, but I think she's lovely."

"Why do I have a hunch that parameters are about to be firmly put into place," Flynn murmured unhappily.

"I find in these situations that it's best to be completely honest," Olivia said matter-of-factly. "What we have isn't working for me anymore. Let's part amicably and continue our book discussions fully clothed in the future."

In the heavy silence, Dixie arrived with Flynn's pancakes. She prattled away as he spread several pats of butter across the surface of the stack and then poured liberal amounts of warm, pecan-flavored syrup on top of the butter. When he failed to laugh at Dixie's joke or take a single bite of his breakfast, she put her hands on her hips and gave him a frank stare. "What's wrong with your food?"

"There could *never* be anything amiss with your fine fare," Flynn answered dramatically. "But Olivia just broke up with me and I'm wishing she'd waited until I was done with my pancakes. I've been dreaming about these all week."

Dixie shot Olivia an accusing look. "Did you put this man off his breakfast?"

Ignoring her, Olivia took some money from her wallet, slapped it on the table, and rose. "Have a nice day. Both of you."

She patted her thigh to stir Haviland, who was dozing contentedly against the diner's wall, oblivious of the mixed emotions filling the air above his head.

Neither Flynn nor Dixie interfered with Olivia's leaving. She reached the Range Rover and felt an immediate and powerful sense of relief. Rolling down all four windows, she turned on the radio and pulled away from her unlawful parking space in front of a fire hydrant and headed for Laurel's subdivision. The combination of Aretha Franklin and the autumn air sweeping into the car's cabin tasted sweetly of freedom.

Laurel welcomed Olivia by promising that the coffee she was in the midst of brewing would be fresh and strong.

"I bought myself a new machine with the money from my first paycheck." She proudly stroked the appliance's stainless steel façade and Olivia agreed that it was most impressive. After pouring two cups, Laurel offered Haviland a bowl of water and several dog biscuits she'd purchased especially for his visit. The two women then settled at the kitchen table where Laurel had laid out three yearbooks on the sticky tabletop.

"That's just some jam leftover from breakfast. The boys get more on their clothes and the furniture than in their sweet little tummies," Laurel said with a laugh, swiping at the surface with a sponge. "Here. You take my sophomore year. I'll go over my wonderful days as a junior. When I was—"

"Why are there only three books?" Olivia immediately cut short her friend's high school reminiscences.

Laurel frowned. "I think my parents have my freshman yearbook. I must have left it behind after marrying Steve and they just packed it with the rest of their stuff when they moved to Florida. I could easily picture my mom looking through it every now and then." Laurel seemed pleased by the thought. "Anyway, I rooted around in the attic as soon as I got back from dropping off the twins this morning but could only locate these three. If we don't find any suspicious photos in here, we'll have to pay a visit to Ms. Glenda at the school library."

Olivia opened the first book and carefully scanned page after page of young faces. The photos revealed evidence of acne, thick glasses, gawkiness, mouthfuls of metal braces, minor facial scars, and one wheelchair-bound student, but nothing struck Olivia as out of the ordinary. Like any group of photographs representing a large population, there were attractive faces, unappealing faces, and altogether unremarkable faces.

Laurel was turning the pages with agonizing slowness, chuckling over the comments written or waxing nostalgic over memories of homecoming or prom. She held one-sided conversations with the smiling visages on almost every page and even giggled a time or two, sounding very much like a teenage girl.

"Slide over your senior year," Olivia commanded impatiently. "I have no doubt it was unforgettable, but we've got a job to do. Stop reliving the glory days as a pompom shaker and search for deformities, would you?"

"Spoilsport," Laurel retorted and pretended to sulk,

but by the time she'd reached a spread featuring the junior class candid shots, she was laughing again.

Olivia finished scrutinizing the second book but found nothing. She insisted on paging through the one Laurel finally set aside. Finding no clues in the third yearbook, she carried her cup to the sink and rinsed a splotch of grape jelly from her wrist. "Let's head over to Pampticoe High. I'll drive."

On the way to the school, Laurel chatted about how much she was enjoying her new career and how comfortable she felt interviewing members of the Oyster Bay Police Department. "Chief Rawlings has been so kind to me. I really hope he can make it to our Bayside Book Writers meeting on Saturday. I loved his chapter! I wrote down so few criticisms that he's going to think I'm buttering him up in order to get information for my articles."

The two women discussed Rawlings' chapter and what progress they hoped to make on their own manuscripts. Olivia didn't tell Laurel that she'd reached a writing roadblock since receiving the vial of blood from Will Hamilton. It was now impossible to dream up plot lines focusing on Kamila, her fictitious Egyptian concubine, in the face of such poignant real-life drama. Luckily, Laurel was brimming with ideas for a contemporary romance novel and discussed these for the remainder of the ride.

Pampticoe High was bustling with activity when Olivia and Laurel stopped by the front office to collect visitor badges. Students were in the middle of changing classes and poured through the dingy hallways, talking, laughing, shouting, and slamming lockers. Half of the teens wore ear buds and listened to music as they moved while another large percentage was talking or texting on cell phones.

Olivia thought back to the boarding school she'd attended—the strict dress code, the rule of silence when in public areas, the insistence on politeness and proper etiquette at all times. Had these students attended Olivia's school, most of them would have been immediately hauled off to detention for inappropriate dress and the use of foul language, their electronic devices confiscated and all privileges revoked.

"This is a different world," she commented under her breath after an oblivious young man barreled into her and then shuffled off without so much as an apology.

Ms. Glenda's domain was refreshingly quiet and orderly. Olivia only had to watch the woman interact with a single student to see that she ruled the library with a blend of softness and steel. She was also remarkably unsurprised by Laurel's request that she recall the names of former students with notable physical deformities.

"A nice young police officer asked me the very same thing yesterday afternoon," Ms. Glenda whispered, removing her reading glasses to clean off a smudge on the left lens. "It was no small feat to consider the unusual birthmarks, burns, scars, missing limbs, additional fingers or toes, and excessive overbites of two decades worth of students!" Having finished with her glasses, she put them back on and gazed at Laurel with interest. "I see your experience with the school paper eventually blossomed into a career. Journalism suits you, my dear. I've followed your recent articles with pride, knowing I once taught you how to conduct research."

Laurel blushed prettily. "You certainly did, Ms. Glenda. Believe me, your coaching has come in handy more than once over the last few weeks."

Ms. Glenda preened and Olivia suspected the woman deserved every accolade she received. It couldn't be easy to instruct the group of unruly miscreants Olivia had seen in the school's hallway. "I don't know why the police were interested in my memories of days gone by, but I suspect it has something to do with the Cliché Killers. Didn't you come up with that nickname? Quite catchy."

Nodding modestly, Laurel held her blank notebook page in the air. "I think we're chasing down the same lead. Were you able to assist the police?"

"Not at first." Ms. Glenda indicated they should follow her into the stacks. She pulled a yearbook from the shelf, found the page she was looking for, and then held it open against her chest with the blue cover facing outward. "I thought I'd be of no help until the officers used the words 'cliché' and 'tease' in the same sentence. Two faces quickly surfaced in my mind." She studied Laurel. "Surely you remember a student being teased for the strange sounds she made when she tried to talk. Does the phrase, 'cat got your tongue' help you remember?"

Laurel began to shake her head, but then stopped. She paled and reached for Ms. Glenda's yearbook. The librarian pointed to a group of photographs featuring the senior class. "See there? It says, 'Absent from this group: Andrew Davis and Ellen Donald.' "

"Ellen Donald." Laurel's words were barely audible. "I remember her now. Oh! I may have . . . I believe I joined in when the older girls made fun of her."

Ms. Glenda seemed satisfied by the admission. "Her older brother was Rutherford. He graduated three years ahead of Ellen and was also severely tongue-tied."

Olivia accepted the yearbook and put her finger on the place where Ellen's photograph should have appeared on the page. "Wasn't their condition reparable?"

"I imagine so." Ms. Glenda reclaimed the yearbook and shelved it, clearly signaling that she didn't want to discuss the matter any further.

"Can you provide us with a more concrete answer?" Olivia demanded, sensing the librarian knew more than she was willing to let on. "Or point us to a faculty member who might have a more complete recollection of the Donald siblings?"

Her pride stung, Ms. Glenda crossed her arms over her chest. "I do not like to gossip, especially when it comes to former students of mine."

"Of course you don't!" Laurel whispered passionately. "You must feel protective of them. I'd never quote you without your permission, but people have been hurt, Ms. Glenda. You could help bring an end to the robberies, to the violence, afflicting *two* counties."

Listening to the plaintive tone of another former student, Ms. Glenda capitulated. Turning slightly, she spoke solely to Laurel. "The Donalds were a Jehovah's Witness family. There were six children in all, Rutherford and Ellen being the youngest. Those two rarely spoke at school, and when they did, it was almost impossible to understand what they were saying. Their words were garbled. The guidance counselor and several teachers attempted to talk the parents into seeking medical treatment, but Mr. and Mrs. Donald refused to listen. It was their belief that their children were perfect in the eyes of God and that they had been born with twisted tongues for a reason."

"Those poor children," Laurel murmured sadly. "They faced ridicule their entire childhoods when it could have been avoided?"

"I've heard that the procedure is fairly straightforward. I don't remember what it's called, but apparently it's performed on infants quite often. A surgeon cuts away the extra tissue the child was born with, allowing the tongue to move more freely. At their age, the Donald kids would have had to go into the hospital. A local doctor offered to do the surgery for free, but the parents wouldn't even consider it." Ms. Glenda pursed her lips in disapproval.

Olivia's eyes had strayed to the row of yearbooks on the shelf. "The robbery victims were classmates of the Donalds. We can safely assume that at least one spouse of each couple contributed to the misery of the Donalds' high school career."

"Let's test that theory before we leave." Laurel pulled another yearbook from the shelf. "I'll try to find Christina Quimby. I know her maiden name."

Laurel found Christina's photo quickly. After that, she looked up Felix Howard, followed by Sue Ridgemont's husband. "Chief Rawlings was a step ahead of us. Unless the Donalds are using false identities, he'll have them in custody today." She glanced at her notebook. "I wonder if their parents are still local. I should try to find their house. It would make the perfect photographic accompaniment for my article on Rutherford and Ellen. Maybe I could even get an interview before they know what their kids have been up to. I could pretend to be doing a piece on Jehovah's Witnesses."

Olivia was more than a little astonished that her friend was able to remain so detached from the story. After all, the crimes had been inflicted on her schoolmates and she knew, if only by distant acquaintance, one of the perpetrators. "Come on, Diane Sawyer. I need to let Haviland out of the car. We can do a search for the parents using your home computer."

Laurel thanked Ms. Glenda and followed Olivia out of the library. After passing through a pungent hallway smelling of sweat and disinfectant, they both exited the school and drew in grateful breaths of refreshing autumn air.

On the way back to Laurel's house, the women exchanged title ideas for the next piece on the Cliché Killers. Olivia's phone rang and her heart fluttered. Was it the lab? At the next stop sign, she looked at the screen. Her contractor had called to let her know the work on the lighthouse keeper's cottage was done and she was free to move furniture back in.

"Our writer's group can meet at its usual locale this weekend. That was my contractor calling with the good news."

"I've heard about him from April Howard. She told me that you'd offered her a job," Laurel said as Olivia parked the Range Rover. "When I'm done breaking this story, I'm going to do an article on you, Oyster Bay's behind-the-scenes benefactor."

"That'll be the end of your career for certain," Olivia growled. "I'll buy the paper and fire you. And I'm *not* joking. In any case, everyone in town is fully aware of every move I make without any help from you or the *Gazette*."

Ignoring her, Laurel told Haviland he was free to take care of business in the strip of woods separating her property from her neighbor's. "Their dog does it on our front lawn all the time and they *never* pick up after her." Laurel glared at the Georgian house next door. "Go wild, Haviland!"

Cocking his head at the sound of his name, Haviland trotted off to the specified area. The women waited until he'd complied with Laurel's wishes and then Olivia called him back into the house, promising to take him to the park immediately after lunch.

Laurel asked Olivia to boot up her laptop while she placed a call to Chief Rawlings, hoping to prime him for information before he made what was sure to become a celebrated arrest.

"No luck," she told Olivia. "He's not answering his office or cell numbers and I can't reach Officer Cook either. He's kind of been my go-to guy. That man loves the idea of having his name in the paper."

As Olivia began a search for the Donald family, the doorbell rang. Haviland, who had stretched out on the tiles under the kitchen table, raised his head and lifted his ears in curiosity. Then, seeing that his mistress hadn't reacted to the sound, he flopped back onto the cool floor and closed his eyes.

Upon hearing more than one set of footsteps in Laurel's hallway, Olivia stopped typing. It seemed odd to her that there were at least two people in the house, perhaps more, and yet no one spoke. The feeling intensified. Sensing something was wrong; she swiveled in her chair and gasped.

There was Laurel—trembling hands held above her head in surrender, face ashen with terror.

She stood shakily between the rigid bodies of a man and a woman. They both had tanned skin and brown hair streaked gold by the sun. They were both armed and their deep-set dark eyes were cold with rage.

The woman held a knife with a sinister black blade and the man held a length of steel wire. They wore identical work gloves with red rubber palms.

Olivia's eyes moved from the bloodred hue to the clenched jaws and icy calm stares of the Cliché Killers. Rutherford and Ellen Donald had clearly not fled town.

The siblings had another agenda. They'd come to exact their revenge on one more Pampticoe High alumnus.

They'd come for Laurel.

Chapter 16

*So comes snow after fire, and even
dragons have their ending.*
—J. R. R. TOLKIEN

"I'm sorry, Ellen!" Laurel cried, turning to face the woman on her left. "I was an idiot to tease you like I did! I was *more* than an idiot! I was cruel but I am so, so sorry!"

Ellen shrugged, indicating that Laurel's apology hadn't moved her one bit. "You were a stupid sheep. You were all sheep, doing what the cool kids told you to." Her words were flawlessly clear and laced with bitterness. The woman who had grown up with a major speech impediment now spoke with the elocution of a Juilliard actress. "Rutherford and me were little bugs for you to step on. You didn't think about anything but your clothes and your boyfriends. Now you're all grown up and you're still the same." She gestured in a wide circle with her knife. "Perfect house. Perfect little family. Sheep."

"And a perfect job where you get to judge other people in print. Do you think you've earned the right to influence people?" Rutherford growled. "We've read what you've written about us, little lamb. Let me ask you, what do you *really* know about us?"

Laurel's face crumpled. "I know you're not wicked! People were mean to you and you both suffered. I played a part in that, but I have two precious boys—"

"Shut up!" Ellen shouted angrily, spittle flying from her mouth. "*My brother and I* never got a chance to have families of our own. Not only did our folks force us to live at home until we were nearly *thirty*, but people screwed with us for too many years before that for us to come out normal. We've waited a *long* time to punish everyone who hurt us. You need to understand"—she brought the tip of her black blade within centimeters of Laurel's eye—"we have nothing to lose."

"You were one of them, Laurel," Rutherford hissed and then, in a frightening singsong, he whispered, "Cat got your tongue, cat got your tongue, cat go your tongue," until Laurel put her hands over her ears, her fingers shaking like branches in a hurricane wind.

Olivia had sat through this charged scene as though made of stone. Her focus was divided by the appearance of the Donald siblings and the absurd thought that if she were a character in a movie or a book, she'd immediately come up with a plan to save her friend. There would have been some useful weapon at hand and the police would have been battering down the front door, moments away from rescuing the women in the midst of a desperate struggle against the villains.

When Ellen raised her knife to Laurel's face, Olivia was able to break the spell of immobility and react. Slowly turning her head, she looked for a weapon that could stop both Ellen and Rutherford, but the only items nearby were Laurel's laptop and two plastic sippy cups belonging to Dallas and Dermot.

Yet, Olivia had two advantages. The Donalds weren't paying attention to her, giving her the element of surprise if only for the next few seconds. And she had Haviland, out of sight beneath the kitchen table. It would only take a single word to subtract from the intruders' advantage and Olivia knew the moment had come to call it out.

"HAVILAND!" Her shout was infused with authority. "ATTACK!"

She jumped up and jerked her chair to the side, giving Haviland the space he needed to bolt out from under the table. In a flash of black fur and bared teeth, he was on Rutherford before the man could even think of slipping his length of sharp wire over the poodle's head.

When Rutherford howled in pain, Olivia lunged forward, grabbing hold of Ellen's wrist. The knife tilted away from Laurel's face and Olivia yelled, "RUN! *NOW! CALL RAWLINGS!*"

Laurel complied. In a flash of blond hair, she raced through the kitchen to the garage.

Olivia had no time to feel relief that her friend had escaped. Ellen, who was younger and stronger, suddenly wrenched her forearm to the side and broke free of Olivia's grasp. Her eyes were wild, glittering with madness and decades of unspent rage.

She slashed at Olivia's chest with her knife and Olivia leapt backward, but not quickly enough. A searing pain screamed along the flesh of her upper arm and Ellen smiled, delighted to have drawn blood from this stranger who'd dared to interfere.

Haviland yelped, and even though hearing his cry was like receiving another wound, Olivia didn't dare take her eyes from her opponent. She struck out with her right leg, her foot slamming powerfully into Ellen's stomach. She heard a grunt and Ellen bent over, the air knocked from her lungs. Olivia used the reprieve to dash into the kitchen, her arm burning in agony.

At a safe distance for mere seconds, she tried to yank open a drawer in search of the biggest knife she could find, but child-protection locks had been affixed on every drawer.

"Damn it!" Olivia had never felt such intense helplessness.

But she did not have time to waste on self-pity. Ellen was coming for her again, knife held out in front of her, lips twisted in a predator's smile. "You're going to pay for hurting my brother!" she snarled. "When I'm done with you, I'm going to carve up your dog like a Thanksgiving turkey!"

"What is with you and all the clichés?" Olivia asked derisively, deliberately backing into a corner. Behind her was Laurel's new coffee machine, complete with a twelve-cup, stainless steel thermal carafe. She'd brewed a full pot of coffee only an hour ago. There were at least eight cups of hot coffee left.

As Ellen advanced, Olivia unscrewed the pot's lid. The motion hurt her arm terribly and she could feel the blood soaking into her shirt and streaming down her skin until it had covered her wrist and fingers, but she couldn't give in to the pain. Across the room, Haviland was also fighting for his life. Rutherford's body had been strengthened by years of physical labor and he could easily break the poodle's bones or punch him hard enough to render Haviland unconscious.

Olivia knew she couldn't waste another minute tangling with Ellen. She needed to end this now.

"So now you're mocking us too?" Ellen hissed. "We didn't get to go to college like *some people*. We taught ourselves what our folks wouldn't and worked shit jobs until we had enough to pay for an apartment and bills and the operation our ignorant parents should have given us when we were kids! But we showed them." She uttered a strangled chuckle.

As much as Olivia wanted to hear every nuance behind the siblings' motives, it was more important to incapacitate Ellen Donald. She waited for the other woman to lunge with her knife hand. At that moment, Olivia jerked to the right and flung the contents of the coffeepot into Ellen's face.

The knife clattered to the floor as Ellen raised both hands to her face, screaming. Mercilessly, Olivia swung the stainless steel vessel with all her strength, landing a debilitating blow to the side of Ellen's head. The woman sank to the ground like a stone dropped into deep water.

Olivia stepped over her opponent's sprawled legs.

A voice shouted, "FREEZE!"

It was Rawlings. He stood in Laurel's foyer, his gun drawn and fixed on Rutherford. Two officers, both of whom had their weapons trained on Ellen's brother, flanked the chief.

Olivia's gaze turned to Rutherford. Her blood turned to ice.

Rutherford had a switchblade in his hand and was pointing it at Haviland's throat. The poodle was growling a low, dangerous growl and was tensing to pounce. If he did, Rutherford's blade would pass straight through his jugular.

"Haviland! Off!" Olivia commanded but terror made her words come out as a croak.

Rawlings stepped forward. "I will shoot you in the leg, Rutherford Donald. If you do not drop your weapon *this instant* so help me, I will shoot you!"

"Come, Haviland!" Olivia heard the desperation in her voice but didn't care. "Come to me!"

The poodle obeyed. Skirting around Rutherford, he reached Olivia's side and nudged her with his nose.

Olivia couldn't stop the tears of relief that fell onto Haviland's fur as she ran her panicked fingers over his body. There was no blood so he had not been cut and he didn't flinch in pain as she examined him. His chest was slightly tender and Olivia suspected he'd taken one of Rutherford's blows to that region, but all in all, he was well.

In turn, Haviland licked her, nuzzled her, and sniffed her wound, whining a little in concern. Olivia waited until

Rutherford tossed his knife onto the rug and was promptly cuffed by one of the officers before she returned to the kitchen. She wound Laurel's checkered dishcloth around her arm and winced as a fresh burst of pain shot up the damaged limb.

Rawlings was beside her in an instant.

He was angry. "You're hurt."

His eyes blazed with threads of green and gold and Olivia realized that they only had that appearance when the chief was struggling to keep his emotion in check. He found another dishcloth in a drawer and placed it over the first, applying pressure to Olivia's wound. "We've got to stop the bleeding."

Don't look, Olivia told herself, but then she did. Blood seeped through both towels, spreading across the material in a wave of red. She felt a surge of nausea and then a rush of cloying heat. She reached out for the countertop to steady herself before she passed out altogether.

"Easy," Rawlings whispered and put his arm around her waist. He eased her to one of the kitchen chairs. "Keep your head down. Breathe deeply." She did as he directed but he wasn't satisfied. "No, slow down. Innnnnnnnn. Now ouuuuuuuuuuut. Better."

They remained like this for a full minute. Olivia had the absurd thought that they sounded like an expectant couple practicing Lamaze breathing techniques. She carefully straightened and looked at Rawlings. His face was inches from hers and his eyes had softened, returning to their muddy, pond green hue. "Thank you," she murmured. "You came just in time."

Rawlings glowered. "Yes, we did. That's our job, remember? When you talked Laurel into investigating the Donald siblings, you put both of your lives in danger. All I asked you to do was to *think* about the meaning of the clichés! I didn't ask you to lure the killers here!"

"They would have come for her anyway!" Olivia protested but silently felt the chief had spoken the truth. After all, the robbery victims were old enough to have attended Pampticoe High with both Ellen and Rutherford. Laurel was two years younger than the others and had only ridiculed Ellen. Her articles about the siblings may have drawn their attention to her. If she hadn't started writing about them, it was likely they would never have remembered her at all. "Where is Laurel?" Olivia asked, needing to know that her friend was safe.

"Sitting in my car. She's both shaken and plenty mad over having to stay behind while we charged in, but she'll get over it."

Olivia gave Rawlings a grateful smile. "I'm relieved she didn't witness how this played out. By the time she comes back into the house, the Donalds will be gone and I'll have this mess cleaned up." She briefly gestured at the blood-splattered floor and countertop.

She and Rawlings watched as one of Rawlings' brawny officers fastened Ellen's limp wrists together in front of her body using a plastic restraint and then the officer sat down beside her to wait for the paramedics to arrive.

"I like Ellen much better when she's unconscious." Olivia stood and wrestled with the child lock of the cabinet beneath the sink, searching for cleaning supplies.

"Get back in that chair. The only thing you're doing is going to the hospital," Rawlings commanded and waited until she was seated again. "This place is about to be invaded by EMTs and an army of cops. The scene must be thoroughly documented."

"Then let Laurel take me to get stitched up," Olivia said. "You know how slow emergency rooms are. By the time I'm finished, your team should be done here."

Rawlings got down on his knees and put his hands on

her shoulders. "Only if you promise to go straight there. No stopping to purchase a pound of raw liver for Haviland, though God knows the dog deserves it." He glanced over at the poodle. "Well done, sir. You could show our K-9 unit a thing or two. Our department might need to look into those advanced canine training classes you took."

Olivia was overwhelmed by the urge to kiss Sawyer Rawlings. She raised her good arm and put her palm flat against his rough cheek. "Haviland's not my only hero," she whispered and pulled his head toward hers. Closing her eyes, she pressed her lips against his lips and felt his hand slide up the skin of her neck. It came to rest at the nape but his fingertips stretched a bit higher, gently grabbing her hair and sending a ripple of heat through her body. She responded by opening her mouth more fully, inviting him to kiss her more deeply and with more urgency.

The tread of heavy footsteps reentering the house ruined the moment. They hastily broke apart, flushed and glassy-eyed with desire.

"Put your arm around my waist," Rawlings directed huskily.

"I am perfectly capable of walking outside without assistance, thank you," she answered stiffly, noting that the officers were watching their chief with interest.

Rawlings frowned. "Do as I say or I will carry you out."

Feigning reluctance, Olivia allowed Rawlings to support her, but in truth she wanted to feel his touch, no matter what the circumstances were. She leaned into him, smelling coffee and soap and the sandalwood of his aftershave, and Haviland brought up the rear, looking as though nothing out of the ordinary had occurred.

Outside, Laurel was pacing back and forth on the lawn. The cruisers bearing the Donald siblings were already gone.

"Oh, *Olivia*! Thank God!" Laurel ran to them, her

eyes puffy from crying. She stared at the bloody dish-towels Rawlings held against Olivia's upper arm. "What happened?"

"She has a deep laceration and needs to be taken to the hospital," Rawlings said with perfect calm. "Can you drive her? I need to stay on site until the other officers arrive."

Laurel nodded vigorously. "Of course!" Taking Olivia's purse from the chief, she sprinted to the Range Rover and hopped into the driver's seat.

As Rawlings opened the passenger door, Olivia leaned toward him and whispered, "Please make sure everything looks normal before she comes home. I know that's not exactly your job, but I'm asking as a favor to me."

With Laurel busy digging through Olivia's purse for her keys, Rawlings felt free to brush Olivia's neck with his lips. "Since you asked so nicely . . ." He then eased her into the car and opened the back door for Haviland.

"No stopping," he told Laurel firmly. "No matter what she says."

Laurel squared her shoulders. "Yes, Chief. I promise."

Olivia had no intention of avoiding the hospital, but she asked Laurel to drop her off at the emergency room and take Haviland to the park.

"He's not allowed inside anyway," she reminded Laurel when her friend began to argue. She insisted on waiting until Olivia had registered and moved back to the triage area before driving off with Haviland.

The entire ordeal took over two hours. Olivia's cut was deep enough to merit a layer of dissolvable stitches to help the rent tissue mend, followed by fifty-some sutures to knit her layers of skin back together. She received a teta-nus shot, instructions on how to clean her wound, and an appointment for suture removal in ten days' time.

During the ride back to Laurel's house, Olivia's arm

throbbed mercilessly. She'd been given plenty of shots to kill the pain while the doctor cleaned and repaired her wound, but now there was a steady ache and her entire arm felt heavy and swollen. The nurse had given Olivia a sling, and though she hated to wear it, she couldn't imagine letting her limb hang on its own.

Not only had Laurel let Haviland dash after the park's squirrels to his heart's content, but per Olivia's request she'd taken him to the vet to ensure he had no injuries. As soon as Diane declared the poodle healthy as usual, Laurel called The Boot Top and asked Michel to prepare something special for the canine champion.

"My mother-in-law is picking up the twins so we can go straight to the restaurant," Laurel said. "I'm in no rush to go home."

Olivia leaned back against the headrest. "Good. I could use a drink."

Being that it was past lunchtime, The Boot Top's bar was empty and the lights were set to their daytime setting. Olivia immediately adjusted the dimmer slide until the room was plunged into semidarkness.

Taking up Gabe's position behind the bar, she checked the ice supply and reached for a tumbler. "What's your pleasure?" she asked Laurel.

"Normally, I'd say it's *way* too early to be drinking, but I could easily slurp down a sea breeze or two."

"Purely medicinal," Olivia said, beginning to mix Laurel's cocktail. "You've had a rather extraordinary morning after all." She glanced at her friend in concern. "What does Steve have to say about all this?"

Laurel shrugged. "He doesn't know yet. His whole office takes a long lunch hour, and when I called his cell, he didn't answer. I told his folks that I was taking you to the hospital, but that's as much information as I wanted to arm *them* with. They'll be chewing me out soon enough." She took a grateful sip of the fruity cocktail Olivia set on the bar.

"I'll have what she's having!" Millay called out as she strolled into the bar, Harris close on her heels.

Olivia paused in the middle of pouring out a generous measure of Chivas Regal. "This is a pleasant surprise. Have you both called in sick?"

Millay glanced at her watch. "I've got two hours before my shift starts and Harris snuck out of a meeting. We had to show up after Laurel called and told us what went down today."

"Besides, my meeting was crap anyway and they'll never notice I'm gone," Harris remarked idly. "The whole staff is there and everyone just sits around and plays games on their phones while the boss yaps about the bottom line. During our last warm and fuzzy get-together, I achieved a new high score on Cannon Challenge. It was *awesome!*" He examined the beer taps and pointed at the one bearing the logo of an area microbrewery. "Amber ale. Perfect. Good thing you can work the tap with one arm, eh?" His voice abruptly lost its levity. "Seriously, Olivia. Are you okay?"

Olivia distributed drinks before answering. "I'm fine, thank you. The Donalds are in police custody and I'm confident that Rawlings will get a confession from Ellen. She wants everyone to know exactly how she and Rutherford turned into monsters. Her anger hasn't been assuaged and I believe she'll enjoy having an audience."

"I hope they both confess," Laurel said with a shiver. "I'd rather not have any more knives pointed at my eye."

Millay slapped Laurel on the back. "Just think of the article you can write now! A first-person account to *totally* wrap up all the groundwork you laid in your earlier pieces. This is Pulitzer material, girlfriend!"

For a moment, Laurel's blue eyes shimmered at the thought, but the light quickly died. "Steve will never let me continue my work after what's happened. He'll tell me that my actions might have endangered the lives of our boys. If they'd been home, that would have been true." She hung her head in shame. "My selfishness could have led to the end of my family. And they're my whole world."

Harris pushed his beer aside and jumped onto the barstool next to Laurel's. He slung a lanky arm around her shoulders. "You're a writer. It's who you are. Whether you write for the paper or stay up all night working on a novel, you can't just stop. It's not selfishness, Laurel, it's how you're wired. You couldn't turn that off even if you wanted to."

Olivia gave Harris a nod of approval. The simple truth of his words alleviated some of the guilt she felt for pushing Laurel into a career in journalism. She took a deep swallow from her tumbler, knowing full well that it was unwise to mix whiskey and narcotics. It was her hope that the alcohol would help numb the pain in her arm enough for her to abstain from taking another dose of medicine before bed.

Laurel put a cocktail napkin to her face and cried silently. Her friends let her be, sensing that she needed the release. They drank and reflected on the Donald siblings, wondering whether the police had collected enough evidence to ensure that the twisted siblings would be in prison for a long time.

Eventually, Laurel's tears ceased and she managed a wobbly smile. "I don't know what I'd do without such amazing friends. Thanks, everybody."

Millay rolled her eyes in disgust, but Olivia knew the gesture was all show. "I'm way bummed I missed the action. Here I am, my finely honed kung fu skills going to waste while Olivia's getting sliced up by some crazy slasher bi—"

Harris cut her off. "Do you really know kung fu?"

"I promise to phone you before the next knife incident," Olivia said and then shot Laurel a questioning look. "Ellen and Rutherford spoke quite clearly, didn't they? They must have gotten the operation they'd always wanted as soon as they were out of the family home."

Laurel twisted her napkin into a white, wrinkled snake. "I called the police station while I was at the park with Haviland and asked Officer Cook to check on Mr. and Mrs. Donald. He said they already had but he sounded funny and got off the phone in a flash. I really hope they're unharmed!"

"They might be okay," Harris tried to assure her. "Ellen and Rutherford's first act of violence was killing that Alan guy and burying him in the sand."

Millay looked doubtful. "As far as *we* know. There could be a trail of dead bodies from here to Arkansas. We don't know that Felix's death was an accident. The Donalds might have been aware that he was at home all along. They could have been gunning for him like they were gunning for Laurel, here."

Fear flickered through Laurel's eyes and Harris scowled at Millay. "How about showing a little sensitivity? The lady's had a scary morning."

Returning his frown, Millay mumbled an apology to Laurel and then focused her energy on consuming the rest of her drink.

Haviland appeared behind the bar, having been fed a selection of gourmet goodies by Michel. The chef fussed and cooed over the poodle even after Laurel explained how Olivia had ended up with her arm in a sling.

"I'd give you oodles of sympathy," he told his employer briskly, "but I know how you'd react, so I'll just skip it and say that I'm overwhelmingly relieved that the person who signs my paychecks isn't left-handed." Michel then tried to be extremely solicitous to Laurel, but she only smiled weakly and thanked him.

Soon, Gabe would arrive to put the bar in order and the kitchen would be filled with steam, noise, and delectable scents. Olivia was on the verge of breaking up their impromptu party when Rawlings stepped through the front door. He nodded at the ensemble and then crooked a finger at her.

"Could you step outside for a moment?" he asked and then turned, giving Olivia no choice but to comply.

Millay shook her head in sympathy and jumped down from her barstool. "Oh, man. You must be in major t-r-o-u-b-l-e. I'll do the pouring until you come back."

"That's fine as long as you answer my cell phone if it rings. I'm waiting for an important call."

"Secretarial services will cost you extra," Millay replied with a saucy curtsy.

Outside, it took Olivia's eyes several seconds to adjust to the afternoon light. Rawlings was waiting for her at the end of the path leading to the parking lot, his cell phone pressed to his ear. Upon seeing her, he quickly ended his conversation and watched her approach with close scrutiny.

Olivia's heart beat faster beneath the intensity of his stare. "Why are you looking at me like that? Am I about to be frisked?"

The chief ignored her attempt at playfulness. "How's your arm?"

"Stitched, sore, and ugly. I won't be wearing sleeveless tops over the next few weeks," she stated airily while her insides churned. Why did the very sight of this man leave her feeling so unsettled?

Rawlings drew so near that Olivia thought he'd kiss her. He didn't. He reached an arm around her back and gently eased her forward so that her sling barely touched his chest. He put his cheek against hers and used his free hand to tuck a strand of hair behind her ear. His fingertips then moved under the lobe, tracing a slow line down the skin of her neck to her collarbone. He breathed into her ear. "We got them. Full confessions. It's done."

He pulled back so that he could look into her eyes, leaving Olivia instantly hungry for his touch. "The moment the Donald siblings were out from under their parents' thumbs, they began to plan their revenge against their classmates. Anyone who repeatedly taunted them with the cliché 'the cat got your tongue' was to be punished. They had an entire list of enemies to terrorize and a dozen more cliché tableaus to create."

"*I'll* certainly think twice about using one in my writing," Olivia joked softly.

Rawlings continued as though she hadn't spoken. "And when the paperwork involving the Donald siblings has been filed and all the press interviews are done and Oyster Bay falls quiet again, I will want one thing and only one thing." His gaze was electric. "I'm here to see whether you will grant me this one thing."

Olivia took his wide, strong hand in her own. "What would that be?"

"An evening. A bottle of wine. Some time to see what this is. In short . . ." His eyes met hers, green and golden brown in the light. "You."

Pushing aside thoughts of the dramatic morning, her blood test, and the fact that she needed to tell Rawlings that she was no longer involved with Flynn, Olivia smiled. "I think we can work something out."

Behind Rawlings, a delivery truck pulled into the parking lot and Olivia dropped the chief's hand. "Come inside. I believe there's a chocolate milk with your name on it."

Millay looked up when the pair reentered the bar. "Gabe's

got a nice setup back here. I could get used to not standing on beer-covered concrete all night long. Chief? What'll it be?"

Rawlings placed his order and then informed the Bayside Book Writers that the case of the Cliché Killers was closed. "I'll grant you the first interview if you're interested," he told Laurel.

"Of course she is!" Harris shouted. "Having one of us being published on a regular basis gives this group some weight. You're our pathfinder, Laurel. You can't stop now!"

Laurel laughed. "When you put it that way . . ."

Millay put both palms on the bar. "Olivia. I need some whole milk. Gabe only has half-and-half in this fridge, so unless the chief wants to clog an artery before he starts giving Laurel here a bunch of stellar quotes, you'd better grab some from the kitchen."

Olivia was about to walk away when Millay called her name again. "And some lab called. I pretended I was you and they told me that your blood test was positive." She grinned. "You're a little old to be getting knocked up, aren't you?" She paused, seeing the stricken look on Olivia's face." Hey, I'm just messing with you. You'd have the smartest, best-looking, richest kid in town. You'd be single mother of the year! Olivia?"

It was all Olivia could do to wave off Millay's ridiculous assumption and continue on toward the kitchen. She could feel every eye upon her as she walked away, yet the simple act of putting one foot in front of another was remarkably difficult.

The entire kitchen staff had arrived and had begun preparations for a busy Friday night. Olivia moved through the activity and chatter like a zombie. The milk was forgotten. Rawlings was forgotten. The throbbing in her arm came at her from a great distance.

In her office, she sank into her chair and struggled to breathe normally.

"My father is alive," she told the room. She looked from the desk to the telephone to the computer. "My father is alive."

The objects remained blissfully mute. There was no living thing to bear witness to the mixture of hope and agony surging through Olivia's heart. For that, she was grateful.

She didn't know when Haviland trotted into the office, but his presence allowed Olivia to function again. She looked up the Okracoke Ferry schedule and calculated how much time it would take to reach the port of departure. The last ferry left from Cedar Island at five. It was already after three and the drive would take over two hours. She couldn't make it.

Olivia signaled for Haviland to follow her. She would go home, pack a bag, and make a few calls. Okracoke was less than fifty miles from Oyster Bay by boat. Confident that she could hire a vessel if she offered its captain enough cash, Olivia planned to be on the island before nightfall.

Someone in the kitchen spoke to her as she pushed open the door leading outside, but the words never reached her.

"My father's alive," she told the September afternoon and wondered how she could possibly process this momentous truth.

As it hit her full force, she did the only thing that made sense. She got inside the Range Rover and sobbed.

Chapter 17

The curfew tolls the knell of parting day,
The lowing herd wind slowly o'er the lea,
The ploughman homeward plods his
weary way,
And leaves the world to darkness and
to me.
—THOMAS GRAY

Olivia sat in front of the instrument panel next to the owner of the *JoFaye,* a sleek, hardtop super-yacht that cut through the waters east of Oyster Bay at thirty-seven knots. The man at the helm was accustomed to taking inlanders out on pleasure cruises up and down the Carolina coast. He'd had a good season and had managed to put away enough money to see his family through the winter, but when Olivia Limoges called and offered him enough cash to cover his monthly mortgage payment, he couldn't refuse. One of her stipulations was that he ask no questions and tell no one of her visit to Okracoke.

"I value my privacy," she'd said firmly. "If you illustrate discretion tonight, I will do my best to send business your way when the tourists return in the spring."

JoFaye's owner knew of Olivia's influence and had no

doubt that pleasing her would result in increased bookings. The yacht's captain attempted small talk at the beginning of the short trip, but he was astute enough to see that she wasn't interested in conversation. With a grim face, she kept her eyes on the horizon, holding her injured arm so that it didn't bounce around too much whenever the boat crossed another vessel's wake. The poodle also struggled to maintain his balance as the *JoFaye*'s powerful dual engines ran full throttle.

Olivia was too busy focusing on the pain in her arm to speculate on her upcoming reunion, but as the island became visible to starboard, she began to feel an increased sense of panic. The urge to tell the captain to turn his boat around was strong. After all, Olivia's father had abandoned her. It would serve him right if she did the same to him as he lay dying. Perhaps he wasn't even aware that his caretakers had contacted her and would be upset to suddenly find the woman his little girl had become standing at his bedside.

Olivia had fled from hardship before, but she wouldn't now. Instead, she swallowed her anxiety and stood tall in the prow of the boat as the shore grew closer and the shapes of houses and trees became visible.

The captain headed for Silver Lake, an inlet south of Mary Ann's Pond. He eased back on the throttle, motoring slowly past the ferry dock.

The sun had moved lower in the sky and part of the island had been cast in shadow. Only the white walls of the lighthouse seemed undiminished by the encroachment of evening and Olivia drew comfort at the sight of the old structure.

Earlier, Olivia had told the yacht's captain that she needed to be dropped off at the dock closest to Hudson's Raw Bar, being that she'd made no arrangements for transportation once she reached the island.

"Hudson's is right in the village," he'd told her. "They've

got their own dock. I'll just let you hold the wheel steady while I throw a line over and get us secured. My wife has a rug on hold over at The Island Ragpicker and they're staying open late so I can pick it up. Think you can man the helm with your arm in a sling?"

Olivia had nodded.

Now, as the yacht's motor decelerated from a deafening roar to a steady drone, the captain deftly maneuvered the *JoFaye* into an open slip, gave Olivia a few instructions, and leapt from the boat to the dock with feline agility. Securing the bowline, he told her to cut the engines as he lassoed the stern line to the dock's iron cleat. He then set out a pair of disembarkation steps and offered his hand to assist Olivia down. She accepted reluctantly, but Haviland disregarded the steps altogether and jumped onto the dock with an anticipatory bark.

"Yes, Captain," Olivia whispered to him. "Another adventure awaits us."

Shouldering her overnight bag, Olivia hastily thanked the yacht's captain, eager to be alone for a moment to gather courage. He said good-bye and hurried off, eager to complete his wife's errand.

From her vantage point on the dock, Olivia could see the brown clapboard walls of the eatery and the second-story windows of the house that the Salters had converted into guest rooms.

Olivia stared at the windows, watching the waning light dance upon the panes. On the other side of one of those sheets of glass, behind the glimmering farewell of daylight, was her father. Her throat tightened and she looked away, taking in the tranquility of the village and the sleepy inlet. She stood like this for several minutes, drawing courage from the clang of mooring lines and the gentle rocking of sailboats at anchor.

Finally, she walked forward, her eyes returning again and again to the lighthouse. It was incredibly strange that her father had taken up residence so close to another lighthouse. He had deserted his home, his daughter, and the memories of his wife. And yet here he was, still tied to the ocean, working in a town interdependent on the sea, living in the lee of another lighthouse.

"Did you really escape?" Olivia wondered aloud. "Or did our voices float to you across the water? Mother's and mine. Did you see our faces in the tidal pools? In the glassy water before you pulled the shrimp nets in?"

Olivia fell silent, knowing that she was describing how she'd been haunted by the ghosts of her past.

She gave Haviland a brave smile and then stepped into the restaurant.

The décor was casual to the point of neglect. There were scarred wooden picnic tables and chairs, mismatched barstools, old fishing nets slung across the rafters. A few customers were at the bar, getting an early start on a long night of drinking. A television set was tuned to ESPN, and a woman stood at the end of the bar, refilling catsup bottles and saltshakers.

Upon seeing Olivia, she wiped her hands on her apron and murmured something to the old man sitting closest to her.

"Can I help you?" she asked with guarded friendliness.

Olivia examined the woman. She was barely thirty, but toil and worry made her appear older. Her brown hair hung limply down her back and her watery blue eyes were wary. Glancing at Haviland, she placed a protective hand on her swollen abdomen.

"Are you Kim Salter?"

The woman nodded. "You must be Olivia. My husband said you would probably come." Her tone was apologetic. She pointed at Olivia's sling. "What happened to you?"

"That's not important." Olivia clenched her jaw, her blue eyes darkening with intensity. She disliked being short with the woman, especially since she was both tired and pregnant, but it couldn't be helped. "I came to see my father and I want to see him *now*."

"I'll get Hudson." Kim turned and hurried through a swing door leading into the kitchen.

Olivia didn't wait around for Hudson Salter to emerge from within. She didn't trust the man and she didn't want to give him the chance to manipulate her in any way.

Bursting into the kitchen, she found him boiling a pot of stone crab claws while a little girl carefully cut a lemon into tidy wedges. Hudson, whose back was to the door, had been speaking to his wife but immediately broke off and swung around to face Olivia. His cheeks were flushed from the steam billowing out of the stockpot and his eyes were hooded and unreadable. He glanced between Olivia and Haviland and then wiped his hands on his apron.

"Caitlyn," he said in a deep, authoritative tone. "Take those lemons out to the bar. Kim, you go on too."

Kim seemed about to protest, but a steely glare from her husband silenced her. Putting a gentle arm around Caitlyn's bony shoulders, she led the girl out of the kitchen. They both gave Haviland a wide berth.

"I suppose we need to come to terms before you'll let me see my father," Olivia stated, dropping her purse on an unused cutting board. She pulled out her checkbook and wiggled it impatiently. "How much?"

Hudson was clearly taken aback. "This isn't the time to talk about money. I've gotta fill this order and then I'll bring you upstairs. And for the record, I don't like animals in my kitchen. I take pride in my cooking." He shot Haviland a distasteful look and then fixed his gaze on Olivia again. "Your daddy's been sleeping most of the time. He's pretty doped on morphine. Got a local lady to watch him while we work. He doesn't have much life left in him now." His voice had suddenly lost its edge. "You should expect the worst."

Olivia put her checkbook away and watched Hudson finish with the crab claws. After draining them, he dumped them into a bowl and then untied his apron. "Follow me."

"As you might imagine, I have many questions," Olivia said, struggling to remain civil.

Hudson continued walking. "He started getting sick about three months back. It came on real quick. Got a bunch of scans on the mainland and found out about the cancer. Those tests 'bout bankrupted us. Kim asked him if there was anything he wanted, you know, before it was all over, and he wanted us to find this lady named Olivia Limoges. So we got on a computer and tracked you down."

Following him through a hallway connecting the restaurant to the first floor of the house, Olivia tried to absorb what Hudson had said. "He asked about *me*?" She hated how much it mattered to her that her father had initiated the chain of events that had led her to Okracoke.

"Yeah. First we ever heard about you—that he had a daughter."

"And how long have you known him?"

Hudson gave a wry chuckle. "My whole life, lady."

Olivia didn't answer. She was trying to rein in her anger, but failed. "So you found me and someone else decided to blackmail me into coming out here just in time for my father's last days on earth?"

Hudson stopped and turned to face her. "I didn't send you that letter. Kim and I were going back and forth over how to tell you about your daddy, but Betty did it for us, behind our backs."

"Who the hell is Betty?" Olivia demanded.

"She's his nurse. The woman we hired to take care of him when we've gotta work." He frowned. "I don't blame you for being mad, but she swears she did it because it's his dying wish. She didn't care how she had to make it happen, she just wanted you here."

Olivia rolled her eyes. "Feed me another lie. She could have just called me. Why did she ask for cash?"

Hudson dropped his gaze to the ground. "For us. This whole place is going down like a ship with a cracked hull. Betty's known Kim and me since we were in diapers. She delivered Caitlyn. She's our closest family friend." He reached out his hand to touch Olivia's arm, but he let it hover in the air near her shoulder without making contact. "I'm sorry about how you ended up here, but you're here, and that's what matters now."

Every muscle in Olivia's body constricted when Hudson put his hand on the knob of the guest room at the very end of the hall. Olivia keenly wished there were no witnesses to this moment, but she knew she had no control over the situation. Pushing aside her dread and fear, she followed Hudson inside, unable to see around his broad back.

"How's he doing?" Hudson asked an older woman seated in a chair against the left wall. She was crocheting a pastel blanket and watching a cooking program on television.

Olivia heard genuine concern behind Hudson's question and she knew he had told her the truth. The woman in the chair was the blackmailer. Hudson was just a cook trying to keep his family afloat while an old man slowly died in one of his rooms.

"Same as this morning," the woman answered. Putting her needles aside, she switched off the TV and scrutinized Olivia. "This his daughter?"

Hudson grunted in assent and stepped aside. "Olivia,

this is Betty. She's a nurse. She's been helping out since he got real bad."

"Who can't spell apparently," Olivia said and shot the woman a hostile glance.

That was all the attention she had to spare for the blackmailer at the moment for the figure in the bed became the center of Olivia's universe. The very walls could have fallen away from the house and she wouldn't have noticed. She hadn't laid eyes on her father's face in thirty years, but she knew that the gaunt and bearded visage on the pillow belonged to William Wade.

Her face was a blank mask but her heart silently cried, *Daddy!*

In a flash, Olivia Limoges was gone, replaced by skinny, tow-headed Livie Wade. She approached the bedside on the balls of her feet, as though the groan of a floorboard would break the spell and her father would disappear once and for all. But her adult eyes knew he was going nowhere. The painfully thin arms, the loose, jaundiced skin, and liquid, labored breaths made that clear. So did the IV bag dripping a steady supply of blissful morphine into his body.

Olivia knelt on the floor but did not touch her father. She cradled her hurt arm and stared at his hand. When she'd last seen it, it had been the hand of a man in his prime. Calloused and weathered, tough and powerful. This hand was all bones and swollen veins. The nails looked ragged and tissue-thin. It was easier to look at this than to gaze upon his sallow, wrinkled face.

Her father was an old man. Though Olivia knew his age and that he was very sick, she hadn't been prepared to see him in such a reduced state. All the strength and forcefulness teeming beneath his skin was gone. He was a shell, a sinking ship, a pitiful thing.

"You can touch him, honey," the nurse said gently.

"That man had plenty of bite in him for most of his life, but he's got none left now."

Without glancing away from her father's hand, Olivia said, "You knew him."

"Shoot, I tended to him when he first came here. Half drowned, concussed, practically pissing whiskey." Betty shook her head. "When he finally came 'round, he said he couldn't remember what had happened and he was sure he didn't want to remember. He sold his boat and started working as a shrimper and then ended up as the caretaker for this place. He met Meg not long after that, back when the grill was just a little hole-in-the-wall—a place to grab a cup of coffee and a sandwich."

Now Olivia did look up. "Meg?"

"His late wife."

Olivia turned to see if Hudson had anything to contribute to this string of revelations, but he was already gone. "A second wife," she muttered.

Betty heard her and chuckled. "That was news to everybody. Meg had no idea. Nobody knew about your mama until a month or so ago. Didn't know about you either. We thought the man was raving, but Willie wouldn't let up and I took it upon myself to track you down. I figured you had enough money to share with the Salters, but I didn't know if you'd part with it willingly. Those two have a precious child to raise and another one on the way and they've worked themselves to the bone trying to do right by the man you see lying in this bed." She sent Olivia a defiant, sidelong glance. "I might have gone overboard with the block print and the weird grammar, but I just wanted to get your attention and I succeeded. I'd do it all over again too, because you're here and that's what Willie wanted." She straightened a corner of bed sheet. "I only hope he wakes up one more time so he can see you in the flesh."

Neither woman spoke for a moment. Olivia listened to the contradictory sounds of her father's labored breath and the industrious, steady clicking of Betty's needles.

"How long has it been since he was lucid?" she asked quietly, deciding that both Hudson and Betty were right. The letter and the doubt had put her through hell, but she was here. She hadn't missed seeing her father, and if she was lucky, there'd still be time to find out the answers to the questions she'd waited her entire life to ask.

"Two days." Betty sighed. "He had some broth this morning, but even then, with his eyes open, he wasn't seeing anything. He's drifting between worlds, confusing the past and the present, dreams and reality. Mumbles all sorts of fishing tales and whispers about some little dog and a storm." Gathering up her crochet materials, she rose. "I'll leave you alone. I'm sure you've got things to say and I truly think he'll hear you. I've seen this kind of thing before." She paused at the threshold. "I believe he's been waiting for you so he can let go. Talk to him, honey. It's not too late."

Olivia accepted the counsel with a nod, but when the door shut behind Betty, she found she had nothing to say. She reached for Haviland, who had sniffed every nook and cranny of the room and was now sprawled at Olivia's feet. He raised his head as she stroked the curly fur on his flank, a question in his ale brown eyes.

"No, Captain. It's not time to go."

She stared at her father for a long time, wondering in angry silence about his life on Okracoke. He'd landed on its flat shores, been received and cared for by the locals, and had come to marry one. Olivia felt freshly abandoned, but most of all she felt betrayed. She believed he might have lost his memory for a time, but eventually he had remembered that he had a daughter and that the woman he had loved was dead. He'd simply decided to do his best to forget them both.

Suddenly, Olivia wanted evidence of his other life. Assuming the room had been her father's before his illness, she began to open drawers. It never occurred to her that it wasn't right for her to rifle through his belongings. She'd had no chance to lay claim to this man for thirty years, but now that she was here, Olivia planned to exercise all the authority that a blood tie granted her.

If she'd expected to find a neat file of important documents, personal letters, or photographs, she was to be disappointed. Her father's room was Spartan. The drawers and closet contained clothes. There were a few books and magazines, but Olivia's father had never been much of a reader. She found a wooden toolbox filled with his whittling tools in the dresser and on top of a nightstand, a tin of tobacco, matches, and a pipe. The walls were decorated with vintage blueprints of famous sailing vessels.

Frustrated, Olivia paced around the room, stealing nervous glances at her father as though he might awaken to find her snooping through his things. She was certain he wouldn't approve of that. Like her, he'd always been fiercely protective of his privacy.

"Didn't *anyone* matter to you? Isn't there a single piece of evidence that you shared your life with other human beings?" she addressed the motionless form in the bed. Strangely, it was all she could say to him. She no longer felt like ranting at him, accusing him, or trying to make him feel guilty for leaving her. She just wanted to know who he was, one adult to another, and it was far too late for that.

Olivia paused at the window, which faced west toward Oyster Bay. She wondered if Rawlings was back at the station tying up loose ends, how Laurel was handling Steve, whether Harris had been missed at his work meeting, and if Millay truly believed Olivia's blood test meant that she was pregnant.

"I'm going to have to clarify that little detail as soon as I get back or Rawlings will think I'm carrying Flynn's child," Olivia remarked drily to Haviland.

Kneeling down to pet the poodle, Olivia furtively stuck her arm under her father's bed. Her hand came in contact with something solid. It was a struggle to pull the object out with only one arm, but once her fingers closed around a handle she was able to drag it into the light.

It was an old suitcase. Olivia tried to pop open the central latch but it was locked.

Undeterred, she grabbed one of her father's whittling knives and began working on the lock. It was difficult going with only one hand and she cursed aloud more than once, but eventually, the knife blade pried the lock loose and the latch snapped open.

She wasn't prepared for what she found. Inside the suitcase, stacked in a tidy pile and tied with a piece of string, was a collection of letters written by Olivia's grandmother. Olivia read the first one, which dated back to her first year in boarding school. Her grandmother had written to her son-in-law about Olivia's recent activities. She'd even included a school photo of Olivia in her uniform, looking lovely and poised but far too serious for a girl her age. And so it went. Every six months there were updates, photographs, report cards, and occasionally, one of Olivia's charcoal sketches or a copy of a poem she'd written for English class.

Olivia was floored by the realization that her grandmother had been communicating with her father throughout Olivia's childhood. A fresh, hot wave of anger swept through her. Why hadn't her grandmother told her that her father was alive? She'd let her grow up believing she was an orphan. It was so cruel, so heartless.

"I bet you didn't want Daddy to get his hands on the Limoges trust fund," she hissed at her grandmother's perfect cursive. "You never liked him. You never wanted him to marry my mother. I bet you told him he could never raise me properly and he agreed. Maybe you were even right about that, but to let me believe, for all those years, that I had no family except for *you . . .*" Tears burned her eyes. "How could you do that to a little girl?"

Olivia sat very still for several minutes, trying to calm the cyclone of thoughts in her head. It was as if all she had known had been turned inside out, yet there was no going back. The past was over and done and the present was steadily slipping away.

She continued to look through the contents of the suitcase.

After her grandmother died, the letters ceased, but Olivia's history lived on in yellowed newspaper clippings from the days in which the media followed her every move, hoping to catch the young and beautiful heiress doing something scandalous. Mostly, they detailed her presence at a museum gala or opening night at the Met, focusing on her escorts, who were usually handsome executives of the *Fortune 500* variety.

There was even a clipping from the *Oyster Bay Gazette* announcing Olivia's revitalization projects downtown. Lastly, there was an object wrapped in an old towel and secured by two rubber bands.

With care, Olivia removed the rubber bands and unrolled the towel on her thighs. A pair of metal objects fell to the floor. Olivia recognized them right away. They were her parents' wedding bands. Forever tied together on a piece of frayed blue yarn, they'd been tucked in a fold inside the towel.

Olivia clutched the rings briefly to her chest, cherishing

the relics of happier times and then set them on the ground in order to continue unwrapping the towel. Peeling back the final fold, one of her father's carvings was revealed. Olivia inhaled sharply, her eyes darting over the lines and indentations, the contours that formed the shape of a young girl standing in the shadow of a lighthouse, her hand shielding her eyes as she stared outward, searching, searching.

It was her girl-self and the lighthouse was not Okracoke's, but Oyster Bay's. The beacon that had guided William Wade home time after time after time.

"I've been so close!" she yelled at her father. "*Why?*"

Olivia began to cry. "Why didn't you come?"

Cradling the carving in her hand, she sat in Betty's chair and, after calming down, began to read her grandmother's letters out loud. She relived a dozen years, explaining her version of events to her father. She spoke for over two hours, until the sun dipped below the waves.

Turning on a single lamp, she eventually stopped talking. She pulled her chair closer to the window and then eased it open a few inches, inviting the ocean breeze into the room.

Her father seemed to breathe easier as soon the sound of the water became audible. The rhythmic chant of the waves was faint, but to a man who'd lived a lifetime in tune to their music, it was enough to coax him into a more restful sleep.

Olivia briefly left the room to let Haviland outside and see to his dinner, but afterward she waved off Betty's offer to stay with the patient through the night.

"I'm not going to give up our last bit of time," she told the nurse.

Returning to the soft chair by the window, Olivia sat as the sky morphed from steel gray to soot black, nodding off here and there but still alert enough to welcome the ochre dawn.

The entire time she sat, listening as her father's exhalations mingled with the lapping of the waves, she never released her hold on his carving. Olivia knew it was the only gift her father would ever give her, and even then, she'd had to discover it for herself.

To Olivia, who'd watched her father whittle dolphins, sharks, and mermaids in front of the fire for countless winters and yet had never carved a token for his only child, it was enough that he'd finally done so.

And he'd put all he had into that last carving; she could feel it in the wood. In the dawn light, it glowed with life, even as her father's began to fade.

Chapter 18

Forgiveness is the fragrance that the violet sheds on the heel that has crushed it.
—MARK TWAIN

Olivia left her father's side only when Betty insisted that she take a hot shower and eat some breakfast. Kim served her toast with cream cheese, bacon, and a bowl of fresh blueberries on the patio while Haviland explored the small garden behind the house.

"Caitlyn's keeping an eye on your dog," Kim said, pouring herself a cup of coffee and sitting down across the table from Olivia. "He won't run off, will he?"

Olivia shook her head. "He's obedient and very gentle. You don't have to worry about Haviland becoming aggressive toward Caitlyn or your guests. He *is* energetic though. I'll need to take him for a quick walk before . . ." She trailed off. She didn't want to say that she planned to spend the rest of the day watching the rise and fall of her father's chest.

"How old is your daughter?" she asked instead.

Kim brightened. "Six. I thought she'd been our only one, but as you can see, we're having a second. Betty says I'm going to have a boy. She's got a way of knowing these things." Her cheeks flushed. "I'm so sorry about the letter, about her asking you for money."

"It's not your fault," Olivia assured her. "And I don't have the energy to be angry with her. There's too much going on in here." She tapped at her chest, just above her heart.

Glancing across the garden, Olivia watched as Caitlyn hesitantly reached a hand out to Haviland. The poodle sniffed her palm and gave her a friendly lick. The girl's face, heart-shaped and covered with freckles, glowed with delight. With the sunlight streaming over her long hair and a secretive smile on her face, she looked like a fairy among the flowers.

Olivia ran her finger around the rim of her coffee cup. "What does Betty say about my father? Does she have a sense about how much time he's got left?"

Kim uttered a sympathetic sigh. "She said it's only a matter of hours now. I wish it wasn't happening so fast."

"I should have been here sooner," Olivia stated mournfully. She thanked Kim for breakfast, carried her plate to the sink, and called Haviland.

He obeyed reluctantly, sulking over having been forced to dine on dog food instead of bacon and eggs, but Olivia didn't feel comfortable asking Kim if she could cook the poodle a meal using supplies meant for the restaurant.

Hudson intercepted Olivia at the garden gate. "Your town's on TV. You might want to see this." He gestured for her to follow him to the bar.

A reporter was standing in front of Oyster Bay's marina. In a carefully somber tone, he gave a brief overview of the robberies and murders committed by the Donald siblings. The image then switched to a taped segment showing Rawlings speaking at a press conference. Olivia's shoulders dropped a fraction in relief as the chief told a throng of journalists that Rutherford and Ellen Donald had signed detailed confessions and were now in the capable hands of the North Carolina court system.

The camera view returned to the docks and the reporter promised an exclusive interview with one of the Donalds' robbery victims at noon. "We'll also be hearing a chilling account from Laurel Hobbs, a staff writer for the local paper, who survived what could have been a fatal visit from Rutherford and Ellen Donald." A photograph of Laurel appeared on the screen. "If not for the heroism of Hobbs' friend, local entrepreneur Olivia Limoges, and officers of the Oyster Bay Police Department, Hobbs might not have lived to share her story with us today. Ms. Limoges could not be reached for comment."

The reporter swiveled slightly as he spoke and Olivia saw that the live shot included her Range Rover. Someone must have tipped off the press about her sudden departure by boat. The media would now haunt the docks until she returned to claim her car. Olivia could already visualize the tabloid headlines: "Heiress Wounded in Knife Fight."

She groaned.

"We've been reading about those robberies," Kim whispered in awe. "Look. There's a big article about it in *The News & Observer*. This reporter must not have known that you were involved, 'cause we sure didn't see your name mentioned until just now." She handed Olivia the Raleigh-based newspaper. "Is that why your arm's in a sling? You were there when that crazy brother and sister went after your friend?"

Olivia tucked the paper under her good arm and picked up her coffee cup. "If you want to know what happened, you'll have to listen to the story upstairs. I've been gone too long already."

Hudson and Kim trailed behind Haviland as he followed his mistress back to the sick room.

Betty had her crocheting out again. The morning light winked off her needles and Olivia recognized that she was making a baby blanket. It seemed unreal that this woman and the couple behind her were preparing to welcome a new life while her own reason for being there was to bear witness to the end of another.

Settling herself in a ladder-back chair in front of the room's other window, Olivia stared at her father. He looked the same as he had before she left to shower, but his breath sounded raspier. She listened to the harsh rattles emitting from between his lips for several minutes. Without taking her eyes off her father's face, she began to talk.

Telling Kim, Betty, and Hudson about the Donalds gave Olivia a measure of closure. The narrative had a beginning and a middle and an ending in which justice prevailed.

When she was finished, her audience was kind enough not to pepper her with questions. The three of them sat quietly, absorbing the unbelievable tale, until Betty's needles ceasing moving. "So what happened to their folks? What did their kids do as payback for making them go through childhood with twisted tongues?"

Abashed, Olivia realized she hadn't given a second thought to Mr. and Mrs. Donald's fate. She'd concentrated solely on reaching Okracoke and had left her friends, her business, and several unanswered questions behind.

"I don't know, but this article is quite long. Perhaps it will tell us." She unfolded the paper and found the story on the Cliché Killers quickly. When she was done reading it to herself, she returned her gaze to her father's pallid face.

"The parents were injured, but are recovering in the hospital. The paper doesn't give any more specifics other than to say that their injuries were inflicted by Ellen and Rutherford." She handed the newspaper to Kim. "Are there any photographs of my father and his life in this room?"

Kim and Betty exchanged nervous glances.

"I've got a couple," Hudson mumbled. "But he didn't like for people to take pictures of him."

That came as no surprise to Olivia. "What of Meg? What happened to her?"

Moving closer to her husband, Kim leaned against his thick arm. "She died of a brain aneurism," she whispered. "It was very sudden."

"What about children?" Olivia asked. "I'm assuming they had none."

At that moment, Caitlyn entered the room. Her eyes fixed on the figure in the bed; she stepped across the floor on her tiptoes like a prima donna ballerina. Her movements were so quiet and unobtrusive that it was clear she was accustomed to avoiding attention, but it was impossible not to take note of her grace. Without looking at any of the adults, she knelt by the bed and took the sick man's hand in her own.

Seeing the little girl's tender affection ruptured something in Olivia's heart. She could feel tears burning in her eyes and excused herself, murmuring something about having to take Haviland outside for a spell.

She headed for the water, but her customary source of solace failed to bring her peace. For the first time since she'd fled The Boot Top, she wondered how her friends were faring.

Brushing away her tears, she opened her purse and checked the messages on her cell phone. There were over a dozen. All of the Bayside Book Writers had called and she recognized both Flynn's and Michel's number as well. There were also several voice mails from local television and radio stations, but Olivia deleted these without bothering to listen to them.

Olivia was torn. She wanted to check on her friends but

didn't feel like talking about what she was going through in Okracoke. Paging through the names on her list of recent calls, she highlighted Millay's number and dialed.

"I hope I didn't wake you," she said when Millay answered.

There was a pause. "You're worried *about that?* What the hell, Olivia? You bolted without saying a word to anyone!"

So much for avoiding explanations, Olivia thought. "I can't go into that now, but I will tell you when I get back. I called to see if the case is really closed and when the media vultures might be moving on."

"Tied up like a Christmas gift," Millay assured her. "There's an extra creep factor to the whole thing though. Did you hear about the parents?"

"Just that they were injured."

Millay made a choking noise. "That's PC code for 'their tongues were cut out by their own children.' Then they tied their parents to chairs and left them to bleed to death."

Olivia drew in a sharp breath. "My God."

"Exactly. A total horror show. If the chief hadn't sent men over there when he did, those people would be dead. Laurel's been to the hospital. She was the only member of the press the Donalds would see." Millay spoke the latter phrase with pride. "A surgeon is going to try to reconstruct their tongues, but even if the surgery is a success, that couple is going to talk funny for the rest of their lives." She hesitated. "We can mull over the irony of *that* little detail later. First, I want to e-mail you the photo Laurel took at the hospital. You will *not* believe what it shows."

Olivia imagined Laurel using her new camera, fearful of being alone in the room with the wounded couple, yet determined to complete her assignment and pursue a career in journalism despite the many obstacles she faced.

"File's been sent," Millay said. After a hesitation, she asked, "Did you skip town because of that blood test?"

"Yes, but I did not test positive for a disease nor am I pregnant," Olivia answered tersely. "I will tell you everything during our next meeting."

Millay grunted in disbelief. "Just call Laurel. She was freaking out over having to see the Donalds without you."

Smiling, Olivia promised to phone her friend. "Laurel needs to discover that she's perfectly capable of doing this job without me or Steve or her in-laws giving her their blessing. Are you doing okay?"

"Yeah. Harris is dragging me to look at the house he wants to buy. He wants me there to see if my BS meter goes off while the Realtor gives him a tour. And before you lecture me on being careful with him, you don't need to worry. He's dating that bimbo we met at the Regatta."

Olivia detected a note of jealously in Millay's voice. "Let's not forget that he built a giant gryphon boat in your honor. And he's looking to you, not Estelle, to help him choose his first house. Just make sure to tell Harris not to sign any papers until I can have one of my contractors inspect every inch of that place."

After giving her promise, Millay rang off.

It took a moment for Olivia to open the e-mail attachment on her phone, and when she saw Laurel's photograph, her eyes widened. "I shouldn't have jested about her winning the Pulitzer."

Laurel had captured Mr. and Mrs. Donald lying in twin hospital beds. Their room held no flowers, no balloons, or any other tokens from well-wishers. The couple looked alike. Short, gray hair, lined faces, pale skin, and gauze bandages protruding from their mouths.

They stared at the camera with fierce conviction, their dark eyes daring the viewer to hold their gaze.

Olivia couldn't look away.

Each of them held out a piece of white paper. On hers Mrs. Donald had written, *LOVE IS FORGIVENESS* in bold, block letters.

Mr. Donald's was shorter. It simply read, *Forgive.*

The photograph was alive with the emotions of the injured parents. Despite their wounds, what radiated from the Donalds' faces was not anger or regret, but a blend of sorrow and defiance. Despite everything that had happened, it was clear by their expressions that they would not be changed by what they'd gone through. No matter what their children had done, Mr. and Mrs. Donald would stand by their parenting decisions. In a sense, they were almost as creepy as Ellen and Rutherford.

It was a powerfully disconcerting image.

Olivia was grateful when Haviland brought her a tennis ball that he'd unearthed beneath a nearby bush. She put her phone in her pocket and tossed the ball away from the docks onto a stretch of grass.

Summer had bleached the color from most of the island's vegetation, but the local shopkeepers had filled wooden boxes and ceramic planters with an abundance of fall annuals so that the subdued colors of the village were punctuated with bright gold and crimson hues.

Olivia had just thrown the ball for Haviland again when Caitlyn came running toward her. "He's trying to talk!" she cried urgently.

The child didn't need to say anything else. Olivia raced back into the house and up the stairs.

In the sick room, Hudson was leaning over the bed. Her father's eyes were blinking rapidly and his mouth opened and closed like a fish on a boat deck. He twisted his head to the left and right, searching.

"Dad!" Olivia cried and grabbed his hand, heedless

of the IV wires or the presence of the other people in the room.

Her voice seemed to puncture the film over his eyes and he found her face, seeing her clearly for the first time in thirty years.

"Livie." It was a whisper, the faintest breath of air.

She'd never expected her name to pass over his lips again and to hear it spoken so softly, so unlike her memories of his constant angry shouting, that she smiled down on him.

His tongue poked from his mouth in an attempt to moisten his lips. Betty dribbled some water from a washcloth over the chapped skin. He shook his head, signaling for her to let him be. "Missed. You. Livie." He swallowed, coughed weakly. Olivia wanted to send her breaths into his body, to give him this chance to say what needed to be said. He struggled, but managed to push out a few more words. "So many mistakes . . . I'm sorry, my girl."

He sank deeper into the pillows. He'd given everything to tell her of his regret. There was nothing left.

Olivia wasn't ready for him to go. There were things she wanted him to hear now. "You can't leave yet!" she yelled, the sound reverberating too loudly in a room where death hovered, filling every space. "You can't leave me alone again!"

There was a tremor from the hand she held. "Not. Alone." He did not open his eyes. The words were barely audible. Olivia leaned in, smelling the rotten odor of his spent body. In one last whisper, an exhalation actually, Olivia's father said the word, "Brother."

And then he died.

Olivia thought something in the room would change, that she'd feel her father's spirit as it left the confines of his body, but there wasn't even a stirring of the air. All was silent except for a sniffle, which came from Kim.

The noise reminded Olivia of the presence of the other people in the room and she swiveled with agonizing slowness to look at Hudson.

How did I not see it before? she thought, taking in the dark, unreadable eyes, the square jaw line, the handsome, rugged features. Hudson was bulkier than Willie Wade had been, but he had the Wade family's height and the scattering of freckles across the nose and cheeks. There was no doubt he was Willie's son.

And Olivia's half brother.

Releasing her father's hand, Olivia stood up and crossed the room. She drew close to Hudson, waiting for some feeling of instant affection to sweep over her, but there was already too much churning inside for her to connect with him at this moment. Shock, grief, disbelief, and a thousand questions crowded her mind.

Hudson's eyes were moist with tears. He glanced at the form in the bed and then at Olivia and bit the edge of his lip.

This small movement gave him the appearance of a little boy, unsure of himself and his future, and Olivia recognized in him the same fears and struggles she'd known as a child.

They were connected after all.

She reached out and brushed the back of his hand with her fingertips before leaving the room, her father's words reverberating in her mind.

Not alone.

Olivia spent an hour sitting on the dock, stroking Haviland's black curls and watching the harbor traffic. A flock of Canadian geese flew overhead and she tracked their flight until their V was just a dark smudge on the horizon.

Later, once her father's body had been collected by the funeral home, Olivia, Kim, and Hudson sat in the garden together. They drank coffee laced with spiced rum and went over the burial details. After that, Kim left the siblings in order to prepare to open the restaurant. Olivia didn't see anything strange in the Salters working that night. She hated the thought of spending her night in idleness. She didn't want to lay herself open to the full force of her grief.

Hudson asked her to stay for supper, his pleading eyes belying his gruff manner. She agreed and was surprised by Hudson's skill in the kitchen.

"It must have been a big shock to you, to learn that you had a half sister," she said as he poured oil into a frying pan.

His mouth curved into the ghost of a grin. "I'd have thought it was a joke coming from another man, but Dad wasn't much for telling jokes."

"Why didn't you tell me when I first got here?"

He shrugged. "He wanted to be the one to do it. I almost told you when you first came in, but it seemed real important to him."

Olivia nodded. She liked that Hudson could hold things close to his chest.

"Have you ever thought of living elsewhere?" she asked him after finishing a delicious dinner of grilled grouper and homemade hush puppies.

He nodded as he plated steamed muscles and handed them off to Kim. "All the time. I want my kids to have more than I had growing up here."

Olivia watched Kim pass through the swing door, a heavy platter in each hand. "And your wife?"

"She doesn't have it easy, but it's all we've got."

Olivia poured Hudson a shot of whiskey and handed him a glass. Raising her own she said, "Perhaps we can change that. Together. I'm turning an old warehouse into the Bayside Crab House. My problem is that I don't have anyone to run the place. Do you think you'd be interested?"

Hudson stared at her and then he grinned. "Hell, yeah, I'd be interested."

"Then let's toast to our father with his favorite drink and after this shot, we don't have to look back ever again. We can start over. All of us."

"I'll drink to that."

"To the future," Olivia said.

The siblings clinked their glasses and drank.

With the whiskey still warming her belly, Olivia stood at the end of the Salter's dock waiting to board the boat she'd hired to take her back to Oyster Bay.

She'd called Rawlings and asked him to meet her at the lighthouse keeper's cottage.

"I really need to see you," was all she'd given him by way of explanation. To her immense relief and gratitude, he'd asked no questions but promised to be there, waiting for her.

All traces of daylight were nearly gone when the small craft motored past Oyster Bay's lighthouse. Olivia had removed her watch and shoes and had her pant legs rolled up, fully prepared to hoist her overnight bag onto her shoulder and disembark near the sandbar. Haviland was quivering with anticipation, eager to get wet and to return to the gourmet fare he knew was stocked inside his house on the bluff.

A figure appeared on the beach and Olivia waved as she recognized Rawlings. He shielded his eyes against the setting sun, mimicking the pose of the carving Olivia's father had made for his little girl.

The man at the helm cut the motor. They drifted gently toward the sandbar.

In the twilight, the only sound was the lapping of the water against the hull. Olivia handed the captain some cash, put her purse in her overnight bag, and slung it over her good shoulder. Accepting the captain's hand, she prepared to put one leg over the side, but Haviland sprang forward, splashing them both as he leapt into the water.

"It's all right, boy, a little salt water never hurt nobody!" the man called out with a chuckle. For some reason, his words caused Olivia to recall the photograph Laurel had taken of Mr. and Mrs. Donald in their hospital beds. More specifically, her mind's eye focused on the word written on their signs.

"Forgive," Olivia whispered.

She fixed her eyes on the lighthouse keeper's cottage, seeking out the window of her girlhood room. The restless spirits had been laid to rest. It was time to forgive and to move on.

Olivia glanced at Rawlings and then at the lighthouse towering above him.

The beacon flashed, forming a luminous path on the surface of the water, welcoming her to the shore.

Turn the page for a preview of Ellery Adams's
next Books by the Bay Mystery . . .

The Last Word

Coming soon from Berkley Prime Crime!

*Home is a name, a word, it is a strong
one; stronger than magician ever spoke,
or spirit ever answered to, in the
strongest conjuration.*
—CHARLES DICKENS

"All houses have secrets."

Olivia Limoges was surprised to hear such an enigmatic statement from her contractor, but there wasn't a hint of humor on Clyde Butler's weathered face. Perhaps the seasoned builder was merely trying to make a point to the eager first-time home buyer who stood nearby, one arm wrapped possessively around the porch post.

Harris Williams gazed toward the front door of the aged bungalow with a look of pure devotion, and Olivia could tell he was already visualizing himself living there.

"Regardless of what you've discovered, Clyde, I don't think you can talk Harris out of purchasing this place," Olivia stated with amusement. "He's clearly fallen in love."

Captain Haviland, Olivia's standard poodle, sniffed around the foundation of the 1930s home and then trotted around the corner, conducting a canine version of a house inspection.

Wearing a hopeful grin, Harris watched the poodle until Haviland disappeared from view, and then picked at a flake of peeling paint with his fingernail. "Everyone thinks I'm crazy, but I can feel that this place has history. That's important to me. There's more character in this rusty nail than in all the other places I've seen put together."

Olivia surveyed the façade of the two-bedroom bungalow. It had whitewashed brick walls and rows of large windows with black shutters. Olivia's favorite feature was the wide and welcoming front porch. Leaves had gathered in between the railings and there were rents and holes in the screen door, but the slate steps felt solid under her feet. She'd been inside with Harris a few days ago and had liked the house. Harris was right. The place had a warm personality. Its modest design spoke of simpler times, of family traditions, of hard work and perseverance. She believed Harris was making a good choice.

Harris continued to defend the bungalow even though no one had argued with him. "I've seen a dozen new houses in my price range and yeah, sure, they all had pristine white walls and stainless steel appliances and shiny light fixtures to go along with the flat lawns and four little bushes and a pair of ornamental trees, but they had *zero* personality." He puffed up his cheeks. "They were all like the straw house from *The Three Little Pigs*, but the wolf doesn't stand a chance against this place. It's a rock."

Clyde nodded. On this, he and Harris agreed. He gestured toward the front door. "If you want strong bones and a solid foundation, you'll find them here. Houses are like women. The new ones might seem attractive because no one's touched them and you feel like they'll treat you well without giving you an ounce of trouble." A snort. "But they're built out of cheap materials and will start falling down the second you move in. This old girl is sagging in places and, yes, she's a bit wrinkled, but she can be made over until she looks like a June bride. She'll be faithful to the end, but it'll take lots of labor and expense on your part, my boy."

Harris's grin expanded. "Did you know that all the houses on this street were moved during the late sixties to make way for the highway's expansion? Twelve houses were trucked right down Main Street and brought back to this stretch of empty land like horses being set free on an open pasture."

Olivia rolled her eyes. "This is one of those times I'm thankful you write science fiction, Harris. If you had put a metaphor like that in your recent chapter, I would have sliced it out with a box cutter."

Harris pushed a strand of unruly, ginger-colored hair away from his eyes. His looks were often compared to those of Peter Pan, and Harris was constantly striving to prove that he was a man, not a boy. Olivia knew her friend believed that being a homeowner would make him appear more of a bona fide adult, and he certainly behaved like he wanted to acquire this house without delay.

As though sensing her thoughts, Harris eased back the sleeves of his shirt and flexed his left bicep. "This property has half an acre bordering on three more acres of woodland. Think of all the manly man activities I can do here. I can chop wood, refinish furniture, spackle walls, grout tile!" He held out his arms, encompassing the house. "I'll be like Ty Pennington. A bachelor handyman with mad computer skills to boot! Before you know it, I'll have my own reality show."

Clyde shook his head. "Before you start rewiring ceiling fans and installing AC units, we'd better go over my inspection list."

The two men moved into the house, which Harris's real estate agent had unlocked a few minutes earlier before retreating to the comfort of her Cadillac. Her daughter, who happened to be nine months pregnant, had phoned shortly after the Realtor had turned the key in the front door. Gesturing for the threesome to enter without her, she'd hurriedly rushed off to take the call in the privacy of her car.

Inside the bungalow, Harris listened carefully as Clyde pointed out flaw after flaw, from the presence of mold behind the wallpaper to wood rot on the stair treads. Pulling back a corner of the stained and faded blue carpet running down the stairs and into the living room, Clyde showed Harris a series of water stains and areas of damage permeating the subfloor. From there, the contractor reviewed every item in his report, explaining how to address each problem and offering an estimate as to what it would cost to fix.

When they were finished, Olivia joined them on the back patio. Haviland reappeared from a copse of trees and settled on his haunches, his warm, caramel-colored eyes darting from one face to another, his mouth hanging open in a toothy smile.

Harris rubbed the black curls on the poodle's neck and then walked over to the brick retaining wall and sat down. He gazed first at the house and then toward the woods, which bordered the scraggly patch of lawn.

Winter's chill had abated for good and the sun lit the pines, dappling the soft needles on the forest floor with a ruddy light. Squirrels raced up and down the rough bark and birds twittered from the branches.

Olivia sat beside Harris on the wall, relishing the peacefulness of the moment. Her life had had little quiet of late, and this patio of cracked flagstones surrounded by a garden of weeds was an oasis of blissful calm.

Clyde's focus remained on the house. He glanced from his notes to the structure and back at Harris. "I know I took some of the wind out of your sails, boy, but I don't want you to think this is going to easy. She's going to make demands of you, but all houses do. In the end, she'll be worth the work you're going to have to put in."

Harris smiled, his cheeks dimpling with pleasure. "And you'll help me find the right guys to do the jobs I can't figure out how to do?"

After a solemn nod, Clyde jerked his thumb at Olivia. "I'd get in here with my own toolbox if my taskmaster would let up on me for just a day or two, but she's hellbent on opening her Bayside Crab House by Memorial Day weekend."

"So *that's* why you've been so interested in real estate lately," Harris said. "You must be scoping out houses for your brother and his family."

"*Half* brother," Olivia corrected tersely. "And it's not for me to decide where they're going to live. I just thought I'd rule out the duds to save time. I need Hudson to review the final kitchen layout for the restaurant, and if he's running all over Oyster Bay comparing three-bedroom properties we're sure to fall behind deadline."

Clyde gave Harris a meaningful look. "See what I mean? We should send her to Washington. She'd have the deficit licked and both our jobs and our soldiers back from overseas before the lawmakers knew what hit 'em."

Olivia grimaced. "I could never subsist on such a paltry salary. Let's go, gentlemen. I believe Harris has an offer to submit before this day is done."

Millicent Banks, Harris's real estate agent, was parked alongside the curb in front of the picturesque bungalow, still chatting on her cell phone as her prospective buyer walked through the house for the third time.

Olivia was pleased to have been left alone with Harris and Clyde. Millicent was a shrewd saleswoman, and Olivia didn't want the Realtor to talk their ears off the whole time. One could only glean the true sense of a house in absolute silence. It was a feeling really. A hunch.

Having stood side by side with Harris inside the sturdy bungalow, Olivia saw no reason to dissuade her friend from submitting a bid, and as the amicable young software designer waved good-bye to Clyde and approached Millicent's Caddy, the look on his face made it clear that his Realtor was about to make a sale.

Olivia smiled as Millicent hastily completed her phone call and sat back against the supple leather of her seat with an nearly inaudible sigh of satisfaction. Millicent was also the listing agent on this house and stood to make a tidy commission on the property, and while Olivia admired the older woman's drive, she didn't want her friend to pay a single cent over what she deemed to be a fair price for the house.

"Can we go back to your office and draw up the papers?" Harris asked as he jumped in the car.

Millicent was about to answer when Olivia leaned against the open passenger door. She gestured for Harris to come close and then whispered a figure into his ear.

"In this market, that's a solid offer," she said firmly and then acknowledged Millicent's presence with a polite nod. "Fixing this place up will put a strain on his savings account as it is," she fixed her sea-blue gaze on Millicent. "The Bayside Book Writers need him to have enough money left over to buy coffee and printer paper, so I've given him my recommendation on what I consider to be a fair price. I'm sure there's wiggle room to be had, seeing as you represent the sellers as well. Am I right?"

"Of course!" Millicent readily agreed and plastered on her best saleswoman grin. "Any friend of yours is a friend of mine."

"That's good to know." Olivia tapped on the Caddy's hood as though giving Millicent permission to drive away. She then whistled for her poodle and strode to her Range Rover, casting one last glance at the house Harris longed to call his own.

Inside her SUV, she noted the time on the dashboard clock and cursed. She was supposed to meet April Howard for a business lunch at Grumpy's Diner to go over paint and carpet colors for the Bayside Crab House, and was now sure to be late. Olivia hated tardiness. She preferred to arrive for any prearranged meeting at least ten minutes ahead of schedule. Now she'd have to rush downtown, search for a parking spot along Main Street, and hope that April had secured Olivia's favorite window booth before anyone else could.

With the onset of spring, tourists had begun streaming back to Oyster Bay. The coastal North Carolina town was already thirty degrees warmer than many northern locales, and the pale-faced, sun-starved vacationers had been counting down the days until their children's schools let out for spring break. Bypassing long flights to Cancun, Caribbean cruises, and the chaos of Disney World, the residents of a dozen snow-covered states opted for the quiet beauty of Oyster Bay instead.

Ditching heavy parkas in favor of T-shirts and sunglasses the moment they arrived, the vacationers hopped aboard rental bicycles and pedaled merrily through town, passing yards filled with blooming dogwood trees, pink and purple azalea bushes, and oceans of daffodils. The lawns were Ireland-green and the buzzing of industrious bees and hummingbirds blended with the tourists' contented sighs.

The locals were equally relieved to see the last of what had been a particularly long and damp winter. Oyster Bay's economy depended heavily on tourism, and a dry and sunny spring meant replenishment for the town's depleted coffers.

Olivia Limoges was landlady to many downtown merchants, but she spent most of her time overseeing the management of her five-star restaurant, The Boot Top Bistro. Today, she drove right by the entrance, searching for a parking spot closer to Grumpy's Diner, but decided on a space in a loading zone.

A middle-aged dwarf wearing roller skates and pigtail braids met her at the diner's door. "As I live and breathe!" Dixie Weaver declared, waving at her flushed face with her order pad. "Miss Punctuality is *late*!"

Frowning at her child-sized friend, Olivia stepped aside as Haviland entered the diner. He placed his black nose under Dixie's palm and gazed up at her in adoration.

"You sure know how to turn on the charm, Captain." Dixie ruffled the poodle's ears and then accepted one of his gentlemanly kisses on the back of her hand. "I know you're just anglin' for a juicy steak or some turkey bacon, but I'm the closest thing you've got to a godmother so I might as well spoil you silly!"

It was unlikely that Haviland had heard anything beyond the word 'bacon' as he'd turned tail and made for Olivia's customary window booth before Dixie could finish speaking, but the diner proprietor gave him an indulgent smile nonetheless.

"You're certainly in a good mood," Olivia said, still holding the door. An elderly couple shuffled in and headed for the *Evita* booth.

Dixie had a strange fascination for Andrew Lloyd Webber's musicals. As a result she'd plastered Broadway paraphernalia on every inch of available wall space. Each booth had its own unique theme, and while most patrons found the décor charming, Olivia did not share in her friend's Webber Worship.

Her eyes gleaming with excitement, Dixie looked over her shoulder and then whispered, "You'd be happy as a cat in tuna factory too, if you knew whose lovely, rich buns were planted on the leather in the *Cats* booth."

Olivia stole a glance at the middle-aged man dining on a chicken salad sandwich and a mountain of fries. He looked vaguely familiar but she couldn't place him. "He's handsome in a bookish sort of way. An older version of Brad Pitt in spectacles. I suppose he's a celebrity since you're *this* flustered. Let me guess. He played the lead in *Jesus Christ Superstar*?"

Placing a hand over her heart, Dixie released a dramatic sigh. "You've got the wrong field, but he does work in the arts. Keep guessin'. He's good-lookin', smart, is in great shape for a man in his fifties, has got the Midas touch, and I just read in *People* that he sold the film rights to his famous *book* for a figure with lots and lots of zeros."

Now Olivia knew the identity of the diner. "Ah, it's Nick Plumley, Booker Prize–winning author of the international bestseller, *The Barbed Wire Flower*. I wonder if he's here conducting research. The Internet's been rife with rumors regarding a sequel, and his groundbreaking novel was set down the road in New Bern."

"You'll have plenty of chances to ask him," Dixie replied enigmatically. When Olivia didn't rise to the bait by asking her how, the diner proprietor gave an irritated tug to her sequin-covered lavender top. "You're about as fun as a preacher at a strip joint, but I'll tell you anyhow. Mr. Plumley's rented a house down the beach from your place. You two can bump into each other on a lonely stretch of sand." Her eyes were shining with mischief. "There'll be an instant spark between you. Passion will ignite! You'll tear off your clothes and have wild, steamy—"

"Dixie! You'd better go. The lady in the *Evita* booth is waving her menu at you. I promise to ogle Mr. Plumley during my meeting with April, but we both have far too much work to do for me to stand here staring at him any longer." Olivia turned away.

"First you dump Oyster Bay's most eligible bachelor, and now you don't give a fig that a gorgeous, unattached, and gifted *writer* is sittin' ten feet away, ripe and ready for the pluckin'." Dixie muttered loudly enough for Olivia to hear. "Maybe what folks say is true: you *do* have ice runnin' through your veins."

"A large cup of your excellent coffee should clear that ailment right up. You can decide what I want for lunch too. You always seem to know what's best," Olivia said over her shoulder and then greeted April Howard, the woman in charge of interior design for the Bayside Crab House.

Olivia and April spread swatches of fabric, paint palettes, and carpet samples across the booth, barely leaving room for their lunch plates. April had chosen Grumpy's famous country fried steak, and Olivia was envious of the lightly battered meat smothered in gravy until Dixie appeared with her lunch—a generous wedge of cheese, shrimp, and mushroom quiche, Olivia only had to taste one bite of the golden crust to know that she'd been given the superior dish.

After serving the two women, Dixie lingered at their booth. She gave Haviland a platter of ground sirloin mixed with rice and vegetables and then asked after April's kids. She voiced her opinion on the array of fabric samples, picking the gaudiest one of the lot and chiding Olivia for being too conservative.

"This place should be lively! Red, white, and blue with a

few disco balls here and there!" Dixie exclaimed. "Where's your sense of adventure? Folks are gonna be crackin' crab claws with little mallets and tearin' at the meat with their front teeth. This isn't fine dinin', you know."

"We'll have checkered tablecloths," April said with a conciliatory smile. "But we need to keep the wall color relatively neutral because we plan to hang dozens of nautical flags in place of framed photographs or posters. Trust me, it'll be bright and busy."

"Bright and busy, huh? Just how I like my men," Dixie joked and skated away to clear dishes from the countertop.

Olivia concluded her business with April, insisted on paying for lunch, and then remained behind while her employee left to make phone calls to suppliers before meeting her kids' school bus.

Watching April jog across the street, Olivia recalled how she'd first met the talented designer. Last September, April's husband had been murdered and Olivia had been involved in the investigation. She'd appeared at the Howard's home in search of a clue and had found one that helped break the case wide open.

Slowly, April was healing from the devastating loss. She often called in sick and on those days Olivia guessed the mother of three had been assaulted by a wave of grief too potent to overcome. Olivia knew plenty about the grieving process and was fully aware that time wasn't the consummate healer people claimed it to be. There were stretches of time in which the pain surfaced with such a raw and unexpected power, that it crippled the grief-stricken until it required an immense feat of strength just to get out of bed.

"You did a good thing, takin' her on." Dixie had appeared bearing a fresh carafe of coffee.

Olivia waved off the suggestion. "I needed an interior designer and she needed a job. Nothing more to it than that."

Dixie snorted. "You're a transparent as a ghost, 'Livia. I know you're payin' for her kids to be on that special soccer team. Fixed it up to look like some kind of sports scholarship, but you can't fool *this* dwarf."

Olivia put her fingers to her lips. "Don't tell anyone about that. April isn't looking for handouts."

The bells above the diner door tinkled and a man wearing a pale blue blazer strolled in. Both women recognized the logo on the name tag pinned to the man's lapel. Engraved with a beach house, a lone wave, and the words Bayside Realty, the tag indicated that Randall McGraw had come to Grumpy's to meet with a prospective client. He headed straight for Nick Plumley's booth and, after shaking the author's hand, pulled a sheet of paper from a yellow folder bearing the realty's name and placed it reverently on the table.

Dixie and Olivia exchanged curious glances.

"What are you waiting for?" Olivia hissed. "Get those wheels spinning! I'm dying to know which property he's looking at."

With a toss of her bleach-blonde pigtail braids, Dixie zipped over to Nick's table, held out the order pad she only pretended to use as she'd never forgotten an order in her life, and beamed at the real estate agent. She then took her time clearing Nick's plate and finally skated into the kitchen.

Before Dixie had the chance to report back to Olivia, Nick was pulling bills from his wallet. He collected the sheaf of paper from the Realtor, folded it in half, and left the booth. Instead of exiting the diner, however, he walked right up to Haviland and stopped.

"Your companion is beautiful. Male or female?" he asked Olivia, his eyes on the poodle.

"His name is Captain Haviland," Olivia answered. "No need to be shy. He's extremely friendly."

The author extended his hand, palm up, and Haviland immediately offered him his right paw in return.

"I miss having a dog," Nick said wistfully. "But I travel so much and it wouldn't be fair to leave a pet in someone else's care all the time."

Olivia grinned, for Nick had given her just the opening she needed to satisfy her curiosity. She gestured at the man in the blazer who was pouring sugar into a glass of iced tea. "It appears as though you might be thinking about staying in one place for a while."

The writer adjusted his glasses and cleared his throat. "I'm renting a place at the moment, but I'd like to put down roots here. I have ties to Oyster Bay and I feel like I can achieve a level of anonymity in this town that I've yet to find in other places."

Playing dumb, Olivia cocked her head. "Should I recognize you?"

Nick laughed and attractive crinkles formed at the corners mouth and eyes. "That'll bring me down a peg." He extended his hand. "I'm Nick Plumley, author and dog lover at your service."

Olivia was pleased that his handshake was firm and that his eyes held a smile as he asked for her name.

"I knew who you were," Olivia confessed after introducing herself. "Still, I couldn't resist giving you a hard time. Consider it one of our new resident initiation rites."

"As long as you don't shave my eyebrows while I sleep," Nick replied smoothly and took a seat across from Olivia. "It's taken me years to perfect this arch."

The pair had begun exchanging ideas for other pranks when one of the local school librarians entered the diner.

She stopped just inside the door and scanned the room. When she saw Nick, her eyes widened and she scurried over to the window booth, clutching a hardcover against her chest.

"I am *so* sorry to interrupt, Mr. Plumley." Her voice was an animated whisper. "But when I heard you were here, *in our little diner*, I had to rush right over. I am *such* a big fan. This book—!" She gently eased the novel away from her body and touched the cover with reverence. "I thought of those German soldiers as my own brothers. Now *that* is skillful character development, to make *me* empathize with Nazis when I lost *two* uncles to that war."

My, but Dixie got the word out fast. What's she doing? Sending out tweets about the diner's guest? Olivia wondered, watching the author's reaction to failing to avoid his celebrity status.

Nick Plumley opened his mouth to thank the elderly librarian, but she didn't give him the opportunity. "And the *murder scene*! Utterly chilling. I researched the actual events, of course. We even had the nephew of one of the Nazi prison camp guards speak at the school's annual fundraiser." She glanced behind her as though the rest of the diners were hanging on her every word. "If you're working on the sequel, you should interview him. He says he remembers all kinds of stories from those days. *I* could introduce you."

Something altered in Nick's expression. The change was subtle. The laugh lines became shallower and a shadow darkened his eyes until he blinked it away. His smile, which had been sincere when the librarian first approached the booth, became stiff.

He recovered quickly, however, and offered to sign the woman's book. She prattled on about area book clubs, wringing her hands in delight as she spelled her last name with deliberate slowness.

"I have *quite* a collection of signed books," she informed Nick. "And this one will be given a place of pride among the John Updikes and the Dan Browns."

Olivia was growing bored with the librarian's fawning and wondered how the man seated opposite her had survived hundreds of events in which he was subjected to an endless horde of such sycophants.

Without regard for the librarian's feelings, Olivia cleared her throat and made a show of examining her watch. Luckily, the older woman took the hint and scuttled off, the book once again pressed against her chest.

"Sorry about that," Nick said, looking strangely weary from the encounter. He sat back, withdrawing into himself, and all traces of the amiable camaraderie that had begun to bloom between them evaporated.

Her curiosity aroused, Olivia tried to draw Nick into revealing more about his personal life, but he politely deflected all of her questions and began to shift in his seat. In a moment, she knew, he'd be gone.

"At least let me see the house listing you've got there. I know the best contractor in town should you need an inspection or repairs." She gave Nick her warmest smile, opening her deep sea-blue eyes wide.

It worked. "Showing you where I hope to live doesn't say much for my ability to guard my privacy, but for some reason I trust you." He slid the paper across the table to her.

Olivia unfolded the sheet and drew in a sharp breath. Of all the houses in Oyster Bay, the wealthy writer wanted to purchase the one Harris was dead set on buying.

As Olivia stared at the familiar bungalow, Nick excused himself and headed toward the restroom. Within seconds, Dixie was leaning over Olivia's shoulder, studying the black-and-white photo.

"I'd have thought he'd go for somethin' fancier." Dixie

frowned. "What's the point of bein' loaded if you don't toss your money around? It's not like you can take it with you."

Olivia jabbed at the paper with her index finger. "Never fear, Dixie. Nick Plumley won't be living here. He'll have to choose something more suitable."

Dixie shook her head. "I don't think so. I heard him tell the real estate broker that he *had* to have this house, so I reckon it's as good as sold."

Handing Dixie some cash, Olivia stood up and signaled to Haviland to follow suit. "You tell Nick Plumley that this house is unavailable. Tell him it has ghosts or asbestos or that it's been condemned. Tell him it's built on sacred Indian burial ground. I don't care what you say, but tell him it's off the market."

Dixie put her hands on her hips. "What on earth has gotten into you, 'Livia? Whether you like it or not, Oyster Bay's newest celebrity is gonna leave that gorgeous place he's renting and set out a welcome mat at this little house by Memorial Day. You just mark my words."

Olivia snatched the paper from the table and opened the front door. As soon as Haviland had trotted outside, Olivia turned to Dixie and calmly declared, "The only way he gets this house is over my dead body."

Without waiting for a response, she left, shutting the door so firmly that the bells were still ringing when Nick Plumley returned from the restroom to find that the woman, the poodle, and his house listing were gone.